Fashionably Hotter Than Hell

Book 6 of the HOT DAMNED Series

By

Robyn Peterman

Acknowledgments

I write alone, but the process is not singular. It takes a lot of people to make a book happen.

Meg, your editing has saved me from myself too many times to count! You rock!

Rebecca Poole, your covers are beautiful and so are you!

My critique partners… I would be in big trouble without you Donna McDonald and Jennifer Madden. Thank you is simply not enough.

Melissa, Wanda and Susan you are the best beta readers around. Smooch!

To my readers, thank you for reading. You are why I write.

Dedication

For my brothers.
You are all nuts and helped make me the tough chick I turned
out to be!
I love you always.

Chapter 1

"If you tell anyone, I will deny it and decapitate you," she said casually as she pulled her panties on.

"Noted," I replied. Watching her through hooded lids, I pondered what it would take to get her to remove the offending scrap of material and go for another round. Was I insane? Yes. Did I have a death wish? Absolutely.

"I just said I would remove your head and that's all you have to say?" she snapped and glared.

"Depends on which head you're talking about."

"Oh my God. You're disgusting," she yelled as she hurled a lamp my way.

Ducking the light fixture, I rolled off the bed and donned my jeans. I winked as I caught her ogling my backside. "I heard you and I raise you one. I will deflower, deny, and decapitate. Damn." I shook my head sadly while grinning from ear to ear. "Already deflowered… two hundred years ago."

"You're an ass. And I wasn't a *virgin* for your information," she hissed as she yanked on the rest of her clothes, covering a body that was made for sin.

However, the mouth left much to be desired. I certainly didn't enjoy hearing about other conquests. The need to kill any man who'd even looked at her wasn't healthy for me or for them. She was much nicer with her mouth closed. Well, not when it was wrapped around my…

"This was a mistake and will not be repeated," she informed me haughtily as she twisted her red curls into some kind of sexy looking bird's nest on the top of her head. "Never going to happen again."

I shrugged and grinned. Who was she trying to convince? Herself? Me? We'd been playing this game for quite a while. I was tempted to make a wager with her due to the fact she had a difficult time passing up a bet or a dare, but that could backfire on me in an enormous way.

"Heard that one before, Red." I slid my shirt over my head and quickly sidestepped a left hook from the insane woman I'd just given eight consecutive orgasms to.

"My name is not *Red*. If you value your jewels, you'll remember that," she informed me.

She strapped a dagger to the sexiest thigh I'd ever seen and headed for the door.

Why were the hot ones certifiable? I slid my katana into its sheath and waited patiently for the next insult. Was I a glutton for punishment? You bet, but it was worth every damned second.

She paused and glanced back with an evil little smirk that made me simultaneously want to bed her and run for cover. She made me feel alive. *In fear for my undead life alive*, but alive nonetheless.

"You know," she purred, "you're not really that good."

"Interesting," I commented as I slipped a knife into my boot. "That's not what you screamed ten minutes ago."

The look on her face was priceless. The next words from her mouth… not so much.

"I faked it."

Rolling my eyes, I wondered for a sickening moment if that was true and immediately decided it was bullshit. I was over two hundred years old. I knew when a woman faked it. Didn't I?

I stretched, flexed my muscles and made sure she saw what she was missing. "Well, that's too bad because I enjoyed the Hell out of it. Especially when you screamed my name and your body clamped itself around my… "

"Enough," she shouted as she practically sprinted to the door. "You're an arrogant son of a bitch and I can't stand the sight of you. You will never touch me again. I will no longer slum it with lowlifes like you and your big mouth and your big ego and your big… "

"Dick?" I suggested politely.

"In your dreams," she informed me over her shoulder as she hightailed it out of my suite like the Devil was on her heels.

I flopped back down on my bed and smiled. Now I *knew* she was lying…

Score one for me.

***

Later that afternoon…

All Hell had broken loose. I hadn't had so much fun in ages. Literally.

The office was in shambles, but I couldn't stop myself. Her anger was as sexy as everything else about her.

"Bet you can't nail my head," I challenged. Riling her up had become my favorite pastime.

"Bet this, jackass," she shouted as she hurled something colorful and large.

The object flew through the air like a bullet out of a gun. I couldn't even make out what it was.

"Shrew," I shot back with a laugh as I ducked. The crash was loud. I winced realizing she'd just annihilated an ancient Ming vase.

"Moor dweller," she hissed as she flung another irreplaceable artifact at my head.

"Very clever," I replied as I dodged the incoming projectile.

"I thought so… *Heathcliff*," she purred.

Her smile was infuriating and lamentably hot. The office was decimated. There was very little else to break, except for her.

It would be far easier to be in a room with the abomination if I didn't want to kill her or bed her. I was torn between which one would give me more satisfaction—tearing her arm off or losing myself inside her body. Unfortunately, neither was a viable option at the present time. Her fiery red curls had fallen out of the mess on her head and fell loosely down her back. Her creamy skin tempted me to distraction and her scent made me dizzy. She was every man's fantasy and my personal nightmare. Even the sprinkling of freckles across the bridge of her nose, which she usually disguised with glamour, were making my pants tight and uncomfortable.

Working as a team had been a tremendously bad idea, evidenced by the rubble that used to be Prince Ethan's study. Ethan was my dearest friend and brother to the nightmare staring daggers at me from five feet away. Thankfully Ethan's son, young Samuel, our one and only student, had not been present for the latest showdown between his teacher, *her*… and his fight coach, *me*.

I could simply leave the office. That was far more mature than throwing her over my knee and spanking her. Or, God forbid, stripping her down and fucking her into submission on the couch we'd destroyed in our melee. Leaving would ensure she lived another day in her long immortal life and that I wouldn't be brought up on charges for killing a Princess—no matter how much she deserved it.

I stiffly turned to go and was shoved right back into the room by my cousin Astrid, the mother of the child we were supposed to be teaching.

"What in Satan's slightly misguided obsession with Journey happened to this office?" Astrid demanded as she stormed into the room and plopped down on what used to be a priceless antique settee. "Motherfucker, this chair just stabbed me in the ass."

"Ask Wuthering Heights," the flame-haired viper snapped as she pointed at me with her middle finger— definitely not an accident on her part.

I glanced up at the ceiling hoping against hope it would give me the strength not to rip an appendage from her body. I'd had enough of the *Wuthering Heights* slams. Yes, I was named after a literary character. And yes, my sister was named Cathy. However, my mother had been friends with Emily Brontë, hence the names. I'd come to terms with it hundreds of years ago—or so I'd thought.

"So Cousin Heathcliff," Astrid said as she grinned at me. "Care to enlighten me?"

"Not particularly," I told her. "Why don't you ask the *lady*?"

My nightmare blushed in fury. Her delicate hands fisted at her sides and her eyes blazed green, which delighted me to no end and made the erection in my pants even more painful. Vampyres didn't blush, but this one did—an anomaly that always fascinated me.

"Raquel?" Astrid questioned as her head bobbed back and forth between us like a spectator at a tennis match.

"He has anger issues," Raquel spat.

"Pot, kettle, black," I muttered.

"Plus, he keeps daring me," she accused as if it were all my fault.

"Well, that certainly sucks," Astrid said. She gave me the stink eye while acting as if the bullshit Raquel just spouted made sense. "While I find all of that fanfuckingfascinating, do you think you guys could take this outside instead of destroying my house?"

"Ask him," Raquel said without looking at me.

"You're buying this crap from her?" I demanded of my cousin.

Astrid shrugged and grinned.

Raquel completely ignored me and went on. "Anyway, he's a chauvinistic pig who clearly comes from a line of pigs. I can't be expected to work with him."

Astrid appeared to be enjoying herself far too much. She found a clutter free spot on the floor and got comfortable. My cousin, too many times removed to remember the number, loved drama—especially drama that she didn't create.

"You do realize you just called me a swine, oh soon-to-be sister-in-law," Astrid announced as Raquel blanched.

No one wanted to incur Astrid's wrath.

My mother had been Astrid's grandmother several hundred years after she had given birth to my sister and me. While at first it had been awkward and alarming, since Astrid and I mistakenly thought we were attracted to each other, it later turned out to be a blessing. The logistics of our heritage were complicated. Easiest and shortest way to explain is that there had been reincarnation on my mother's part.

"I didn't mean you," Raquel replied contritely.

"Heathcliff is my thirty-fourth or seventy-eighth cousin," Astrid told her as she played with the shattered pieces of a vase that was older than dirt. "So while he may be all those other things, his line is pristine."

I had to roll my eyes at that one. I was a Vampyre and Astrid was half Vampyre and half Demon. Pristine was pushing it.

"Raquel, come with me," Astrid said as she got up and stepped on an ancient scroll. Both the bane of my existence and I winced at that one. "We'll find Samuel and you can teach him quantum physics or some other equally redonkulous bullshit like algebra."

"My pleasure," Raquel said as she waved goodbye to me with her middle finger and flounced out of the room.

That would definitely be the first body part I would remove.

"Heathcliff, you wait here. Ethan wants to talk with you."

The sound of Raquel's laughter as she sped down the hall made me grind my fangs. She wouldn't have the last laugh. Nope, I'd make sure of that.

***

"She's a pain in the ass and as difficult as they come, but she's brilliant and she's my sister. You will make this work. And for God's sake, stop betting her or daring her to do things. She can't stop herself," Ethan said tersely.

My oldest and closest friend ran his hands through his hair in frustration as he took in his office. I glanced around at the disaster and looked down at the floor. I never lost control. Ever. That woman was knocking me off my game and I didn't like it.

"She not difficult. She's a fucking menace," I told him. There simply had to be another way.

"Correct." Ethan grinned, enjoying my pain. He was just as bad as his mate, Astrid. "You two are the best qualified. Astrid and I trust you with the life of our son and that is not something we do lightly."

"She blushes," I said.

"I'm sorry, what?"

"Raquel blushes," I repeated.

Ethan busied himself with trying to piece together a statue that had been the victim of his sister's wrath. He ignored my query.

"It's not normal," I went on, glaring at his back.

"Nothing about my sister is normal. Most of what I know about her defies logic. However, that's her story to tell. Not mine. Furthermore, you are both related to my son by blood. And unfortunately, the two of you are the most qualified to teach him what he needs to know," Ethan snapped as he tossed the statue into a wastebasket. "My child is six months old. He's the size of a four year old. He can turn people's skin all colors of the rainbow, not to mention he can conjure Trolls and Gnomes." Ethan shuddered. "He's been kidnapped by Fairies and he needs to be trained to defend himself. Not sure how much clearer you need me to make this."

"Let me teach him to fight and send her back to the rock she lives under," I shot back. "He doesn't need to know his multiplication tables to kill a Troll."

"And that is where you are wrong, my friend," Ethan said. "His mind is a wonder. We need to feed it and keep it occupied so he stops animating stuffed animals that have death wishes."

"You're joking."

"No, I'm not joking. Not even a little fucking bit," Ethan ground out. "Have you ever been attacked and almost decapitated by an army of orange and blue teddy bears?"

I was speechless.

"I thought not," Ethan said wearily. "Add to that a fire breathing purple plastic dragon and a dagger throwing headless doll. My son thinks these sorts of things are funny."

"It actually is kind of funny."

The glare I received made me bite back the tasteless dragon joke on the tip of my tongue. Samuel was not just a Prince and the child of Astrid and Ethan. He was a True Immortal—one of nine. God was Good. Satan was Evil. Mother Nature was Emotion, her husband, the father of Satan was Wisdom. Hayden, the Angel of Death was Death. Elijah, the Angel of Light was Life. Dixie, Satan's daughter was Balance, and her half-sister Lucy was

Temptation. Astrid was Compassion and Samuel was Utopia—a combination of all of them.

That kid had one Hell of a row to hoe.

"I knew this would be difficult," Ethan admitted, "but it is what it is. You'll do this because I have asked you… and you will do it well."

"Yes, of course I will. But I won't be responsible if your sister loses a few limbs."

There was no choice in the matter. I had no issue with training the child. I adored Samuel and it was an honor to have been asked. But getting along with his shrew of an aunt was difficult at best and impossible at worst.

"As long as it's not her head she loses, then I'm fine with that. Just don't do it in front of my child," Ethan said. "Clear?"

"Clear."

It was a promise I didn't know if I could keep.

Chapter 2

"Me can't eat pie. Me a Vampyre just like you," Samuel explained to Raquel as I watched from my seat at the desk in Ethan's newly renovated office. I pretended to be absorbed in a folder filled with fighting techniques, but in truth, I was fighting to keep my eyes off Raquel.

She was a witch and I was determined to break the psychotic spell she had on me. Clearly screwing her out of my system wasn't working. I'd been doing that for two hundred years with no clear end in sight. My pants were killing me at the moment. Embarrassing as it was, not even Samuel's presence could quell my desire.

The furniture in the office had been replaced with finds from yard sales since we had destroyed a small fortune due to our skirmishes. The ragtag desks and chairs looked ridiculous in the grand office with the marble floors and cathedral ceilings, but it was a wise move on Ethan's part. Raquel and I obviously couldn't be trusted around priceless objects.

"It's not the kind of pie you eat," Raquel corrected him with a giggle and a kiss. "It's math. You can't eat math."

Why didn't she ever giggle at anything I said? *Why in the Hell did I care?*

I pressed my fingers to the bridge of my nose and went back to the paperwork in front of me. Astrid, my only, and least favorite, cousin right now, had decided Raquel and I would work with Samuel together. She reasoned it would force us not to kill each other.

She was wrong.

I knew if need be, I could distract Sammy with something shiny and dismember my foe in two seconds flat. The major problem with the scenario was that she could potentially do the same. I might outweigh and outmuscle her, but Raquel's rabid desire to maim couldn't be discounted.

She was equally dangerous to my concentration, my life and most definitely my libido.

"Do you remember what I told you about pi? What a big number it is?" she asked Samuel as she pointed to a passage in a book.

Sammy closed his eyes and slammed his chunky little hands over the numbers.

"The first fifty numbers in dethimal digits are 3.1415926535 8979323846 2643383279 5028841971 6939937510. Is me right?" he asked as he peeked under his hand.

"Um, yes," Raquel choked out. "How did you know that? We haven't learned that yet."

"Me debided some stuff in my head, silly Raquel." He laughed and pulled on her red curls as he popped his thumb into his mouth with satisfaction.

"Very good," she whispered as her eyes caught mine in shock.

Did this kid even need us? Well, he needed me, but his brain was a sponge. Maybe Raquel could go back to her dungeon and leave me to work with Samuel.

"Looks like he's smarter than you," I said as I got ready to duck in case the textbook came flying.

"Looks like you're still an ass," she shot back.

"Ass ass ass ass ass ass ass," Sammy chimed in gleefully as Raquel closed her eyes and dropped her head to the table in defeat.

Damn it, that was my fault, not hers. She would not get in trouble for teaching him the word ass when I goaded her into it.

"Samuel, an ass is a donkey—an animal similar to a horse. Aunt Raquel was referring to me as a strong and masterful horse with all of the massive parts that a horse has. She has *hung* a great honor on my *head*. Do you understand?" I asked.

My double entendre was not lost on my enemy as she bit back a laugh and pretended to throw up. Grinning, I shrugged and blew her a kiss. Furthermore, I was not in the mood to be chastised for expanding his swearing vocabulary. His mother was doing just fine with that on her own.

Raquel rolled her eyes dramatically and swallowed her grin. Amazingly, she threw nothing at me. Astrid had threatened to remove tongues if her boy learned new *potty words*. I liked my tongue... and God knew I liked hers.

"Yes, Sammy," she agreed with me. "Heathcliff is a donkey. Donkeys are much smaller than horses in every way. In fact, many would call them puny—tiny, puny and inconsequential. Unable to satisfy the needs of anything."

"That no make sense," Sammy said as he looked at me strangely.

"Trust me, little man." Raquel laughed wickedly. "It makes perfect sense."

It was a tie. God, she was fun to spar with. I couldn't remember the last time a woman had challenged me both in and out of the bedroom. Only problem was that we despised each other outside of the bedroom. Well, she despised me.

"Let's get back to work, little man," she said as she cuddled him and opened a thin volume of poetry.

"Raquel," Sammy whispered as he captured her face in his small hands. "Me love you so much."

He covered her cheeks in wet kisses. I froze and I watched the adoration shine from her eyes. She was childlike in her delight—innocent and young.

Something in my gut clenched. I didn't like it or want it. Raquel needed to stay cold and inhuman to me. I couldn't deal with anything more than what I perceived and wanted her to be—if I did it might destroy me. She pressed her forehead to his and held him tight.

"You no have to sleep anymore," he told her. He traced the sprinkling of freckles on her nose with his little finger as she paled and gaped at him.

"What?" she asked softly.

"You can love and not sleep. It be okay. You have to trust, silly pretty auntie." He grinned as she shook her head in confusion.

My eyes moved back and forth between a nodding Samuel and a shocked Raquel. *What the Hell was going on here?*

"Samuel, what are you talking about?" Raquel's mood changed abruptly. She turned tense and extremely uncomfortable.

"*You know*." He giggled and buried his face in her neck. "It be time to stop sleeping. Too dangerous now."

Her manner altered dramatically. She went from vulnerable and scared to strong and somewhat cold. Putting Samuel in the chair beside her, Raquel stood and paced. She stopped dead in her tracks when she saw me watching her.

"You're still here," she stated with unhappy surprise.

"Never left," I replied wondering what had just happened.

Samuel watched us both with curiosity as she circled the room. He cocked his head to the side and winked at me.

"Heathcwiff be the one to wake you up," he announced with conviction.

"No," Raquel barked as Samuel ignored her and giggled. "Enough, Sammy. We are done for today. Heathcliff, please return him to his parents."

With a mumbled goodbye, Raquel raced from the room.

Closing the folder, I sat for a brief moment and pondered how to go about getting the information I wanted. *No sleeping? I would wake her? What exactly did that mean?*

I slowly crossed the room to a very calm and composed Samuel. He looked quite pleased with himself. The puzzle was killing me.

"Would you like to tell me what that was about?" I asked as I squatted in front of the boy genius. He raised his eyebrows and gave me a look so reminiscent of his father I had to stifle a laugh.

"Is not Sammy's story to tell," he said as he put his thumb back in his mouth and watched me with narrowed eyes.

"But you might save Raquel some time if you let me in on the secret," I said logically. How hard was it to pry something out of a six month old child?

"You try to be tricky, Heathcwiff," Sammy yelled gleefully. "You no get me! Me too smart for you!"

"That you are, my little man. That you are."

***

"You've got a pole up your ass," Astrid said. "And you need to pull it out."

"I beg your pardon?" Raquel asked, shocked.

The voices halted me. I stilled in the hallway and backed away before I was discovered. They were in Astrid's art studio with the door wide open. After having delivered Samuel to his father, I'd planned on sparring in the gym to release some of my pent up aggression. However, eavesdropping was far more fun.

Rude? Yes.

Inappropriate? Again, yes.

Was I going to do it? Absolutely.

Quickly cloaking myself in invisibility and hiding my scent, I joined the hen party and took a front row seat.

"You need to loosen up and have some fun," Astrid recommended.

"I have fun," Raquel protested.

"Really?"

"Um… yes," the bane of my existence huffed.

Astrid was on a mission and Raquel was her objective. I didn't envy either of them at the moment—insane taskmaster and certifiable, albeit sexy, subject.

"What do you do for fun? Astrid inquired as she poured over a Prada catalogue and dog-eared various pages.

"Well, I…" Raquel stuttered. "You know, I… um"

"Yep, well that's definitely fun," Astrid said with an exaggerated eye roll as she tossed the magazine aside.

"Fine," Raquel relented. "You're correct. What do you suggest?"

"Shopping," Astrid stated firmly.

"I'm a fabulous shopper," Raquel shot back, clearly insulted.

"True, true, true," Astrid conceded. "What we need here is something more creative."

"Cooking?"

"Dude, we're dead—we don't eat," Astrid said sorrowfully.

Invisibility let me react without fear of losing my head, so I grinned and rolled my eyes. We'd all heard ad nauseam about the massive hole that not being able to eat had left in Astrid's life.

"I've got it! Swearing," Astrid shouted.

Holy God Almighty, this was going to be good. I got comfortable and waited for the show to begin.

"Swearing?" Raquel asked with a giggle.

"Yes," Astrid insisted as she stood to make her ludicrous point. Her excitement was contagious and it was all I could do not to reveal myself by laughing.

"Umm, I'm not so sure…" Raquel said as she stood and gave Astrid a quick hug. "I have a few things I need to do."

"Sit," Astrid commanded.

Raquel did so with great reluctance. Unfortunately, she sat right next to me and her scent almost made me groan aloud. My need to touch her was dangerously close to becoming reality. That would certainly not go over well—at all. Slowly I eased myself up and planted my feet by the door in case the need to make a quick escape was necessary.

"You need to let her rip. It's invigorating and uses up tons of calories," Astrid explained with a smirk and a covert wink to me.

God damn it, I'd forgotten Astrid could see through cloaking. I sent her a pleading look and she winked again. I was clearly going to owe my cousin a big one.

"We're Vampyres—we don't eat. Remember?" Raquel reminded her.

"Damn it you're right. But still it's a good way to start."

"I already say inappropriate words," Raquel argued and tossed her red curls.

Astrid groaned and plopped down beside her in the seat I'd just vacated.

Thank God I'd moved. She would have shoved me over and given me away for certain. Her evil little smirk was not lost on me—at all.

"Right there is your first problem. They are not inappropriate words—they're cuss words, dirty words, good old no-no's."

"Profanities!" Raquel added with clasped hands and a blush, trying hard to please the nutbag guiding her.

"A little better," Astrid replied as she wrinkled her nose.

It was fascinating to watch Raquel wrack her brain to come up with something that would impress her teacher. She was always so damned self-assured. I both liked and hated this carefree side of her, but I didn't want to see her lighter side. It made everything even harder than it already was—pun intended.

I waited to see what she would say. She'd most definitely sworn before—mainly at me—but she was nowhere near as creative and profane as my dear cousin.

"Ass, damn it, hell," Raquel recited hesitantly with another lovely blush.

"Nope, nope, nope." Astrid shook her head and took Raquel's hands in her own. Repeat after me. *Assmonkey, douche canoe, motherfucking turd knocker.*"

"Those are swear words?" Raquel asked with a wince.

"No. Those are cuss words—the kind that makes your mother wash your mouth out with soap."

"I don't have a mother anymore," Raquel said quietly.

"And thank God, Satan and Mother Nature, neither do I," Astrid responded with a shudder. "But you get the gist?"

"I do," Raquel answered slowly. "But I think we need to find something else. I'm quite afraid I'd laugh if I said any of those things."

"You could practice in front of a mirror," Astrid suggested in all seriousness.

"That would be a fine idea if I had a reflection."

"Shit mother fuckballs," Astrid shouted. "I always forget that one. Certain aspects of being a Vamp suck asscranks."

"Is that a real thing?"

"Is what a real thing?" my cousin asked perplexed.

"Um… asscranks," Raquel replied with discomfort.

Astrid thoughtfully considered her answer. "Nope, but it rolls off the tongue like butter, which is something else I *really* miss."

"Astrid, this won't work."

"Probably not, but I dare you to let four cuss words fly from your mouth daily. It's a scientific fact that those who *swear* are more trustworthy," Astrid informed her.

"It's not nice to dare me and where did you read that? National Enquirer?"

"Nope, I heard it on Housewives of Whateverthefuck, so that means it's true," Astrid said with a laugh. "Seriously, try it—you'll like it."

"Four a day?" Raquel asked.

"Yep."

"You're on."

I slipped from the room with a stupid smile on my face, thankful my cousin didn't reveal my pathetic stalking. What I wouldn't have given to have been part of that conversation in corporeal form. God damn it, I wanted Raquel to see me—like me—laugh with me.

I was an idiot. A huge fucking idiot.

Chapter 3

"If you stopped playing hide the salami with her, daring her to do stupid shit, and actually got to know her, you'd probably save us a lot of money in home furnishings," Astrid groused as she pulled me toward the Grand Ballroom. "I hate these fucking cocktail parties. I have several hundred years to go before I can drink anything but blood, so getting drunk is out. And most of these damn Vamps bore me to tears."

"I have no clue what you mean," I insisted as I picked up my pace and tried to drag her into the ballroom so the conversation would end.

Every so often Ethan threw formal parties for his people. With Raquel's European assembly visiting, the soirees had been nonstop. However, Raquel rarely attended.

"Give me a break. Anyone with ears, bionic or not, could hear you two boinking this morning. Quit yanking on my arm," she snapped. "You know you like her. I can tell. I noticed it when we offed all those Demons at the Caves a couple of months ago."

Jesus, I didn't need this. "I do not like Raquel. She is rude and violent and... "

"And smokin' hot and you totally like her. Nothing gets by me," she informed me with a huge grin. "I think she's your mate."

"And I think you're smoking crack," I shot back.

My mate? Bullshit. I didn't need a mate who would joyously kill me when my back was turned. I didn't need a mate who threw Ming vases for a hobby. I didn't need a mate at all. Period.

I was single, lonely, and loving it. No. Wait. I was single and loving it.

"I am not smoking crack, my very handsome cousin with the to-die-for dimples." Astrid grinned and punched me in the arm. "Can't breathe—can't smoke. That's how I got into this shit show to start with."

Astrid had been turned into a Vampyre when she'd gone to a hypnotist to stop smoking and ended up undead. One of the strangest turnings I'd ever heard of, but what was done was done. She was clearly meant to be one of us because she was a True Immortal.

"Astrid," I said with a smile through clenched teeth. "While I appreciate your concern, Raquel is not my mate. I don't like the woman and she most definitely doesn't like me. I'd even go as far to say that she hates me. So I can assure there will be no mating any time in the near future."

"You know, my cousin," she purred as we entered the ballroom, effectively ending our appalling talk. "There is a very thin line between love and hate."

I sighed as my gaze travelled a full room. I despised it when Astrid got the last word in.

***

The ballroom was filled with Vampyres dressed to kill. No pun intended.

Many were leaving the compound in Kentucky tomorrow and going to France to attend a yearly Summit with the Angels. I expected Raquel to leave with them as she was the Princess of the European territory.

The thought of Raquel leaving left an unsettled feeling inside me, which I decided to ignore. A bare bones contingency of fifty would stay behind to protect Prince Ethan, Astrid and Samuel. I was happy to have an excuse to get out of meeting with the Angels. Angelic? Yes. But were they pleasant? No.

"Sweet cousin Jesus in a hula skirt," Astrid muttered as she glanced around the ballroom. "This clusterfuck makes me want to chew glass and swallow it."

I had to agree but stayed mum. Vampyre politics were a bore. Watching the sucking up and posturing had grown tiresome over the years. But Astrid and I were both expected to deal.

"There's a band," I observed. "I suppose there will be dancing."

"Thank God. I should have invited Mother Nature. She would have twerked and scared the shit out of everyone. That would have cleared the room in a minute flat," she said with an evil grin.

Astrid's grandmother on her father's side was Mother Nature—the most delightfully insane woman in existence. Of course, there would have been twerking *and* pole dancing, but there would have also been a forest exploding out of the marble floor and a zoo of animals in her wake. Ethan had just repaired the compound from her last visit. A new visit would not be welcome.

"I have to go stand next to Ethan and pretend I'm listening to all the Vamps kissing his ass. They're all vying for an invite to the wedding even though they think it's ridiculous," she said.

Vampyres mated. They didn't marry. Marriage was a vow that could be broken, while mating was not. Most Vampyres ridiculed the human tradition of marriage, but not my cousin. Astrid was a newly turned Vampyre and her human traditions were still important to her. She played it off well, but I knew the derision hurt her.

"Astrid," I said as I took her hand in mine.

25

"Yes, Heathcliff?" she asked with an eye roll.

"I don't think it's stupid at all. You should have what you want."

She stopped and glanced at the floor for a moment, then up at me gratefully. "I don't think it's stupid either," she whispered. "I want to marry Ethan more than I've ever wanted anything."

"More than Prada?" I teased.

She barely missed a beat. "Yep, more than Prada, Gucci and Stella McCartney. You gonna be okay on your own, my devastatingly handsome cousin?" she inquired with a sly grin.

"Aren't I always?" I replied.

"You know," she winked at me as she walked away and said, "If you'd get your head out of your ass, you wouldn't *have* to be on your own."

Ignoring her, I made my way into the crowd. Astrid was insane. I was happy alone. Being mated would keep me from… all sorts of things I needed to do.

God damn it, I was going to avoid my cousin for a while.

I was greeted respectfully by many and checked my watch repeatedly. How long did I have to stay? A brief appearance should be sufficient. As Prince Ethan's second in command of the North American Dominion, I was expected to attend all formal functions. I grabbed a blood laced scotch from the bar and leaned against a column. I would stay until I finished my drink and then I was out.

"Heathcliff, darling," an exquisite Vampyre named Christina purred as she placed a perfectly manicured hand possessively on my chest. "I called you three times and haven't heard back. Are you avoiding me?"

She was stunning, but for some reason she left me cold this evening. We had dallied on and off for years. She was safe—wanted nothing but sex. But sex with her was not what I craved at the moment.

"Christina, lovely to see you," I said as I removed her hand and stepped back. "I've been quite busy, but I assure you I haven't been avoiding you."

Her eyes narrowed slightly, but she covered it quickly with a seductive smile. "Well then, what say you we meet after the party?"

"We'll see," I said distractedly as I became aware of an unwanted presence close by.

What was Raquel doing here? She never came to parties at the Cressida House. She was above the American need to socialize at the drop of a hat. Apparently, she was slumming it tonight. I felt my blue eyes turn green with desire and Christina very mistakenly assumed it was for her.

"I'll meet you at my place after the gathering," she whispered excitedly as she placed a wet kiss on my lips.

"Not tonight," I replied tersely. "I'm busy."

Her eyebrows rose in surprise and she stiffened. "Your loss."

"I'm afraid it is," I said as politely as I could muster. I moved away from her. She was becoming a bit too clingy which I didn't want or need. I had enough problems.

Where the Hell was Raquel? I could feel her and I was certain she could feel me. We were in a public setting and I was somewhat certain I was safe from flying objects—or so I hoped. She was a fucking flame and I was a moth. My thoughts were wild and I wanted to kill my cousin for putting them there.

"Hi Heathcliff, you hot sexy dead dude," a small voice announced from my shoulder. "Can me touch your butt?"

On my shoulders sat four Baby Demons: Beyoncé, Abe, Rachel and Ross. They stood about three inches high and caused more trouble than beings ten times their size. The miniature hellions belonged to Astrid and she let them have free rein of the compound. They were menaces with a fondness for ass grabbing and breast grazing.

"No, Beyoncé. You may not touch my butt," I said as I plucked them off my shoulders and put them on the bar.

"You no fun," she chastised me as she dove into a blood laced margarita.

"You a pooper party," Rachel added as she walloped her buddy Ross in the head. He went flying into Abe and the melee began.

"It's a party pooper," I said as I pulled Beyoncé out of the drink and separated the little nuisances. "If you can't behave, you'll have to go back upstairs."

"But you need me help," Abe insisted as he took a covert swipe at Ross' head.

"And what exactly do I need your help with?" I asked as I quickly swigged down the rest of my scotch. Unfortunately, it was incredibly difficult for Vampyres to tie one on. It would take at least ten strong scotches for me to feel even slightly inebriated. I was going to have to deal with the Baby Demons and Raquel as a sober man.

"To help you get the girl," he answered without a grammar issue and without suggesting I touch a butt.

"What girl?" I asked as I signaled the bartender for another. This was turning out to be a long evening—and it wasn't even the evening yet. The sun still shone through the skylights in the ballroom. They were muted with protective glass since many Vampyres couldn't handle direct sunlight.

"You know what girlllllllllllllll," Rachel said slyly as she hopped over my shoulder, latched onto the tail of my tux and slapped my ass. "The one you luuuuurrrrrrvvvvvvve."

"I love no girl," I insisted and retrieved her before she took a dive into my pants. "And if I did, I am quite certain I could handle her on my own."

"Me no think so," Abe said as he spastically slapped at his lips.

The others joined his lip slapping antics and I watched perplexed. What the Hell were they doing?

"Me think you need loooooootssssss of help," Ross added.

"But if you no like girl here we take you to Big Sean's Booby Barn," Abe told me as he continued to slap his mouth. "Lots of girls be there."

"Um, thank you, but no." I said as I picked up my new scotch and downed it.

"Me wanna go to Booby Barn," Rachel squealed with bloodthirsty excitement. "Me hungry for bad Demons!"

"Outstanding idea," I said quickly as I scooped them up and walked them to the foyer. I did not need or want their help. The farther away they were the better.

"You suuuure you no wanna come?" Abe asked with a huge grin on his face.

"Quite," I replied.

"You suuuuure you no want our help? You might beeeeee one of the prettiest Vampyres me ever seen, but you no smart," Beyoncé added as she blew me loud kisses.

"I really don't think I need any help."

"Me really think you do, but it be your *hot pink* bloodbath," she added gleefully.

I was mute as I had no clue how to reply to that one. The Baby Demons were odd little creatures. It was definitely time for them to go.

"Don't do anything we no do," Abe screamed as they poofed away to the strip club. I chuckled and shook my head. This day needed to end, but I had still had one more thing I needed to do.

As I made my way back into the gathering, I saw her and stopped in my tracks. Raquel was poured into a sexy black halter dress that made her pale skin and red hair exquisite. My gut tightened and every instinct I had was wildly inappropriate. She was surrounded by her entourage of Vampyres from her European Dominion. All men. All entirely too close. Especially the red headed one who couldn't take his eyes off her.

The American Vamps were paying respects—literally falling over themselves to get close to her. Raquel was both gracious and beautiful. She held the crowd in the palm of her hand. I observed jealously as she smiled and exchanged pleasantries with the besotted group of Vampyres. I ground my fangs and fought my desire to barge in, take her in my arms and lay claim. She shouldn't be here. She should be in Europe. Who in the Hell was running Europe while she was away? Only one way to find out.

The band had started and the music was slow and sensual. The thought of holding her in my arms without being decapitated was appealing. It would be in bad taste for her to turn me down in front of an audience and worse for her to attack me. Win—win.

Her eyes narrowed dangerously as I approached and I hoped my tux jacket hid the growing bulge in my pants. The Vampyres stepped back out of respect for me and I grinned at the alluring blush on her cheeks.

"May I have this dance?" I asked.

"No, you may not," the red haired goon, who had a seriously annoying French accent, said as he stepped in front of Raquel.

The gasps and titters of our audience only served to deepen her blush. Her normally golden eyes had narrowed to slits and blazed green.

"Interesting," I said in a deadly quiet voice as the idiot guard dropped his gaze from mine. I could destroy him in a second flat but knew that really wouldn't go over well. "I don't believe I asked you to dance. You're not my type."

The titters were now full blown laughs.

"My Princess does not dance," he insisted as he raised his eyes back to mine and glared.

Part of me admired his vigilance. However, he was in the way of what I wanted, which was not working for me.

"I find it fascinating that Raquel can't answer for herself," I said softly as I stared her down. "She was quite vocal this morn... "

"Enough," she snapped. "It's fine, Jean Paul," she assured her henchman as she touched his shoulder. "I shall give him one dance."

"Are you sure, my liege?" he asked doubtfully as he glanced up at the skylights. "It's almost time to leave."

Raquel followed his gaze and gave him a curt nod. "It will be fine. One dance," she informed me as she placed her hand in mine. "Only one."

"That's all I asked for, Princess," I said smoothly as I led her to the crowded dance floor.

Her small hand in mine and the feel of her hip beneath the other was almost my undoing. Although, it was her scent that made my head spin—like a spring breeze mixed with desire.

"It's quite ballsy of you to ask me to dance," she said as she stared hard at my mouth with displeasure.

I grinned and pulled her tighter against my body. "Why would you say something like that?"

"Well, I assumed from that shade of lipstick you're wearing that you've already been quite busy with someone else," she said.

What was she talking about?

"Or you've become a metrosexual jackassmonkeydouche. You know, hot pink really isn't your color. With your dark hair you could easily pull off red," she explained with wide eyes, clearly surprised that she'd taken Astrid's advice on creative profanities. "Sorry about that jackdouche thing, it slipped out. However," she continued caustically, back to her lovely self, "I have a difficult time with red because of my hair. I do have a few tubes I bought hoping I could make them work. I'd be happy to give them to you."

"What the Hell are you talking about?" I asked as I stopped dancing and pulled her closer, making it impossible for her to run or knee me in the balls. The appalling insult was funny the accusation—not so much.

"Your lipstick. It's simply the wrong shade or you're actually a man whore." Her eyes spat fire and she tried to pull away.

Not happening.

God damn it. I should have listened to the Demons. My hot pink bloodbath was the leftover lipstick from Christina's kiss. Not good form. The insane lip smacking now made sense. I quickly swiped my lips and made a mental note to listen to the ass-obsessed menaces next time. However, Raquel's obvious jealousy made my pants even tighter.

"Overzealous greeting," I muttered with a shrug.

"Right," she said with a discreet elbow to my gut.

I deserved that. "So I assume you'll be leaving for Europe in the morning," I said, praying I'd removed all of the lipstick and desperately seeking a change of subject.

"Never assume… it makes an ass out of you and me," she said as she stiffly moved to the music.

"You're not going?" I asked, surprised. She was the Monarch of Europe. She would have to be there.

"No."

"Why?"

"I don't see how that's any of your business," she snapped and purposely stomped on my foot.

God, that was hot. "Everything you do is my business, Princess."

"Since when?" she demanded.

"Since I was balls deep inside you and you were screaming my name a couple of hours ago."

"Oh my God," she hissed. "Your ego knows no bounds. We've been having meaningless sex for hundreds of years. You have no rights to me. You should find yourself a nice uncomplicated Vampyre mate and... "

"Why haven't you mated?" I asked in a deadly quiet voice.

"Heathcliff, I'm not going there." She blushed and tried again to pull away. "The subject is not up for discussion."

"You brought it up, beautiful. Tell me why," I ground out.

"Because I..." she stammered.

Her avoidance of my question was a repeated thorn in my side—a thorn that had been imbedded and festering for centuries. My anger rose quickly and I wanted to hurt her.

"It can't be because you haven't been asked," I whispered as I reminded her of a moment we shared in time, two hundred years ago. I ground my erection into her as she gasped and went soft in my arms.

"Stop," she pleaded desperately. "We can never be."

"Because it's more fun to lead me on, play with my pathetic emotions, and then rip out my heart?"

"Is that what you think?" she whispered.

"It's what I know, Red. I'm good enough to fuck but not to mate. You made that abundantly clear a very long time ago." I knew my eyes had gone green with fury and desire. My grip on her body tightened and my need to take her was almost debilitating. Glutton for punishment didn't even come close to describing the new low I'd hit, but she made me weak and I hated her for it.

"You know nothing of me," she hissed.

"I know every inch of your body," I shot back.

"That's just the shell. The part that matters will never be yours."

She ripped herself from my arms and glared at me with rage and a tinge of what appeared to be sorrow. Her body shook and her cheeks blazed with color. She was magnificent. Did she regret saying no to me all those years ago? I laughed at my wishful thinking. She felt nothing and the sooner I accepted it the better off I would be.

"My apologies," I said tonelessly as I gave her a formal bow and felt my chest clench in pain. "What we have had is now over. It should have been over a long time ago, but this lovely dance has truly ended it for me. I wish you the best with your life, Raquel."

"Heathcliff, I…" She trembled and wrung her hands. Her expression went from unsure to resigned.

I waited for more, but no more came. Time to cut my losses and maintain a semblance of pride.

As I turned to walk away, her goons immediately replaced me. She glanced at me, then up at the skylights and nodded quickly. The red headed one I wanted to kill held her sagging body up as the European group exited the ballroom. He looked at me strangely and shook his head in disgust. The need to tear him apart was overwhelming, but I refrained. Ethan would be furious if I killed a guest at the party and I needed to let go of anything that had to do with Raquel. Forever.

Not a problem. Not at all.

I made my way purposefully across the ballroom. The distraction I searched for stood in a group of Vamps gossiping about things I couldn't give a shit about. But I wasn't looking for brains. I was looking to forget. She would do.

"Christina, are you ready to leave?" I asked, ignoring all the giggling and curtsying female Vampyres around her.

She glanced up in surprise and then slithered over seductively.

"I knew you'd come to your senses," she purred as she locked her arm through mine and winked at her friends.

If it were only that simple.

Chapter 4

"Well, this is disappointing," Christina said flatly as we both stared at my flaccid cock. "You're a Vampyre. You can direct the blood where you want it to go."

She was correct, but for the life of me, I couldn't direct it to my dick at the moment. She was beautiful, horny, and mine for the taking. It didn't matter that she couldn't carry on an intelligent conversation. Talking was quite unnecessary. I wanted to blame it on alcohol, but that would be ludicrous. I wasn't drunk, but it would have been a far better excuse than the truth.

"It's not you, it's me," I muttered as I grabbed my pants and pulled them on.

"Oh my God," she whined. "You are not getting out of here that easily. Let me suck on it."

I closed my eyes and pinched the bridge of my nose. If it wasn't so tragic I would have laughed. I had to get the Hell out of here. Now.

"Mate with me," she begged as she grabbed my arm and rubbed her naked body against mine. "It will be just fine if we're mated. And if you still can't do it, I won't tell anyone. I promise. I'll find a discreet lover and we can still be an important couple in society."

"As wonderful as that sounds, I'll have to pass," I quipped sarcastically. She was nuts. "You deserve a mate who's besotted with you." I stepped into my shoes and put some distance between us.

"That's bullshit. I want you. I want to be rich and powerful. You've always gotten it up before. I swear if you let me suck on it I can get you off. And if my having a lover bothers you, I just won't ever talk about it. You need someone like me at your side," she pleaded. "A man is judged by how his woman presents herself."

"I'm sorry. What?"

"I'm beautiful. You're stupidly gorgeous. We'll be the envy of all if I'm yours. We look perfect together. Everyone knows it's just a matter of time before we mate."

That was news to me.

"Christina, this has never been more than sex. I have always been upfront with you. I never promised anything more." How much fucking worse could this day get?

"Of course," she purred, "but I knew you didn't mean it."

"Actually... I did."

How had I not realized she was far more into this than I was? And how did I miss that she was certifiable?

"I call bullshit," she said as she ran her hands over her voluptuous body and tried yet again to entice me.

We both glanced down at my crotch.

Nothing.

Time to cut my losses and get out. Damn Raquel straight to Hell. I couldn't have her and now I was letting her stop me from having someone else.

"I have to go. It was lovely seeing you again," I said as I bit back a groan at the ridiculous pleasantry that had just left my mouth.

"This is not over, Heathcliff," Christina hissed as she rummaged through her bedside drawer and pulled out a vibrator. "You're mine and I will have you and your limp dick. You'll see."

She punctuated her insult with the whirring of her sex toy. I shook my head and did my damnedest not to laugh. She was a piece of work. Thankfully she wasn't my piece of work.

Alone for eternity was starting to sound very appealing.

"It's over, Christina. You're a wonderful woman," I lied. "You deserve so much more than me."

"Yes, I do, Mr. My Dick Doesn't Work Anymore," she hissed nastily.

Her crazed smile of triumph made my skin crawl. I crossed casual sex off my list of hobbies. This had to be one of the worst days of my long life. All I wanted was for it to end.

"Goodnight, Christina," I said as I made my way out of her house.

"I'll call you, darling," she yelled after me.

I walked to my Mercedes CL65 at a fast clip just in case she felt the need to follow me out and negotiate some more.

Done.

I was done with women.

***

The party was still in full swing when I arrived back at the Cressida House. I wasn't inclined to be alone with myself so I made my way back to the bar and ordered a scotch and then another and then another.

The thought of going to my suite didn't appeal. However, the thought of drinking my cares away and then punching someone certainly did.

Hitting people was always a good distraction.

***

"You really don't want to fuck with me right now," I ground out as another Vamp hit the wall with a thud. Vamps-zero. Heathcliff-eight. This was too easy. Damn it. I wanted to be challenged—not wipe the floor with warriors.

Not sure what led me to her suite. I'd like to think it was the alcohol, but I wasn't that drunk. Even the ten scotches I had consumed couldn't be blamed for what I was doing. If I had to explain my actions, I'd have to say it stemmed from the way the red headed bastard had looked at her so possessively earlier in the evening—not to be outweighed by my lack of erection with other women besides her.

The bottom line was that Raquel wasn't his. She was mine… at least in my semi-inebriated state she was.

"I just want to talk to her," I insisted as I threw the outer door to her suite open and tried to push past him.

I'd taken care of the guards in the hallway outside her suite without any problem at all. It felt good to punch a few faces. The sound of bones crunching under my fists satisfied the rage burning inside me.

Watching them fall to the floor in agony just fed my need. I wasn't out to kill. I simply wanted to maim. I knew they'd heal quickly. They were old and quite powerful. They had been chosen to protect the Princess after all. Clearly, European Vamps were pussies. Personally, I would have chosen stronger guards but Raquel was not my concern. She had made that very clear.

"She does not take visitors in the evening," Jean Paul informed me as he stood in a defensive stance, ready to have a go at me.

"Do I look like I care?" I asked as I sized him up.

"No, you do *not* look like you care," he said derisively. "And that, my friend, is your main problem."

His words confused me, but I was certain I didn't like them or their meaning at all. How could chasing someone for two hundred years equate to not caring? The man was an ass and I wanted a piece of him.

"Just move away from her door and I won't hurt you," I reasoned. He knew what I had done to his buddies. Surely he didn't have a death wish.

"You'll have to kill me to get to her," he replied calmly.

"As you wish." I grinned and popped my knuckles. He was an idiot. We both knew I could take him. There were very few Vampyres in the world I couldn't destroy. Why was he being so obtuse?

"*Jean Paul*," I drawled. "You seem like a nice little French guy and I really don't want to kill you. All I want to do is talk to Raquel."

Why hadn't she come out here with all of the ruckus? Was my presence so abhorrent to her?

"You upset her greatly earlier," he snapped and drew a vicious looking sword. "And I do believe I already stated that she does not take evening visitors."

"Except for you?" I demanded. Fuck, I sounded like a jealous fool.

He paused and stared hard at me. His head cocked to the side as I watched him consider his answer. Finally he shook his head.

"No. Not even me, you ass," he said snidely.

"Did you just call me an ass?"

"I did," he replied with confidence.

"While that may be true, men have died for far less offenses," I told him with a grin as I contemplated removing his weapon and decapitating him with it. The fact that he'd called me an ass was amusing. Against my better judgment, I liked the little French bastard.

"How about this," I suggested casually. I relaxed my stance but stayed on guard. His sword was lethal and I wasn't stupid. My deadly reputation hadn't been earned by being careless. "You take ten steps to the left and I walk through the door and have a little chat with Raquel."

"How about this," he countered. "*No.*"

I laughed. He was good, but I was better. He knew it and so did I, but his dedication was impressive. He was truly willing to die for her. For that reason alone, I would not kill him.

"Okay, I see I'm getting nowhere with you. You're refreshing. Not many stand up to me."

I eyed him and debated my next move. I couldn't just walk away—it wasn't in my nature.

"You don't scare me," he said. "You might scare my Princess, but you don't scare me."

What the Hell did that mean? My hands clenched to fists at my sides and I itched to rearrange his face—not permanently. Temporarily.

"Fine. Lose the sword. You have my word I will not enter her room. However, I need to release some aggression and your face is an excellent spot for me to do so."

"Bring it," he said as he dropped his sword and waited for me to make the first move.

Very smart. Little Frenchy wasn't going to be impulsive or careless. His demeanor was casual and alert, but I could scent his excitement and it energized me. Finally a challenge.

And so it began… and continued for a very violent and satisfactory hour.

By the time we'd finished, the room was destroyed and we were both the worse for wear. Blood and smashed furniture were everywhere. We admired our cuts and bruises. He was a worthy opponent. I hadn't enjoyed a fight that didn't end in death so much in a long time.

"Several of your moves were outstanding," I said as I rolled my neck and popped out a few kinks.

"Coming from you, that is a great honor," Jean Paul said as he mopped the blood from his forehead. "I wouldn't mind sparring and learning some more while we are here."

"It would be my pleasure. How long are you here?" I asked as it occurred to me that I could potentially learn what I wanted to know from my new friend.

"As long as the Princess deems fit," he answered carefully.

Damn it, why in the fuck was nothing easy for me today?

"How about I train you and you answer a few questions?" I suggested as I watched him closely.

"No," he replied with a grin and a shrug.

"Outstanding." I laughed as I stood gingerly and straightened my torn and bloodied tuxedo. This was going to be fun. I needed some fucking fun. "I'll meet you in the fight training center tomorrow at eleven."

"I'll be there," he said respectfully.

I glanced up to see an irate Ethan standing in the doorway. "Anyone care to explain why there are eight bloody and passed out European Vampyres in the hallway? And why does this room looks like a goddamned tornado hit it?"

"We were testing the reflexes of our guards, Sire," Jean Paul mumbled and bowed.

"I see," Ethan said. He crossed his arms over his chest, raised his eyebrow and waited for my explanation.

"Jean Paul is correct," I added as I took in yet another room in the compound that I'd had a hand in destroying. Raquel was going to have a fit. Where in the Hell was she? She couldn't possibly have slept through the brawl that had ruined her living quarters.

"In that case, meet me in my suite. Now," Ethan said to me as he turned and walked away. "And pick up these idiots in the hallway and send them back to Europe. If they can't defend my sister, they're not welcome here."

I observed my new friend as he stood and walked to the hallway. "You need help?" I asked as he dragged one of the unconscious Vamps into the room.

"No, I have this," Jean Paul said. "You should probably go get your ass chewed out by your Prince."

"Good point," I replied, admiring his spirit. "I'll see you in the morning. Bring Raquel if she feels up to some sparring," I added.

"I'm sure she will be busy repairing the mishap we've had in here, but I will extend the invitation," he said with a twinkle in his eye.

"Very well then. I'll be off."

"Have fun," Jean Paul called after me as I made my way to Ethan's floor.

I grinned and shook my head. The little fucker had balls. I thoroughly enjoyed people with balls... and I enjoyed those who might have the potential to help me get what I wanted.

Even if what I wanted didn't want me.

Chapter 5

Astrid was grinning from ear to ear when I entered their living room. Ethan and Astrid's suite consisted of the entire top floor of the compound. It was more down to earth since Astrid had arrived and it was baby proofed within an inch of its life. Samuel slept contentedly in her arms as Ethan paced the room and waited for me to come clean.

"Sooooooo, I hear you can't get it up anymore," Astrid commented casually as her grin grew wider.

"Jesus," I muttered as I dropped down on the couch next to her and stretched my sore legs. Jean Paul had gotten a few excellent kicks in. "Good news travels fast."

"Considering it came from the ho-skank Christina, I don't think many will buy it," she said sweetly raised eyebrows and with a shit eating smirk.

"What has gotten into you?" Ethan asked as he seated himself directly across from me.

"Not sure," I replied. I let my head fall into my hands.

"I am," Astrid volunteered. She hopped up, crossed the room with the sleeping Samuel, and tucked him into his big boy bed. His baboon slept contentedly under it on the floor. I was still surprised they'd kept the animal due to the destruction it had caused, but Samuel adored the beast and the feeling was mutual.

"Astrid," I warned as I heard her giggle.

"Out with it," Ethan said tightly, "unless you want my mate to do your dirty work. And trust me, it will sound far worse coming out of her mouth."

"I resent that," Astrid said as she flounced back over and sat on Ethan's lap.

"I, ahhh…" I didn't know where to start—or if I even wanted to.

We all sat in strained silence and waited to see what I would say. I was more curious than anyone about what might come out of my mouth.

"Well, it's like this…" I began slowly.

"Oh, for shit's sake," Astrid interrupted. "He's in love with Raquel. They've been doing the horizontal hula for longer than I've been alive. I mean, my Uncle God, the entire compound heard them bumping uglies this morning. I'm quite sure she's his mate and he keeps fucking, *pun intended*, everything up by sleeping with her and not dating her properly."

Ethan was shocked to silence. He had also been correct. The facts were definitely more heinous coming from Astrid's mouth.

I watched Ethan closely, inwardly seething. His eyes were closed and his lips were thin. My gut clenched and my instinct was to attack. What the fuck was wrong with me? He was my prince… and my friend.

I tamped down my fury with difficulty. I'd had enough of being judged and denied. Did he think I wasn't good enough for her too?

"Is this accurate?" he demanded in a choked voice.

I was unsure if his loss of voice was from Astrid's choice of words or if he believed I was unfit to be his sister's mate.

45

"Not exactly," I mumbled.

"What *exactly* isn't accurate?" Ethan asked as a small smile pulled at his lips.

"Mine's not ugly," I replied evenly.

Ethan's smile was now full blown.

"And neither is hers."

Oh fuck me. Did I say that out loud? If their large eyes and Ethan's pained wince were any indication… I had.

"Okay, that's information I could have lived without—forever." Ethan groaned and buried his face in his mate's neck.

"That was a little much," Astrid agreed gleefully.

The statement was amazingly alarming coming from my cousin. Astrid had no filter whatsoever. With my behavior as of late, I supposed I now qualified for the same club.

"Look, it doesn't matter. Raquel doesn't want me. She's made it clear," I stated.

"Have you made you intention clear? Ethan asked.

"Very," I shot back. Under no circumstances would I share my humiliation from two hundred years ago. That was between Raquel and me.

"Do you think it's because you ripped Raquel's legs off all those years ago?" Astrid asked as she sat forward and clasped her hands together in excitement.

"Possibly… and it wasn't her legs. It was her arm. Only one arm," I added. For a brief moment I contemplated Astrid's theory and then brushed it aside. "No, how could she be mad about that? She deserved it and it grew back."

Again with the silence.

"She was trying to kill me at the time," I protested. "We're Vampyres. This sort of violence is normal."

"Hmmm… there's a lot you don't know about women," Astrid muttered with an eye roll and an unladylike snort.

"Fine," I relented. "It was a thoughtless move, but I've apologized numerous times over the years for that one."

"Did she ever accept your apology?" she asked.

"No."

"Then she's still pissed. I would be fucking furious if someone ripped off my legs," Astrid declared.

"Arm," I corrected her.

"Whatever," she snapped. "I say you offer up your leg, or at least a foot, and let her tear it off. It's not really normal dating protocol, but we're Vampyres. I think it might just work."

"Are you insane?" I hissed.

"Define insane," she said.

"Enough," Ethan said. "I believe she's your mate. So does our father."

My eyes shot to Ethan's and my chest constricted. Why did all of this have to be so complicated? Mates were supposed to recognize each other. Why couldn't I find someone who wanted me as much as I wanted them?

"Now you just have to convince her," Astrid said logically. "I still think a dismemberment would go a long way."

"Sweetheart?" Ethan said.

"Yes?"

"I'm quite positive we can come up with a better idea than maiming Heathcliff," Ethan suggested.

"Fine," Astrid huffed, put out that her bloody horrid idea had been shot down. "How can he convince her?"

"It won't be easy," Ethan muttered. "She has…"

"What?" I demanded. "She has what?"

"Issues," Ethan replied cryptically. "Issues I'm not at liberty to talk about."

"Wait one fucking minute," Astrid griped. "Why don't I know about Raquel's issues?"

"Because it's truly not my tale to tell. It's hers and it's not a pretty one," Ethan said as he put Astrid on the couch and began to pace the room again. "Here's what I will say... Raquel has given up her Monarchy of Europe. She has turned her rule over to our brother Gareth."

"But he rules the largest section of Asia." I was completely shocked by the news. "When did this happen?"

"Right before she came here. My father's fine with this. He has given his blessing. Gareth is a solid and honest leader, even if he can't seem to keep it in his pants," Ethan said with shrug.

"Will he be at the wedding?" Astrid asked.

"My father?" Ethan asked confused.

Astrid smiled. "No. Your manwhore brother."

"He wouldn't miss it," Ethan replied. "He adores American Vampyres."

We were getting off track. "I'm a little lost here. Why would Raquel do that? She's one of the finest and deadliest leaders in the world. She's beloved by her people and completely insane. They would die for her," I said as I tried to figure out what would make her give up her birthright.

"That was all really good except for the insane part," Astrid coached.

"Did I say insane?"

"Yep." She nodded.

"Interesting. Well, I meant that, but I didn't mean to say it," I told her.

"I'll let it go this time, but if you say something stupid again, I'll have to zap you. The pain will train you to be more of a gentleman where Raquel is concerned. I'm doing this because I love you, Heathcliff—not because it will be fun to electrocute your ass."

I nodded warily. It was surely a very bad idea. However, I did need to rebuild a filter when I spoke to Raquel.

"This is all well and good," I said as I ran my hand tiredly through my hair. "Everyone in the world can believe we are destined to be together, but if Raquel doesn't—it's not happening."

"I agree. You certainly have your work cut out for you." Ethan shuddered and grimaced. "Good luck."

"Anything else you can tell me?" I asked hopefully.

"Nope, hers to tell."

"That's bullshit," I snapped.

"As is much in life," he replied.

I nodded curtly in frustration and stood to leave.

"Heathcliff, don't worry. I know she wants you too, but something's holding her back. I'm going to help you get her," Astrid promised.

"I really don't think that I…" I stuttered.

"No, don't thank me," Astrid said as she gave me a hug. "It's my duty as your cousin. I will help you kick ass and get the girl."

I hugged her back and was able to hide my look of sheer horror over her shoulder. Of course Ethan saw it and just grinned. I flipped him off and his grin became a laugh. It wasn't funny. It was my *life*.

But since I obviously hadn't done too well on my own with it… Hell. Maybe Astrid *could* help me.

***

"God damn it," I bellowed as my cousin flicked her fingers and almost set my ass on fire. "I didn't say anything bad. Why in the Hell are you zapping me?"

"I'm practicing. It would be a fucking shit show if I zapped your nuts, now wouldn't it?" she snapped.

That shut me up.

I was early to the fight training center. Jean Paul was supposed to meet me at eleven and Astrid had sent word for Raquel to bring Samuel at eleven as well. I had no clue what her plan was, but I didn't care. I wanted to see Raquel. I wanted to know the mystery… and I just plain wanted her.

"Take off your shirt," Astrid instructed.

"What?"

"Your shirt. Take it off. Now."

"Why?" I asked.

"Because Raquel will be here in a few and we need to show off your assets," Astrid explained as if she'd just made a perfectly reasonable request.

"I will not take off my shirt. I'm going to charm her with my wit," I said, right before an electrical volt hit my backside. "*Son of a bitch*," I shouted as I hopped around in pain.

Grabbing my ass, I shot my cousin a look that had brought armies to their knees. Astrid simply narrowed her eyes.

"Retaliate and your balls are next," she threatened.

"Fine," I grumbled as I removed my shirt, leaving me barefoot and in my low riding sweat pants. "Should I oil my pecs?" I asked sarcastically.

"Oh my Cousin Jesus," she squealed. "That's an awesome idea."

"I was joking."

"Well, I'm not. Do you want me to magic up some oil?"

"Absolutely not," I said.

"You are being an asshat," she muttered. "I'm here to help you."

She punctuated her remark with another zap to my backside.

This brand of help was not working for me.

"They're coming," she whispered with manic excitement. "Act normal."

"If I act normal, you're going to zap my ass right off of my body," I growled.

"Right," she said as she wrinkled her brow in thought. "Then just flex your muscles and stay quiet."

"Not happening," I mumbled and quickly jumped out of the way as another electrical current zoomed toward me.

"You do realize that if you move, I might blow up your balls and your Johnson," she informed me as the rest of the group entered the training room.

"Balls," Samuel yelled as he pointed at me from Raquel's arms.

"That's right, baby boy," Astrid said as she took her child from Raquel. "Nice to see you, Jean Paul and Raquel. Let's get this party started."

"Thank you for rearranging my suite last night."

Raquel was not pleased. It was evidenced by her raised eyebrows and an *I'd like to kick your ass* look on her face.

I opened my mouth to counter her attack with something rude and brilliant and noticed Astrid's twitching fingers. Fuck.

"Yes... well, I'm, ummm... sorry about that," I mumbled and almost laughed at the puzzled look of shock on Raquel's face.

"Why am I here?" Raquel studiously avoided my intense scrutiny of her. She was dressed casually in yoga pants and a t-shirt that hugged her breasts to perfection.

"Because… " Astrid started uncertainly.

"Because we decided that after I train Jean Paul for a bit, you and I could show Samuel some more intricate moves," I explained, pulling the first thing I could think of out of my very sore ass.

Astrid's covert nod of approval made my tense body relax.

Raquel's eyes narrowed slightly but she shrugged and took a seat next to the mat. "Fine. It's your funeral," she mumbled with a charming smile.

"That it is," I shot back with a grin of my own. I also prayed my libido stayed in check while we sparred. I didn't really need to explain erections to Sammy. "You ready, Jean Paul?"

"I am," he said as he bowed formally to me. "Weapons or hand-to-hand?"

"Hand-to-hand," I replied as I returned his bow. "Center of the mat. Relax and blindfold yourself."

"Blindfold, sir?"

"Yep. It's all about feeling the energy. If you want to be the best, you need to be able to feel your enemy, not just see them," I said as I handed him a blindfold and put one on myself.

There were two reasons I did this. One—I would be more focused if I couldn't see Raquel. Two—if I couldn't see her, the potential problem in my pants was more likely to stay calm.

Win—win.

"Begin," I instructed quietly.

Jean Paul was less sure of himself without his sight and became aggressive and sloppy. His punches were strong, but it was easy to take him down.

"Feel me," I commanded. "Don't punch air. Don't waste one single movement."

I demonstrated my instruction with a jab to his head that left him disoriented and on the floor.

"This is foreign to me," he grunted. I felt him stand back up and take a defensive position. "I need to see."

"No," I admonished him. "You don't. Trust your senses and find me. There is power in stillness. Stop flailing about."

He stood quietly and centered himself. To an average observer, it would seem as if nothing was happening. However, they would be very wrong. Jean Paul had found his inner sight and the power that welled from him was impressive. Not enough to make me shudder, but I was the very best. Very few stood a chance against me. Not ego—just fact.

"Take me down," I taunted. "If you can do it, I'll give you a favor of your choosing."

"A rare gift." Jean Paul chuckled and his body tensed. "And if I fail?"

"You'll owe me a favor."

I felt him consider the offer. Then he struck. And it was glorious.

Violent and balletic, we fought with aggression and purpose. With each punch and roundhouse kick, I felt him grow stronger. I back flipped out of the way as a vicious right hook came at my face. I came right back with a scissor kick to his head that brought him down.

Pinning him to the floor, he struggled and tried to regain the upper hand, but it was over.

"A fine try, but not good enough," I hissed in his ear.

"I want to go again," he grunted as I let up on his throat.

"No... no more today. Wear the blindfold when you aren't on guard and find your center while you're without sight. If you can't... you're worthless."

"I am not worthless," he spat as he removed the material from his eyes.

"We shall see," I countered with a grin.

He was correct, but telling him would be counterproductive. The over protective Frenchman had balls, and training him would be a good distraction. Plus, it would ensure some time to grill him for information—he owed me a favor. Again... win—win. "You're excused, Jean Paul. Go shower and think about what I've said. Tomorrow at eleven again?"

"I will be here, sir. Thank you." He bowed to me and then checked in with his Princess. With a few quietly exchanged words and a quick nod, he left the training room.

Raquel stood and watched me. Her eyes strayed from my face to my body. Color suffused her cheeks and I could scent her desire. Suddenly Astrid's shirtless directive seemed like a brilliant idea—not that I would ever admit that to my cousin. She'd become a bossy monster.

"Are you ready?" I inquired, meaning so much more than the simple question.

"I'm always ready," she said calmly. "P.S.—I like my arm. You remove it again and you lose your head."

"Noted." I grinned and bowed to her. "I'm not guaranteeing that I won't go for your overactive middle finger."

"This one?" she asked as she flipped me off with a grin on her face.

I chuckled and willed my dick to stay asleep. "Yep, that's the one."

"Oh shit," Astrid shouted.

"Shit," Samuel yelled with joy.

"Sammy," Astrid reprimanded him. "Shit is a filthy fucking word. We don't say shitty words like that. You got it?"

"Yep, Mommy. Me got it."

"It's the Baby Demons teaching him that crap," she muttered as she stood up and headed for the door.

"Crap," Sammy shouted and lifted his middle finger to me and Raquel.

"Oh Hell no," Raquel whispered in horror as she watched him wave his chunky little birdie finger all over the place.

"Where are you going?" I called after Astrid as she hightailed it out of the gym.

"I forgot I had a meeting with the motherfucking wedding planner at noon. I'll be back when I can. Don't you two do anything I wouldn't do," she shouted as she left the room.

Well, that certainly didn't leave much.

"Motherfucking," Sammy squealed as they exited the facility.

We stared at each other in silence. Her beauty humbled me. I wanted her to stay. I wanted to throw her to the floor and kiss her senseless. However, that was not the gentlemanly thing to do.

Fuck. What would Astrid do? Grinning at the absurd thought of taking advice from my insane cousin, I decided to stick to the plan already made.

"You still want to fight?" I asked Raquel.

"Sure. I would love to kick your ass," she purred.

"I'd love to bite yours," I shot back.

"If you win, I'll let you… but if I win you have to do my bidding for a day."

Holy Hell—either way I won. "That works for me, Princess."

"Excellent, my bathroom is filthy," she purred with an evil smile.

I chuckled and shrugged. She was full of it. The cleaning staff at the compound was outstanding. Her effort to rile me was moot.

"Show me what you got."

"My pleasure," she said as she centered herself and took a defensive stance on the mat.

"No. Trust me—the pleasure is mine."

All mine.

Chapter 6

I was inclined to go easy on her. My mistake.

"After last night I thought I wouldn't see much of you anymore," she said as she violently kicked my legs out from beneath me and tried to pin me.

"You thought wrong," I shot back as I flipped her to her back and held her immobile.

Her body beneath mine was a temptation almost impossible to ignore. However, her need to best me or tear a limb from my body made me push all thoughts of stripping and fucking her to the back of my brain.

"Can we use magic?" she asked as she twisted and attempted to pull free.

"Nope."

Her hips were in line with mine and I could have sworn she was grinding herself against me. Son of a bitch.

"Are you cheating?" I whispered in her ear. Her breasts were smashed against my bare chest and the evidence of my arousal was impossible to miss.

"Possibly," she whispered back with a soft giggle. "Is it working?"

Pressing my erection against her stomach and nipping at her earlobe was my answer. Her groan almost set me on fire. Next move was hers. My fangs had descended from my gums and I knew my eyes blazed green. I studied her lovely face and was delighted to see that her eyes and fangs matched mine. We were both in need.

Leaning into her, I traced her full lips with my tongue. She tasted like Heaven and sin and woman. She opened her lips and invited me in. My head spun and I lost sight of the fact we were in a public place. Actually, I didn't give a damn.

Her eyes fluttered shut and it took everything I had to explore gently. Every instinct I had was to make her mine for eternity, but she needed to be with me on that one. I would wait until she wanted the same thing. I knew in my gut she wanted it—had known for hundreds of years she wanted it, but something stopped her. This time I would find out.

I wanted her body, her heart and her soul. I was going to win. I always won my battles. I'd just never fought one this long.

The burning desire to be buried deep inside of her was all-consuming, but sex was a bad idea. God damn it, wait… Why was it a bad idea? Her body writhing beneath mine had my brain spinning out of control. Yet I knew I had to stop. I would win the skirmish but lose the war if I banged her on the gym floor. Fuck.

"Can't play hide the salami today," I muttered as I disengaged myself. "Can't do it."

"What did you just say?" she asked. Her cheeks were flushed and she was grinning. "Did you just refer to your equipment as a salami?"

"Of course not," I mumbled. Then I groaned as I rolled off her and ran my hands through my hair in frustration. "All right, I did, but it's entirely Astrid's fault. We're not supposed to bump uglies or do the horizontal hula anymore."

"Ummm… okay," she said as she tried not to laugh. "Can I ask why?"

"No."

We both stared at the ceiling for a while. What was my next move here?

"Are we done fighting?" she asked.

There were several ways to answer that one. "Literally or figuratively?"

"That's kind of loaded, don't you think?" she replied.

I glanced over at her on the floor beside me. Her hair was a mess, her cheeks were pink and her eyes sparkled. She had never been more beautiful and I'd never been more at a loss as to what to do.

"Astrid bet me that we couldn't be friends," I lied. *Fuck, where did that come from?*

"What did you bet?" She sat up as her eyes grew wide with excitement.

Lying was never the best policy, but knowing Raquel was a sucker for a bet or a dare spurred me on. "My fleet of cars," I answered, compounding the lie tremendously. I figured I should just phone Satan and reserve a suite, but she giggled and I couldn't stop myself. "My *entire* fleet of cars," I added as I hoped God and Astrid would forgive me.

"Holy shit," she muttered. She knew my car collection. "What do you get from her if you win?"

"She has to pole dance with Mother Nature at the next formal gathering," I said as I imagined my cousin ripping me from limb to limb. Astrid was going to kill me dead.

"Piece of cake," she said as she laughed. "You will win and Astrid will dance."

"Really?" Could it be this easy? Did lying work? "You'll be my friend?"

"What exactly does being your friend entail?"

"Well, we would talk and be civil instead of trying to kill each other," I said slowly, wondering how much I could get away with. I was headed to Hell anyway, might as well make it worth it.

"I could probably make that work," she said as she pulled her knees to her chest and wrapped her arms around her slim thighs.

"We would hang out and get to know each other better," I added and waited for her to belt me.

"How much?" she asked suspiciously.

"Probably a lot in the beginning. How long are you here?"

"Not sure yet," she said as she rested her chin on her knees. "So no sex?"

"No, no sex," I croaked as we both stared at my raging erection. "Well, maybe if we talked the entire time and got to know each other while we fucked."

"You mean like in between each thrust, you ask me my favorite color or favorite board game?" she inquired with a raised brow and a smirk.

"That sounds somewhat complicated," I said.

"And mood killing," she added.

"How about after each orgasm we ask three questions?" I bargained.

"I get two and you get one?"

"No, we each get three." I shook my head and grinned.

"Two," she negotiated.

I pretended to consider her counter, but I would have said yes to one question after every tenth orgasm. The deal was pretty damn good.

"I can work with that."

"My suite or yours, *friend*?" she asked as she stood and offered me her hand.

"Mine. I hate filthy bathrooms."

She rolled her eyes and laughed like a carefree girl. "You got yourself a deal."

Her laugh was music to my ears. We raced each other to the exit of the training room. I knew I'd get busted for lying at some point. I just prayed it would be after we had mated.

***

"Blue," she said as she tore off her shirt and went for my pants.

"My balls?" I asked as I helped her. Then I picked her up and threw her on the bed.

"No, idiot, my favorite color. Yours?" Her laugh went all through me and I grinned.

"Red," I said as I dove on top of her naked body. "I thought the questions were after each orgasm."

My hands found her breasts and her nipples pebbled beneath my fingertips. She was fucking perfect.

"I know," she said as she ran her hands up my chest and tangled her fingers in my hair, "but I realized there are some things I want to know. Can't you multitask?"

She ground her hips against my erection and I saw stars. I was *not* going to blow my wad like a high school human—at least I hoped not.

This felt different than all the times we'd fucked over the years. Normally we insulted the Hell out of each other and then screwed until we were almost for real dead. This was far better, but there was no way I was going to articulate that. She'd run.

"Do you have any pets?" I asked as I ran my tongue along the underside of her breast.

"Cats. Two," she said as she shuddered and arched her back, silently begging for more.

I happily obliged and scraped my fangs over her firm round breasts.

"You?" she whispered.

"No, but I like pussies."

"Oh my God," she burst out. "You suck at this."

"Nope, but I can," I murmured as I took her distended nipple in my mouth and did just that.

Her hiss went straight to my balls and the need to be inside her was almost debilitating, but I held back. Don't hide the fucking salami until I know more about her than just how to make her body sing.

"Favorite singer?" I asked in a muffled voice due to her breast being in my mouth.

"Johnny Cash," she squeaked as I nipped and then stopped.

"You're kidding."

"No," she snapped. "What's wrong with Johnny Cash?"

"Nothing. It's just surprising," I said as I trapped her arms over her head and got nose to nose with her. "Favorite TV show?"

"*True Blood.*" She narrowed her eyes and waited for me to jump on that one.

"I'm hotter than those fuckers," I said with a smirk.

"Possibly." She grinned back. "Favorite place in the world?"

"Right here. Right now," I said and waited for her to make her escape.

She looked away and the color in her cheeks heightened. "Too personal," she whispered. "Too fast. Hardest thing to kill?"

I would play it her way because she was correct. My plan was to make her fall for me permanently, not run away again. "Trolls," I said firmly. "Or possibly Gnomes."

"I haven't had the pleasure of fighting either one of those," she said as she rotated her hips beneath mine.

My eyes rolled back in my head and I bit down on my lip to keep from coming. "It's not a pleasure. Trust me on that one." My lips found the spot on her neck that made her whimper.

"Truth or dare?" she asked hoarsely as I made my way down her body toward the auburn curls between her legs.

"Dare," I said as I flicked my tongue over her most sensitive parts.

Her hips jerked and I held her firmly in my hands so I could have my fill and make her beg. The beginnings of her orgasm made me slow down. I was going to make her work for it. Prolonged anticipation—prolonged pleasure.

"I dare you to stare into my eyes when we fuck," she said recklessly as she writhed under my lips.

"That's kind of personal, Red," I said gruffly, loving the thought.

"You're right. I take it back," she recanted quickly.

"Nope, a dare is a dare and I accept," I said as I moved with Vampyre speed back up her body, licking and nipping every place that I wanted. "Truth or dare, Princess?"

"Dare," she gasped out as I positioned myself at her entrance and teased her with the swollen head of my cock. She was so wet and ready I almost forgot to play the game.

"I dare you to make love with me. No fucking," I challenged.

Her body stiffened and she tried to turn away. I was having none of it.

Taking her chin in my hand I forced her to see me. "I want you to know it's me inside of your body. I want you to watch what you do to me—what you have done to me for two hundred goddamned years and I want to watch you come apart in my arms. I want my name on your lips when you come and I want… "

"You want too much," she ground out as she began to struggle. "You can't have everything—no one can. Let my body be enough for you."

"I can't. I want all of you," I hissed as I pushed the head of my cock into her. She tightened around me like a vise and it took every ounce of control not to bury myself to the hilt in her body. "I want what's inside and what's outside. I need everything."

"I don't have it to give," she cried out as she rocked and took more of me into her.

"Tell me that you want me," I demanded as I held my body still with gargantuan effort. "Tell me that you recognize me as your mate. Let me in."

She tilted her head and tears filled her eyes. I lowered my lips to hers and kissed her with such tenderness that I felt a sting in my own eyes. My hands splayed her rib cage and I cradled her curves reverently.

The deep-seated ache in my balls was painful, but I wanted her to see me. I needed her to see us. Whether she admitted it or not, it had always been this way when we came together. Our bodies and souls recognized each other as one.

"Why, Raquel? Tell me why."

She closed her eyes and put her hands over them. "I recognize you, Heathcliff," she whispered brokenly. "I have always recognized you."

My chest tightened. The light at the end of the tunnel was dim, but at least it was there. "You're mine," I said as I took her hands off her face and trapped them over her head. "Say it. Stop destroying both of us."

"I can't."

"Can't or won't?" I demanded angrily. How in the fuck could she deny what was meant to be?

Her mouth moved wordlessly and I tried to enter her mind, but she blocked me. I read her lips, but I wanted to make her say it. I needed to hear it even if it devastated me.

"Say it," I ground out.

"Both," she yelled. "I can't and I won't," she said harshly as tears poured from her eyes. "It's not you. It's me."

"Jesus Christ," I muttered as I rolled off of her onto my back and stared sightlessly at the ceiling of my bedroom. "We're not in high school. This isn't a crush. You're my mate—the other half of my soul. You are slowly killing me—killing us."

"I'm broken," she whispered. "I won't break you too."

"Is that really your decision to make?" I asked without looking at her. It was too difficult.

"It has to be," she said woodenly as she rose from the bed and gathered her clothes.

"No," I countered harshly. "It doesn't have to be this way. You know I'm your mate and I know you're mine. It's not complicated. You. Are. Mine."

She stared at me sadly and shook her head. "Even if I explain, you won't understand. You'll never see things the way I do."

"God damn it, just give me the chance. You owe me that."

"No," she whispered as part of me broke for good.

She turned away and began to dress. I longed to run my hands over her smooth skin. I wanted to squeeze this elusive secret out of her, but I knew it wouldn't work. She'd kept it close to her chest for over two hundred years. One would think I'd learned my lesson by now. It was time to force myself to swallow it and move on. I was dying inside and I was letting it happen because I wouldn't let her go. Fate was a bitch and I hated her.

"I can't do this anymore, Raquel. I can't be with only part of you—it's not enough. I'm slowly going insane."

"I know. I am too," she said so quietly I almost missed it. "I'll leave here and not come back again. There are other tutors for Samuel. It was selfish and wrong for me to be here. I'm sorry."

I wanted crawl out of my skin. I wanted to shake her and make her understand or at least make her hurt as much as I did. The agony I felt was unbearable. Her future and her happiness were right in front of her and she was too scared or proud to see it.

"You're an icy woman, Raquel, and fate has destined me to Hell by making me your mate."

My tone held no expression. I had nothing left to give. The hopelessness made me a hollow shell. I loved her as much as I hated her.

I felt her stare but refused to look.

"You're right, Heathcliff. I'm cold and unfeeling. I'm sorry about what fate has destined, but sometimes fate makes mistakes."

"Apparently," I said coolly. "You have pretty words and a pretty facade. I suppose I should be grateful that you only showed me your outside and hid your insides because they are as black as the heart you don't have."

Her sob caught in her throat and I felt ill. I rolled off the bed and sat on the edge with my back to her. Seeing her would make me beg and I'd already done that. I would not do it again—ever again. Her quiet crying shredded me. The cruel words had left my lips willingly and now I would give my undead life to take them back.

"Raquel, I… "

"No, Heathcliff. What you said is true. Believe it always —at least you'll be alive to do so." With that she left.

I picked up the first thing my hands touched and smashed it against the wall. Her words held such irony. I wasn't alive and neither was she. We were undead. We were fucking Vampyres and we would live for eternity… alone.

Because she was too much of a coward to be mine.

I pulled on some pants and went looking for a fight. Getting beaten and bloody was the only thing that was going to work for me and I knew just where to find it.

Chapter 7

"What the Hell is wrong with you?" Ethan roared.

It was somewhat difficult to see and hear him as my ears were still ringing and my eyes were swollen nearly all the way shut. Somehow I'd found my way to his office... or maybe I'd been dragged here. It was all slightly jumbled at the moment and I really didn't give a shit.

"Nothing is wrong with me," I growled.

"Let me recap," he snapped. "You took on thirty Vampyres barehanded and let them have weapons. You decimated the training room with magic and you left twenty of those Vampyres without limbs. I would have to argue that there is something very wrong with you."

"I needed to blow off some steam," I shot back unsteadily as I tried to stand and thought better of it. "And most of the bastards are old. The limbs will grow back immediately."

"Irrelevant," Ethan hissed. "And just so you know, I'm not your biggest problem at the moment. Astrid is on her way up here."

"Bring it," I said. Nothing could faze me now—not even the wrath of my cousin. Maybe she would kill me for real dead. It would be a blessing. There were so few who could do it, but she was one who possessed the power to kill almost anything.

"Heathcliff, you're a fucking mess. You're a Master Vampyre with a death wish—a bad fucking combination."

Ethan was disgusted and I didn't blame him. I was his second in command and I'd just wiped out most of the Vamps who were staying in the States to guard him, Astrid and Samuel. The group of injured would have to regenerate here and others would have to forego the summit with the Angels in Europe.

Fuck. I didn't think my need to release my aggression all the way through.

"My bad," I said as I stood and grimaced in pain. I'd gotten the shit beat out of me and loved every minute. However, in hindsight it didn't seem the wisest move I'd ever made.

"Understatement," Ethan said as he tossed me an icepack. "You're healing already. I should beat the Hell out of you so you stay in pain longer."

"Sounds good to me," I agreed.

I felt her before I saw her. Instinct made me duck as the air in the room changed and my cousin's furious power filled it.

"You bet *what*?" Astrid shouted as she stormed into the room.

Unfortunately, even with the ringing in my ears I could hear her as clear as day.

"No clue what you're shouting about," I replied calmly.

"You bet I would pole dance with Mother Nature at a formal gathering?" she screeched.

"Who told you?" I inquired as I backed away from her. She was literally glowing and sparks flew from her fingertips.

"Every maimed Vampyre in the infirmary told me, you asswhack," she yelled. "I do not pole dance in public. I only do it for Ethan when he gets down on his knees and begs."

"Alrighty then," Ethan cut her off quickly. "That is entirely too much information, my love."

"You're right," she admitted sheepishly and then turned her wrath back to me. "If you weren't so pathetic right now, I would kick your sorry ass into the next century. Why would you bet something that could get you killed?"

"It doesn't matter now," I said as I eased my torn up body onto a couch. "The bet is off."

"Who was the bet with?" she asked as she got in my face.

"The bet was with someone I no longer know or acknowledge."

The silence in the room was deafening except for the annoying ringing in my ears. I waited for the next round of obscene name-calling and wasn't disappointed.

"Oh my Uncle God, you are such a douche canoe," she groused before she shoved me over and sat down next to me. "You made the bet with Raquel?"

"What did I tell you about betting with my sister?" Ethan said as he shook his head.

"It doesn't matter anymore. She's leaving and we are not mates."

"I call bullshit on that and anyway, she can't leave," Astrid said. "She's tutoring Sammy and he loves her."

"Let her leave," Ethan said softly. "She can't stay here if she can deny fate. It will destroy Heathcliff."

"Fate makes mistakes," I informed them and then laughed without humor.

"No, it fucking doesn't," Astrid snapped. "This is all such a clusterhump of doodoopoopcaacaa."

"What did you just say?" I asked, confused. Had my hearing been damaged?

"Shut up," Astrid hissed grumpily. "I'm trying to use words that won't land me in the *I have to duct tape my mouth* Hall of Fame. Just fucking go with it, buttwind."

"Will do," I said as I bit back a grin. I was surprised I could still smile. Life would apparently go on even if I didn't want it to.

"This is redonkulous," she muttered as she examined my mutilated face. "Raquel is your mate. What is her balleating problem? And don't you dare tell me it's her tale to tell," she said as she turned away from me and narrowed her eyes at Ethan.

"Fine," he said. "I won't say it."

"But you won't tell either," she said.

"Can't."

"I can withhold panty privileges," she threatened.

"But you won't," Ethan replied with a grin.

"You are such a… sexy piece of hot Vampyre man meat." She giggled and blew him a kiss.

"Can't listen to happy people in love," I said as I stood and made my way to the door of their suite. "Need to go sleep for a week. I'll be fine when she leaves. I'm sorry for the damage and for removing the appendages of half of our army. Won't happen again."

"See that it doesn't," Ethan said as he walked me to the door. "You'll get through this, my friend."

"Not sure I want to," I told him honestly as I left.

Never had I uttered a statement so true.

***

I sat bolt upright in my bed that still smelled of Raquel and slammed my hands over my ears. My body had healed in the time I'd slept. The ringing inside my head was gone, but a new one replaced it. The warning alarms

71

in the compound blasted shrilly. It felt as if I'd only slept for a minute, but a quick glance at my watch proved me wrong. I'd slept for five hours. It was late afternoon and something was very wrong. Yanking on my clothes and grabbing my sword and knives, I raced from my suite toward the strategy room.

In the hallways, I passed dozens of armed Vamps headed to the first floor. It was utter chaos.

"What the fuck is going on?" I asked several as we sped along the hallway.

"We don't know yet, sir," one yelled from behind me.

"I heard we're being attacked by Trolls," another shouted.

Fuck.

***

Ethan watched the screens that monitored the grounds of the compound closely as several of our top generals gathered what troops we had in the ballroom. The strategy room was as high tech as they came. The walls were covered in screens that showed every inch of the thousand-acre compound. Astrid held Samuel and examined the monitors over Ethan's shoulder. The Baby Demons floated around her head and chattered with excitement. Martha and Jane, two old, profane, and offensive Vamps Astrid had unwittingly allowed to be changed over when she found them dying, flanked her and stared at the pending drama with beady eyes. Everyone made room for me as I approached.

"Trolls?" I asked as I sat down and put on an earpiece.

"At least ten," Ethan said as he closed his eyes and mentally communicated the information to the generals in the ballroom.

"Do we know what they want?" I asked tersely.

"They want Samuel and the one who dies," he answered.

"That makes no sense," I muttered as I tried to make out the background noise coming over the headset.

"What kind of idiots are they?" Astrid demanded as her hair began to blow around her head—a sure sign of an impending shit storm. "We're all dead. We're Vampyres, for fuck's sake."

"Fuck cake," Sammy yelled and clapped his hands.

"No, baby, I said fuck's sake," Astrid corrected her son. "Oh my Hell," she shouted. "I said Buck's rake... Buck's rake. Do you understand? Not fuck cake... which doesn't even make any sense. Buck's rake. Got it?"

"Yep, crazy potty word Mommy. Me understand." Sammy grinned like a loon and gave his mortified mother a wet raspberry on her cheek.

Martha handed Astrid a roll of duct tape and she promptly put a large piece over her lips.

"Did the contingent already leave for Europe to go to the Summit?" I asked Ethan.

"Yes, four hours ago," he said in a clipped tone.

I thanked God Raquel had left to go home. The thought of her being in danger made me sick. My love for her outweighed my hatred. I never wanted to see her again, but I needed to know she was safe.

"Jesus Christ, I picked a bad day to deplete our army," I muttered with self-loathing.

"Actually, you may have done us a favor," Ethan said as he studied the screens with laser focus. "Most of them have completely healed and I held thirty back from the Summit as backups. We have more fighters here because you had a smackdown on them."

"Should I say you're welcome?" I asked.

"No, you shouldn't," he shot back.

"My liege," a large and deadly Vamp named Bennett quickly bowed to Ethan and me. "The Trolls have surrounded the compound. We were wrong on the numbers. Venus cloaked herself and went out among them. She counted at least forty."

"Is she still out there?" I asked as I mentally calculated our odds against forty Trolls.

"Yes, she is, sir."

"Get her back inside," I snapped. "There is something else out there that I can't identify."

"I see nothing else out there except trolls," Ethan said.

"I can't see anything either. I hear it. Put on a headset."

Ethan and Astrid quickly put on earpieces.

"What the fuck is that?" Astrid asked as tore the tape from her mouth.

"Never heard it before," I admitted. It was eerie and unsettling—it sounding like screaming wind and it certainly didn't bode well.

"God damn it," Ethan snapped. "They're not smart enough for this."

"You recognize the noise?" I asked as I played with the volume and tried to adjust the sound in my ear.

"They brought Wraiths," Ethan spat as he threw off his headset and began to pace the room.

That stopped me dead. How did one kill a ghost?

"Oh shit," Astrid yelled. "You mean to tell me there's another motherhumpincowballsackofshitasswhacking species I've never heard of? What the Hell is a Wraith?"

"A bad poopy nasty ghost that be mad," Sammy volunteered and then popped his thumb in his mouth.

"How do you know this?" Astrid asked him with an alarmed expression.

"From me dreams," he explained as he rolled his eyes and giggled.

"Wraiths have entered your dreams?" I asked as I snatched the child from his mother's arms. "Sammy, you cannot let them into your dreams. Ever. They can take you. If anything or anyone tries to take you somewhere in your dreams, you scream and say no. Do you understand me?"

My tone was harsh and his eyes grew huge, but this was some serious shit.

"Wraiths can dream walk?" Ethan was puzzled. "Only sentient beings can dream walk. Wraiths have no corporeal body and only take on the feelings of those that have summoned them."

"I've about had it with new species coming up every other Tuesday—especially those that are trying to take my son in his dreams," Astrid muttered as she took Sammy back and held onto him tight.

"Daddy and Mommy are poopoo silly crazy. Ghosts no walk in my dreams," Samuel squealed. "Sammy go walking in all sorts of people's dreams."

Well, that certainly shut everyone up.

I stared. Samuel was a Dream Walker? They were as rare as they come and a clusterfuck waiting to happen. In my two hundred years, I had never come across a Dream Walker. Most tended to believe they didn't exist. Dream Walkers were few and far between, coveted and hunted. You could start world wars and topple governments by Dream Walking—not to mention you could get information that could destroy an entire species.

"Have you walked in any of the Trolls' dreams that are here today?" I asked carefully. If he had, we had to kill them all. Word of Samuel's power could not get out. Hell forbid if it already had.

"Yep," he announced proudly. "Me walk in Tommy's dream. He a bad, bad Troll. He want me to come and play, but me say no and run."

"I'm gonna hurl," Astrid choked out.

"Vamps can't puke," Martha reminded her and patted her on the back. "Can't fart either, but those fucking Baby

Demons have some anal acoustics that could make you wanna tear your nose off your face."

The Baby Demons, Abe, Beyoncé, Rachel and Ross flipped through the air and slapped each other high fives while shrieking with glee.

"Not to worry though… if you rip your honker off your head it grows back," Jane added as she swatted at a dive-bombing Ross. "I've ripped mine off twice hoping it would come back smaller. I'd swear on my dead ass Uncle Joe, the fucker came back bigger."

"Martha and Jane," Astrid said in a calm voice that made my hair stand up and the Baby Demons freeze in midair.

"Yes?" they answered in unison.

"If you speak again, I will shove your heads up the Baby Demons' asses and feed them beans and Brussel sprouts for a year."

They took the duct tape and quickly put large pieces over own their mouths.

"The Trolls have to die," I said as the door of the strategy room burst open.

It was Venus. A warrior and as vicious as she was beautiful. Black as night with a force that few could handle. She was one of Astrid's closest friends and I was lucky to call her friend as well.

"There are forty. To kill them you need to pierce the left side of their necks and go clean through with a sword," she said wearily as she took a seat and ran her hands through her wild hair.

"And you know this how?" Ethan asked as he checked his sword.

"Let's just say there used to be forty-two," Venus said with a wicked gleam in her eye. "I did a little experiment and it was successful."

"Magic won't work?" I asked.

"Nope, tried it." She shook her head and popped open a bottle of blood. "But the Trolls aren't the main problem. There are at least a hundred Wraiths and no one can kill a Wraith."

"I can," said a hauntingly familiar voice from the doorway.

God damn it, she was supposed to be gone. My gut clenched and my fury made my eyes go green. I whipped my head to Raquel and she took a step back. There was no way in Hell I would allow her to be part of this. She needed to stay alive—gone and alive.

"No," I snapped. "You will not be involved with this. I forbid it."

"I didn't get the memo about you being the boss of me," Raquel said flippantly as she sauntered into the room.

"Check your mail. I laid claim to you two hundred years ago. You're just too much of a coward to step up to your life," I said as I walked toward her and backed her up against the wall.

"Stand down," Jean Paul growled at me as he drew a knife.

"I wouldn't do that if I were you," I said softly to Jean Paul as I kept my eyes trained on Raquel's. "It would be a shame to lose a good warrior before the fight even begins."

No one moved and no one spoke. The silence was charged. I knew every eye in the room was glued to my back and I didn't give a shit.

"Back off, Jean Paul," Raquel told him as she stared daggers at me. "He won't hurt me."

"No one can hurt you, Princess," I said as I placed my hands on either side of her, effectively caging her in. "Your outer shell is so hard it's impossible to break. God knows I've tried."

Her scent and her eyes trapped me more than my arms trapped her. Her lips were a breath away from mine. My fangs descended and my cock stiffened painfully.

Maybe it was time to take the decision out of her hands and make it for her.

She placed her hands on either side of my face and slowly pulled my mouth to hers. The feeling of being home shot through me and my need for her burned so intensely I forgot we had company.

"Ummm… while this is all kinds of awesome, we have a Troll and a motherfucking Wraith problem at the moment. Maybe you guys can work this out a bit later," Astrid chimed in gleefully.

"Oh my God," Raquel mumbled as her cheeks blazed red.

"This is not over," I whispered as I ran my thumb over her swollen mouth. "I'm taking this out of your hands. We clear?"

She nodded quickly and slipped from my embrace.

"I'm the only one that can banish the Wraiths," she said as she regained her composure. "I would never ask anyone I cared for not to be who they are, or to forgo using their power to save the ones they love."

"Ohhhhhh snap," Astrid shouted as she danced around the room. "Guess she busted your ass, Heathcliff."

I nodded absently at my certifiable cousin and kept my gaze on Raquel. Was I one of the ones she loved?

"It's one of my gifts," she said.

"It's almost sundown," Ethan said tightly to his sister. "You're no good to me."

She was flanked by her guards who looked ready to do battle. The only one who was unhappy was Jean Paul. He was positively furious.

"I can last through the fight if I have the blood of three Master Vampyres," she said evenly and stared hard at her brother.

"It might be helpful to know what happens to you at sundown as we will all be counting on you," I said in what

I considered a reasonable tone. Apparently I was the only one who thought I was reasonable.

"Get off her ass," Astrid grunted as the others nodded their agreement. "She's got some whopper super uper duper mother humper of a secret, but if she can suck the ghosts back into Ghostville, I'm good with cryptic right now. You can get the goods on her when you get into her pants later."

Ethan made a guttural noise of disgust and pinched the bridge of his nose. He then sighed and shook his head… resigned. He couldn't possibly be considering her offer. Ethan stared at the ceiling for a long moment and then shrugged.

"Today must be my lucky fucking day," Ethan muttered, barely hanging on to his composure, "because we happen to have three Master Vampyres in the room. Astrid and Heathcliff, roll up your sleeves. Raquel needs to feed." He rolled up his own and approached his sister. "Are you sure about this?" he asked as he took her face in his hands.

"Do we really have any other choice?" Raquel asked as she took his wrist. "Let me be good for something."

"This really is completely fucked up," Astrid informed the room as she rolled up her sleeve and offered up her wrist. "After Heathcliff finds out your secret identity or that you're really a man or something more frightening than that, I get to be let in on the secret too or else I'll go gangster on your ass. Sound fair?"

"Perfectly," Raquel said as she bit back a small grin.

"Heathcliff, start reciting baseball stats in your head and bring your sorry fighting ass over here. We're going to feed your mate so she can obliterate a hundred invisible evil asscankers."

"I'm not his… " Raquel started.

"Enough of that shit," Astrid snapped. "I'm right and you're wrong." She got in front of Ethan and shoved her wrist in Raquel's face. "One Master Vampyre coming up."

Raquel glared at her. It was clear she wanted to clear up any misconceptions, but Astrid was having none of it. Her hair was flying all over the place and she was starting to glow. Even Raquel knew better than to screw with a pissed off Astrid.

"Bite me and then go kill the fuckers. Now."

"As you wish," Raquel muttered before she bit down.

I stood next to Ethan and watched as I waited my turn.

It was one of the hardest things I'd done in my very long life. However, it was not my place to question my Prince or defy him. My duty was to him and my people.

"I don't want you to do this," I told Raquel as my fists clenched at my sides.

"I know," she replied quietly. "But it's what I do. It's what must be done."

I closed my eyes and willed myself not to grab her and run—to take her to a safe place where no harm would come to her, but it wasn't my right or my privilege.

Not yet.

Chapter 8

I went last. As she took my blood, Raquel refused to make eye contact. The pleasure and the pain of what she was doing almost undid me. My fangs descended and the moment became so personal and sexual all in the room looked away. This was more damaging to me than the fight with the thirty Vamps I'd indulged in earlier, but it was part of what needed to be done if we were all to see tomorrow.

She finished and stumbled back. Jean Paul caught her. Her skin took on an iridescent glow and she'd never been more glorious. I realized in that second that Raquel wasn't just an ordinary Vampyre who needed my protection. She was a deadly force of nature—a ruler of an empire and not someone to be fucked with. It gave me some solace, but my irrational need to shield her would not disappear.

"The timing of the attack is interesting," Raquel said as she rolled her neck and shuddered with the sheer amount of power she now held within her body.

"Why do you say that?" Ethan asked as he armed himself with several more long swords. "Bennett," he instructed, "have the men and women get rid of their daggers and strap on swords. Short blades are useless with the Trolls."

"Yes, Sire." He bowed and left the room.

"It's at the same time as the Summit and your troops being depleted. What did the Trolls ask for?" Raquel inquired as she slid a katana into a holster on her back.

"Samuel and the one who dies," Astrid replied as she hooked several grenades to her belt. "They're stupid motherfuckers. We're already dead."

"They want me," Raquel said simply.

Ethan froze and the rest of the occupants of the room looked around in confusion.

"Why do you say that?" I demanded in frustration, staring at the Vampyre I loved.

Raquel exchanged a look with her brother and turned back to me. "I am the one who dies. I am the one they want."

"What the fuck does that mean? Tell me."

"I can't," she said.

"You won't," I shot back.

"She can and she will, but not now. Not here," Ethan said. "There is no time for debate."

"Correct," Raquel said, avoiding my stare. "It's odd that the Trolls would know."

"There is no way they could have the information without someone betraying you," Ethan said angrily. "Who knows?"

"Our brothers and sisters, our father, Pam, and Jean Paul," she told him.

My eyes immediately narrowed on Jean Paul. The bodyguard took several steps back, but held his head high. I stepped forward to kill him but stopped as Ethan held up his hand.

"I would rather die than betray my Princess," he said levelly. "It was not me."

"Bastard's telling the truth," Martha said as she ripped the tape from her mouth.

"And how would you know that?" I demanded in a tone that made the old Vampyre cower.

"It's the damnedest fucking thing," she croaked out. "Since I've become a bloodsucker, I can tell when people are lying."

"She can and it sucks ass," Jane volunteered. "I can't cheat at cards anymore or give her the wrong change or have sex with her boyfriend or… "

"Oh my Hell," Astrid snapped. "First of all, you two are asexual. I refuse to picture either of you getting it on with anything. And second, if this is a joke you are both going to die violently today."

"No joke," Jane said truthfully. "It's real and it sucks donkey balls."

"True that," Martha added, holding up her right hand.

"Fine," Ethan said. "But I have no idea who it could be. This makes no sense."

"While it would be helpful to know what the fuck you are discussing, I beg to differ about not knowing which family member could have revealed a secret," I said tightly as I watched the realization hit. Raquel's mystery was killing me, but she clearly didn't want me to know. This ate at me viciously, but it was what it was.

"No freakin' way," Astrid shouted as sparks flew wildly from her fingertips. "I am going to kill her this time. She is screwing with my child. Of course it would be lovely to know what she blabbered to the Trolls, but I'll leave that for her to tell me when I torture her ass."

"Juliet?" Ethan asked as he paled even further and shook with fury.

"It has to be," Raquel added with ire that made her skin sparkle.

Juliet was the half-sister of Ethan, Raquel, *and* Astrid-- complicated and bizarre, but what in our world wasn't? Astrid and Juliet shared the same mother. Raquel, Ethan and Juliet shared the same father. Bottom line, Ethan and Raquel were blood related. Astrid and Ethan were not.

Juliet had been the one who had changed Astrid into a Vampyre against her will. It was a fucked up plan of their mother's to take over the world. But it had failed. However, Juliet had gotten away and now it appeared she was back with more deadly trouble. No matter. Her time in this world was getting short, if I had anything to do with it.

"The Trolls aren't intelligent enough to summon Wraiths. She knows I can send them back to Hell so she came at sundown."

"Samuel I get, but why does she want you?" Ethan asked as he scanned the monitors again and studied a map of the grounds.

"Of course she wants Samuel because he's a True Immortal. From me? She wants my blood—all of it," Raquel stated pragmatically. "She can only summon Wraiths. She would need to drain me to take my power so that she could banish them."

"Juliet is so fucked up... and so fucking dead," Astrid muttered as she handed Samuel to Martha and Jane. "Take him to the Panic Room and lock the door. No swearing. You open it for no one except me or Ethan. Take the Baby Demons too. They'll kill anything you can't. Do not under any circumstances let Sammy nap. He can't go walking in anyone's dreams right now—too fucking dangerous. If we don't come back to you by morning, have the Baby Demons summon my Uncle Satan. He'll know what to do."

Both Ethan and Astrid went to their son and hugged him tightly. My throat knotted with anger that they had to leave him.

"He's a Dream Walker?" Raquel asked, shocked. "Impossible."

"Not impossible," Astrid said wearily. "He's a full-on, out of control, magical nightmare."

"Yay me!" Samuel yelled as he pumped his little fists in the air.

"Yep baby, yay you," Astrid said as she hugged and kissed him again. "You be a good boy and I'll get you a present when this clusterhump is over. Okay?"

"Another baboon for Blobbityflonk to play with?" he asked with wide eyes and a grin.

"Ummm... sure," Astrid mumbled.

Ethan's gasp of shock made me smile despite the impending shit show we were about to walk into. I caught Raquel's eyes and she giggled. For a moment I pretended what had passed between us hadn't happened, but she turned away quickly and reality came roaring back.

"If we're going to do this we need to go now. My Princess has limited time," Jean Paul said.

"Until what?" I inquired coldly. "Until she has to go and destroy a few more lives elsewhere?"

"Stop," Ethan commanded harshly. "Leave the personal out. No room for distraction. If we all come out of this alive, then we will have a sit down. Am I understood?"

"Yes," I said respectfully. He was correct. Loss of focus would be deadly.

"The Trolls aren't moving," Astrid said as she studied the monitor. "Why are they all just standing on the perimeter?"

"Because they're inherently cowards," Venus said as she stepped forward and took Astrid's hand in hers. "They will wait for the Wraiths to weaken us and then attack."

"She's correct," Raquel said in a brisk, business-like tone. "Each time a Wraith goes through you it will drain some of your power. Everyone needs to keep moving constantly. It's difficult for them to attack a moving target."

"I'll communicate that to the generals," Venus said as she raced from the room.

Ethan closed his eyes and telepathically sent a directive that went to every Vampyre in the compound as he also spoke his thoughts aloud.

"We will go out in three groups. We will exit the compound from all sides since we are surrounded. We will enter the battle in units separated by five-minute intervals. It's best we don't show all our troops at once. The second group will cloak themselves and try to get behind the Trolls so we can take them from both sides. The Wraiths are clustered to the north. Raquel, you will take the exit through the sunroom. Heathcliff and Jean Paul will go with you along with Astrid and me. Raquel will have to stand still to banish them, so make sure we are all moving targets around her to distract them," Ethan instructed.

"God damn it, we're sending her out there to die," I ground out through clenched teeth as I held on to my sanity by a thread.

"We may all be walking out there to die," Ethan stated calmly. "Raquel is our only chance of eliminating the Wraiths. I don't know about you, but I prefer to go out fighting."

"That's my hot, sexy Vampyre," Astrid said with a wide grin as she patted her grenades and checked her sword. "I'm ready to go kill some fugly bastards and rip an unwanted sibling from limb to limb."

"You're hot when you're bloodthirsty," Ethan said as her laid a kiss on his mate that should have been done in private.

"I know. Right?" Astrid giggled and grabbed his ass.

"If anyone gets their hands on Juliet, it would be best to take her alive," Raquel said tersely. "I have quite a few questions for her."

"As do I," Astrid said, going from giggly to deadly on a dime.

"How long do you have, Raquel? Sundown is in about thirty minutes," Ethan said to his sister.

"Then I should have about forty-five minutes to an hour, give or take," she replied.

"Is that enough time?" I demanded, still not understanding what she was up against.

"It will have to be, now won't it?" she said cryptically.

Again I was tempted beyond reason to snatch her up and lock her in the Panic Room with Samuel and the others, but it was a dream that would not come true—similar to all my dreams where Raquel was concerned. I shook off my dread and glanced around the room. Aside from my father and my sister, it was filled with the people I loved most. If we were going down, we were going down together. I couldn't let my worry keep me from being effective.

"Okay. Are we ready?" I asked in a clipped tone. My warrior side had at last taken over. I was now ready for the fight and I had no plans to lose.

"Yes," Ethan said. "We are."

"Then let's go have some fun," I said as I led the way out of the room.

***

The rolling hills around the compound were eerily quiet. Ten foot high Trolls stood as still as statues peppering the hills menacingly while the Wraiths looked like a swarm of bloody bees in the distance. They hovered around a lone figure with wild blonde hair and piercing red eyes.

"Son of a bitch," Astrid swore. "It *is* her."

Juliet's arms were raised and her fangs were bared. She appeared to be deranged and ready to snap. She was clearly controlling the Wraiths. They moaned and screamed impatiently as they floated around her in a frenzy.

"I'd say it's nice to see you," Juliet yelled. "But it's not." Her laugh pierced the air and the wailing of the ghosts increased to deafening levels.

"Jesus Christ, she's a fucking nut bucket," Astrid hissed.

"She always was," Raquel said as she watched her sister with disgust. "She used to steal my clothes and then burn them after she was done wearing them."

"What the Hell?" Astrid griped. "I hear you. The hag stole my really expensive nail polish. She's going down."

"Because she took your nail polish?" Ethan asked, completely confused.

I had to admit I was a bit confused too.

"No," Astrid snapped. "Because she's still trying to take what isn't hers. She can't have my baby... or my damn sister-in-law. They're mine," she yelled as she started to glow.

"Got it," I said as I put a calming hand on her shoulder. It would be a clusterfuck if Astrid started blowing up the hillside. It wouldn't kill the Trolls or the Wraiths and it would make our job much more dangerous than it already was.

"Heathcliff, you will talk to her. She'll be more volatile and less reasonable with her blood relatives," Ethan instructed under his breath.

"You're kidding yourself if you think Juliet's going to be reasonable with anyone," Raquel muttered. "She's completely lost her shit. Look at her."

I had to agree with Raquel, but Ethan made a good point. She didn't know me like she knew her family. I was an unknown to her. It might throw her.

"What do you want?" I shouted up the hill as I stepped forward, making sure I'd blocked Raquel from her sightline.

"And who are you?" she demanded shrilly. "You're very pretty. Maybe we can spare you."

Raquel's hiss of furious jealousy behind me was music to my ears, but the insanity in front of me was my focus.

"My name is not of importance and looks can be deceiving. Are you here to negotiate or are your terms as we have heard?"

"I really like you," she bellowed with a grunt of animalistic pleasure. She ran her hands over her body and cupped herself between her legs. It was all I could do not to turn away in disgust. Pissing her off right off the bat would not bode well.

"Terms?" I shouted again, knowing she had none. However, treating her like a sane equal might help.

"No terms," she shrieked. "No negotiations. I want the baby and I want my sister. Now—or else everyone dies… and I still get my sister and the baby."

The Trolls watched the insane woman with narrowed eyes. Were they a joined enemy or were we dealing with two separate factions?

"No can do, Juliet," Astrid shot back. "You don't look like the motherly type and Raquel thinks you're an assjacket."

"Love what you've done with your hair," Juliet snarled. "The red streaks make you look like a whore."

"What the fuck?" Astrid stomped her foot and the ground beneath us shook. "How many different immortal whackjobs can call me a whore? I mean, I have plenty of faults, but loose morals are not one of them. I'm sorry guys, but I have to kill her."

"Fine by me," Raquel hissed.

"Not yet," I said calmly. "Let her make her move. We don't know if she's controlling the Trolls too. If we keep her talking there's more of a chance of taking the Trolls from behind."

"Mother humper," Astrid complained. "I hate it when you make sense."

"Getting bored up here," Juliet screamed and began to pace in tight erratic circles. "Get the baby. I want the baby.

And send that bitch Raquel up the hill before the sun goes down. I'm hungry."

The Trolls were grumbling and examining Juliet with detached hatred. Were they with her or against her? It really didn't matter in the end because they definitely didn't like us either.

"How many Wraiths have you sent back to Hell at one time?" Ethan muttered to his sister as we all watched the deadly ghosts shimmer and shriek.

"Ten."

"I will pretend I didn't hear that," I ground out as my stomach lurched. "That might have been a good fucking question to ask while we were still in the planning stages."

"I'm your best bet for getting out of here alive," Raquel snapped. "Ten or a hundred—what does it matter? If I fail, we die. If I try, we might not."

She was correct but I was furious. I had no ability to help her or save her. It didn't sit well with me and it went against everything I knew as a warrior.

"Fine," I growled. "What do you need? How can I help you?"

"I need them to come closer. They need to be within twenty feet for me to banish them."

"Not a problem," Astrid informed us. "Watch this… Hey, you skanky douchebag," she shouted at Juliet. "You're not getting anything except a visa to the bowels of Hell. You're stupid and shortsighted and you look like you've gained about ten pounds. Your ass is huge."

The shriek from the hill was insanity personified. Juliet was coming unhinged and the Trolls began to tremble with rage.

"I will kill you, you bitch," she screamed at Astrid. "You're a worthless nothing. I should have eaten you when you were born."

"Now that's just fucking gross," Astrid said and then laughed, which sent Juliet into a psychotic break.

"Enough," one of the enormous Trolls bellowed.

Trees bent and snapped at the root from the sheer volume of his voice. The Wraiths shot up into the air and tore at each other in confusion.

"The woman is not in control here. We are. We will kill her for you, if you give us the child. We don't care about the one who dies. She means nothing to us. We have come for the child. He is our Savior. We will not harm him."

"Shut your ugly mouth, you filthy beast," Juliet screeched. "The baby is mine and so are the rest of them. We have a deal and you will abide by it."

"The baby is ours," the Troll bellowed as smoke and fire blew from his nose. "You only get the one who dies… or you will die—violently."

"You stupid fucks," Juliet roared. "The Wraiths can kill you too. You watch what you say or it will be your bloodbath."

I shook my head as I listened. Clearly a thin thread connected our foes. This was interesting.

"Since when did people start showing up and thinking I would hand my child over?" Astrid demanded.

"I'm afraid this is just the beginning," Ethan said angrily.

"Well, they're smoking crack if they think this will be easy. And what in the Hell is Sammy supposed to save the Trolls from? Being butt ass fugly?" Astrid snapped. "I can't believe I'm going to say this, but we might be safer if we lived in Hell. Satan would never put up with this bullshit."

"And neither will I," Ethan said.

"Astrid, shoot her with magic like you shot me in the ass. Piss her off enough to release the Wraiths. If the Troll kills her first, there's no telling what the Wraiths will do," I directed urgently.

"My fucking pleasure," Astrid said with delight. "You ready, Raquel?"

Raquel grabbed my arm and turned me to face her. She reached up and pulled my face to hers. With no wasted movement, she kissed me like it was the last time she would ever do so and let me briefly into her mind. Her desire, love, and need for me almost sent me to my knees. "If we don't make it out of here, I needed to do that. If we do, this will go down as one of the most awkward moves I've ever made," she said as she pushed me away.

"Awkward works for me," I muttered as I licked my lips to savor her taste.

"Guys," Astrid cut in. "We gotta kill some shit now. You with me?"

"Yep. Zap her ass," Raquel hissed.

And Astrid did.

Then all Hell broke loose.

Chapter 9

"*Move,*" I shouted as the Wraiths expanded grotesquely and started their descent down the hill straight toward us.

"Distract them from Raquel," I commanded as we began to sprint around her with Vampyre speed.

Astrid's electrical strike did exactly as we planned. In her pain and deranged fury, Juliet released the Wraiths and the battle exploded.

The roar of the Trolls shook the entire valley and they began to charge like freight trains from the bowels of Hell. The cries of the Wraiths reached ear-splitting decibels and some of the Vamps in my sightline fell to the ground in agony.

"Move. Keep moving," I bellowed at Jean Paul as the wind around us picked up and made staying on our feet difficult. Ethan and Astrid ran forward with swords drawn to counter the attacking Trolls as they barreled toward us. Thankfully, Unit Two had gotten behind the beasts and were wreaking havoc and confusion.

Raquel stood frozen to her spot with her arms raised above her head and began to chant in an ancient language that was both melodic and macabre. Her red hair whipped wildly in the wind and her eyes rolled back in her head.

Gold and peach gusts of glitter burst from her open palms and her body swayed violently.

The Wraiths flew at us en masse as if they knew Raquel was their target. That left the rest of the Vamps free to attack the Trolls, but a hundred Wraiths to three Vampyres was looking pretty grim at the moment. Death was on our heels.

Glancing quickly to my left as I sprinted around Raquel. I saw Astrid. She was lit up like a fucking inferno and plunging her sword through the neck of a Troll. Ethan was faring just as well, so I turned my attention back to the ghostly specters trying to invade our bodies.

"Merde," Jean Paul gasped out. "So fucking cold."

He was correct. As the Wraiths ripped through our bodies, it felt as if our veins turned to ice. Generally speaking, Vampyres were impervious to temperature, but the ghosts carried a blistering wind with them that shot through us like frozen daggers. Jean Paul was slowing down, clearly affected by the frigid temperatures. I was barely able to make out the battle beyond as the Wraiths cocooned us in a deadly blood red haze of light.

From a distance, they had looked like a swarm of bees. Up close was another story. Dead eyes and gaunt faces with papery skin and open wounds raced around and dove through our bodies. The nearly transparent specters screamed and moaned as they flew in circles with no goal other than to create as much pain as they were in themselves. I repeatedly fought the urge to fall or slow down. I'd been run through several times by the Wraiths and was surprised to see open cuts on my body where they had entered and exited. How in the fuck did a spirit rip skin?

Amidst the chaos, Raquel's chant grew louder and more intense. Her body convulsed with the unearthly rhythm. Her words controlled her more than she dominated them. The golden glow around her burned brighter. I prayed to all the entities I could think of to keep her safe.

"Jean Paul," I shouted. "Don't fucking stop."

"Never," he growled as he pushed his bleeding body far beyond its limit.

Then she screamed. The shriek that left Raquel's body was filled with so much rage, pain and power it stopped me in my tracks. The ground around us split open and tendrils of blazing fire reached out and began incinerating the Wraiths one by one.

Raquel's body lurched forward and she fell to her knees in the middle of the flames, but she continued to chant through the billowing smoke and fire. Seizures wracked her slim frame and the Wraiths fought wildly to invade her and end her magic. She was torn and bleeding, but she forged on.

In a fit of fury and panic, I threw my body over hers and took the brunt of the attack as the fire continued to dance its deadly tango with the ghosts. Raquel's voice stayed strong though I was positive she had no firm grasp on reality at that point. Instead she was lost in her spell and nothing could pull her out.

She rolled out from under me and rose shakily to her feet. Blood poured from open jagged cuts all over her body. "No more," she screamed and waved her hands in a circular motion. "Be gone."

The fire roared and exploded into colorful flames as it choked the life out of the remaining Wraiths. I was thrown at least ten feet back and immediately began to fight my way back to her.

Raquel had collapsed by then and lay lifeless on the ground. The shrieks of the Wraiths as they were sucked into oblivion were something I knew I would never forget for the rest of my eternity. Nightmares couldn't begin to touch this shit.

"Get her," Jean Paul begged as he tried to stem the blood flow from his head. "She's dying. Have to get her out of here."

I crawled to her prone form and shook her gently. There was no time to lay there. Trolls were everywhere and I had no clue who was winning. Her skin still glowed a golden peachy color, but there was something very wrong. Her body stiffened in rigor mortis and her eyes opened sightlessly and stared into nothingness. What the fuck was happening?

"What's wrong with her?" I shouted above the din of the battle as I shook her harder. Her frame was like an unbendable board and my head felt like it was going to explode.

"She's dead," Jean Paul hissed as he yanked her stiff body from my arms and began to run to the compound with her.

In my confusion I let him take her…

However, without her body in my arms I snapped out of my shock. Jean Paul had taken what was mine and it was unacceptable. I took a running start and flew through the air at a speed he could only hope for. I dropped to the ground in front of them and tackled him violently.

Raquel's dead body fell to the ground as my fists connected with Jean Paul's face.

"Stop," he pleaded wildly. "Let me take her inside. There is still danger out here."

He was desperate and attempted to crawl back to her.

"She will turn to ash within the hour," I growled like an insane animal. "You will bring her to my suite and lay her on my bed. Her ashes are mine. Do you understand me?" I hissed as I punctuated my instructions with a right hook that dislodged his jaw. "She is mine."

"You don't under… "

"Do not defy me," I shouted in a voice I barely recognized. "She's my mate. Her ashes are mine. You will do as I say or I will kill you with my bare hands right now."

I wanted to crawl out of my skin. This could not be happening. Jean Paul tried to speak again and I moved in to kill him. He shook his head in frustration as he glanced at the bloody war closing in on us and gave up.

"As you wish," he grunted as he picked her up and sprinted to the compound.

The roar of agony that left my body was wrenched from my soul, blurring my vision. I felt the heat of the still burning fire and heard the screams from the battle that raged around me.

I had nothing left to live for. My purpose for life had just died before my eyes and the need to destroy consumed me.

I pulled my sword from its sheath and went back into the fray without any concern for my safety. The only thing driving me now was revenge. The Wraiths were gone. They took the life of my mate and I would avenge her death by finding Juliet and killing her.

For the next hour, I killed without remorse as I searched the area for Juliet. I had no clue who I fought beside and I didn't care. As claws ripped through my skin, I simply went forward, piercing the necks of Trolls and shoving their dead bodies out of my way. I vaguely heard my name called, but the roar in my ears made hearing clearly impossible.

I hadn't found my target and I wouldn't stop until I had completed my mission.

Death meant nothing unless it stopped me from my goal.

"Heathcliff," Ethan bellowed as he tackled me to the ground. "It's over. The Wraiths are gone. The Trolls have retreated."

His words made no sense and I tried to fight him off. The Trolls meant nothing to me. I wanted Juliet. I needed to rip her head from her body and then burn her to ash.

"Get off of me," I demanded as I fought him like a wild animal. "I'm not done."

"We *are* done," he hissed as he trapped me in a spell of magic that felt like my body was burning from the inside out. "Get control of yourself. Now."

I fell to the ground in agony and he released some of the spell he had cast. Rolling on the ground to try and put out the fire that consumed my insides did nothing.

"Stop. I will listen," I gasped.

With a wave of his hand the burning ebbed and I sat up weakly.

"Juliet," I ground out through clenched teeth. "I have to find her."

"We already have her," Ethan said tersely as he squatted down beside me. "She's been chained and locked in the interrogation room."

I stood unsteadily and began to walk toward the compound. "She's mine," I said. "Her head is mine."

"No, her head is mine," Astrid cut in.

She was battered and bleeding and sparks flew from her body like fireworks.

"She is the reason my mate is dead," I shouted. "Her head is mine."

I didn't care if Astrid blew me to smithereens. Juliet's head belonged to me and I would have it unless someone killed me before I got to her.

"Raquel is not dead," Ethan said quietly as he put his hand on my arm.

"I held her. She's *dead*," I shot back viciously as I shook him off. "Give me the respect of avenging my mate. You can destroy me for defying you after I do what I have to do. Just give me that."

"She is not dead," he insisted as he touched me again. "Hear me before you do something that will force me to end you."

"I don't care if you end me. I held her. I saw her. She's dead. Ending me will be a favor."

"What the fuck is happening here?" Astrid demanded. "I am so confused."

"Give me an hour," Ethan said. "I have a story for you. If, after the story you still want to defy me and force me to kill you, I shall grant you your wish."

"Do I get to hear this story?" Astrid demanded as the light show around her amped up dangerously.

"Yes, my love, you do," he said to his mate as he stared at me and waited.

"You can have an hour," I told him coldly, knowing very little could dissuade me from the path I'd chosen.

"Come with me," he said as he walked back toward the compound.

I would give him an hour. No more. No less.

Chapter 10

Astrid had insisted on choosing my attire, which was why I was in low riding sweats and no shirt. My wounds had healed in the hours I sat waiting.

Juliet was still alive and being interrogated by Ethan and Astrid as I sat in my suite and waited. Each minute ticked by with excruciating slowness.

I'd been invited to participate in the questioning but declined. I knew they would handle the situation in the way it should be handled.

My conversation with Jean Paul had included an apology, which was something I did not give to anyone often. However, it was the right thing to do in this instance and I did it regardless of the hit to my pride.

I also made several important phone calls and now felt at peace for the first time in ages.

As I impatiently marked time until sunrise, I thought back on my very long existence and it seemed like a mere blip in time. The moment my life would start would soon arrive. Like any birth or rebirth it would come with some pain, but it would be worth it. Hopefully, there wouldn't be much blood or broken furniture.

Raquel stirred on the bed as the sun rose. If I had any breath to take I would be holding it. Slowly her eyes opened and she peered around the room in alarm.

"Where am I?" she muttered as she glanced around wildly.

"Right where you're supposed to be," I said sternly as I rose from my darkened corner and approached her.

Raquel watched me like an animal watches a predator and backed away until we stood on either side of my bed. Her gaze fell from mine and she stared nervously at the rumpled bedding.

"Did Ethan tell you?"

"Yes. He did."

"Now you know why, now you understand," she whispered sadly.

"No, actually I don't," I replied.

Her eyes shot to mine and she shook her head in confusion.

"I die, Heathcliff. I die every night and don't live again until sunrise," she spat angrily. "What's not to get? I'm like a Vampyre from a fiction novel. I'm not worthy of anyone. I'm a liability to my race—to you. I may as well have a coffin and a black cape."

"That's an interesting take but I have to disagree. Although you do look hot in black," I said calmly as I rounded the end of the bed and backed her up to the wall.

I gave her some room, but not enough to run. She was going nowhere this time.

"You've lost it," she said as she looked around for an escape route.

"Nope, I do believe I've finally found it."

"Found what?"

"The last wall I have to break," I answered. "I told you before…you're mine."

"I'm no one's," Raquel insisted weakly as she closed her eyes and clenched her fists at her sides. "I will not risk doing this to you. You could end up dying every night or just simply dying."

"Or we could both live out our immortality together—happily."

"There are no guarantees about how the story will end," she insisted. "I'm a freak. There is no explanation for me. There is no telling what could happen to you."

"Tell me why you die every night."

Her chin dropped to her chest and her shoulders sagged forward. "It's a spell—a punishment I suppose. All I know is that I'm cursed. It was cast by someone shortly after I was turned."

"Who?"

"Ahh, there's the conundrum," she spat with hopelessness and fury. "I don't know. No one knows."

"Can it be broken?" I asked, not caring either way.

I would take Raquel any way I could get her. If I died at night with her, it would be a small price to pay. And if we died for real, we would still be together. Win—win.

"Some believe if I mate the spell will be broken," she admitted cautiously. "And some believe if I mate, the spell will kill my mate and myself. No one knows… and I can't take that chance with you. I won't."

"Look at me."

"No," she said as she squeezed her eyes shut even tighter. "I can't."

"Fine," I replied lightly and closed the distance between us. The relief of touching her almost undid me.

I pressed my lips to her ear and breathed in her scent. "You are my mate. You will mate with me," I whispered.

Her body shuddered with desire and I ran my tongue along her delicate jaw.

"Did you not hear anything I just said?" she demanded as she tried to push me away. "I have denied you for hundreds of years because I'm wildly, insanely in love with you. Nothing you can do or say will change my mind."

"Again, I have to disagree," I said as a smile pulled at the corner of my lips.

"Oh my God," she hissed as she tried to bite back her inappropriate grin. "This is not funny. At all."

She pushed against me again. I grabbed her wrists and wound them around my neck. We were nose to nose and our lips were a breath apart.

"Kiss me," I begged gruffly. "If you don't, I'll lose it."

"I'll kiss you, but if you bite me, I will beat your ass," she said as her eyes turned from silver-blue to green.

"Do it. I dare you."

"You suck," she whispered as she bit back a giggle.

"I've been known to," I agreed with a grin and a shrug as I leaned in even closer.

And she kissed me.

My head spun and my need for her intensified to proportions I'd never known. Her lips were soft and her taste intoxicating. While I wanted nothing more than to throw her on the bed and lose myself in her body, we still had a few more things to get straight.

I pulled away, but stayed close enough that escape wasn't an option.

"I have lived half a life for hundreds of years," I told her. Her lips opened to argue and I gently put my finger over them. "I no longer want half a life. It's the same as no life at all."

"That was kind of brave," she said with a smirk.

"My words?"

"Nope, putting your finger over my mouth so close to my teeth. I could have bitten it clean off."

"I'll remember that in the future," I said with a grin. "Raquel, I don't care if you die every night. I don't care if I die every night. I don't care if this kills both of us because we'll be together—in Heaven or in Hell. I just don't give a fuck as long as I'm with you."

"It's not your call," she said as tears pooled in her eyes. "It's mine."

"No, it's *ours*. In your quest to save me, you've almost destroyed me. A mate will eventually go insane without their other half. Death would be kinder. I already feel the pull toward madness. Is that what you want for me? For you?"

"No," she whispered so softly I had to lean in.

"Missed that, Red," I said with a raised brow as I tucked a strand of hair behind her ear.

"I said no, but wouldn't you have done the same?" she demanded harshly as her eyes rose defiantly to mine.

That stopped me. Would I have done the same thing? Possibly.

"A little space here?" she inquired.

"Will you run?" I asked.

"No. I won't. Not this time," she promised.

I gave her the space to think as I walked back to the other side of the room. Arguments raced around in my brain. I would not lose. I couldn't lose.

"I don't know what I would have done," I answered honestly, even though I didn't want to. "I might have tried your method for a while, but if it came to this—this moment, right here right now—I would give myself to you."

She made a noise of disbelief. "You're too noble. You would do the same thing I'm doing."

"Look at me," I ground out. "You think you're broken? You have no clue what broken is until you walk in my shoes. I have chased you for two hundred years. I can't stop. Now that I know what the problem is, I will never stop. If you won't mate with me today, I will chase you to the ends of the world and wear you down until you do. I mean it when I say my life is no longer worth living without you. If we only have today as mates, then this will be the best goddamned day of my life. To hold you and know you are truly and willingly mine will complete me in ways you can't begin to understand."

"I'd rather see you alive and whole." Her body trembled and tears streamed down her beautiful face.

"I'd rather be broken and happy."

She watched me with wonder. "You really mean that, don't you?"

"Never meant anything more in my life."

"Your father. Your sister," she said with hesitation.

"I have spoken with them… and your father. They've all given their blessings," I told her.

"They've given their blessings for you to possibly die?" she asked as she shook her head angrily.

"They've given their blessings for us to find happiness. With each other—as fate has destined. Even if it's only for a day."

The silence was charged with her emotions. In her indecision, she let down her walls and I was able to enter her thoughts. Flashes of my face ran through her mind wildly. Her love for me was so evident it was difficult to watch. Her years of tears and pain matched my own. I pulled her into my mind. My gift was reading thoughts. I was capable of sending thoughts as well. My words were not enough—maybe my memories would be.

"Watch," I said quietly. "See me."

She closed her eyes, dropped to the bed and rocked like a child as I let her into my head and my soul.

Thousands of scenarios of us together, and me alone and pining for her, entered her mind. The depths of my feeling and need for her blasted into her head as tears poured from both of us. My loneliness and hopelessness invaded her and her own shot back at me. My worry at her seeing every corner of my mind was outweighed by my need to make her believe me.

"See me, Raquel. Please see me," I said quietly as I knelt on the floor next to her and took her in my arms. "I have nothing without you."

Her body softened and her crying subsided to sniffles. "I have nothing without you either," she whispered.

"Mate with me. Be mine," I said.

Her pause felt like a knife in my gut. Her eyes searched mine and I stared back steadily, willing her to give me the answer I wanted.

"Yes," she said as she buried her face in my chest. "Yes, Heathcliff, I will mate with you."

Chapter 11

We both sat in silent shock for a few moments as we watched each other carefully.

"My instinct is to bite you really fast in case you change your mind," I said as I held her tightly to my body.

"You're smooshing me," she said with a giggle.

"Sorry," I muttered, relaxing my hold but not letting her go. "Kind of excited here."

"Will it hurt?" she asked as she traced my dimples with her finger.

"No clue," I answered with a grin. "Never done it before."

She straddled my legs and pressed her forehead to mine.

"I love you, Heathcliff. I still don't know if this is the right thing to do. I'm scared, but I have never wanted anything more in my life."

"Do you think after we're mated we'll be able to stop throwing shit at each other?" I asked as I tangled my fingers in her hair.

"Oh my God." She laughed. "I'm being serious here."

"Me too," I said with a smirk. "I feel happier and more free than I've ever felt in my very long life. This is the right thing to do. Scary? Yes. Scary enough to stop me? Absolutely not. Come what may. I want you more than I want to go on alone. You ready?"

"Ummm... yes. I think. Oh shit, this is terrifying," she said as she let her head drop back on her shoulders.

I lifted her up and laid her on the bed. I settled in next to her and pulled her close. "Think about it this way. I'm scared every time I go into battle. Do I show it? No. Do I feel it? Yes. If I didn't feel trepidation, it would mean I'd gotten careless or didn't care at all. Nothing in our world worth having should be easy to get. It should be worth dying for. You are worth dying for. With everything I am, I mean that."

"You're worth dying for too," she said. She took my face in her hands and kissed me—opening up to me like she never had before. It was glorious and humbling. I knew we had only scratched the surface of being one.

"This is the beginning of our love story. Whether we are on this plane or some other, I will love and worship you for eternity."

"Back at you, sexy pants. Let's do it."

Her laugh went all through me and my grin practically split my face.

"I thought you'd never ask," I said as my fangs descended and every muscle I had tightened to the point of pain.

We slowly leaned into each other's necks and bit down. The explosive feeling that rocked my entire being was unlike anything I'd ever known. It went straight to my cock and the orgasm was mind blowing. Her blood ran sweet down my throat and her body writhed in a sensual dance against mine.

In a frenzy, we tore the clothes from our bodies. It was inhuman and sexier than Hell. There was no way to be close enough. Her moans of desire made my head spin.

Her curves felt like Heaven beneath my hands. I ran my open mouth from her neck to her breast and licked and sucked until she was a whimpering mess underneath me. It took everything I had not to plunge into her body immediately. I intended to worship every inch before I pounded into her.

"Oh my God," she screamed. "I need you."

"You've got me," I hissed through clenched teeth as my fingers found her wet channel and the heel of my palm pressed down on her throbbing clit. "You have all of me."

"Make love to me," she begged. Her hips met the thrusts of my hand and she cried out in pleasure as an orgasm ripped violently through her body. "I need more."

I positioned myself between her legs with Vampyre speed. My cock ached and the tingling in my spine dictated my actions. Slow was impossible. I needed her like I needed blood to live.

"I love you," I growled as I entered her body, not stopping until I was fully seated inside her.

I paused for only a brief second to enjoy the feeling of her tight body wrapped around my cock, but the look of lust and love in her eyes set me off. She was mine—body, mind and soul. Finally.

"Mine," I shouted as I slammed into her body at a speed that would have destroyed a human. She met me with wild abandon, thrust for thrust, and her fingernails raked down my back, tightening my balls to the point of agony.

"I love you. I love you," she muttered over and over as our bodies melded together.

I couldn't figure where she stopped and I began, but I didn't care. I wanted everything she had to give.

I knew I was close, but I needed her to go over with me. I reached down between her legs as I pistoned into her like a wild man. I squeezed her clit between two fingers and she detonated under my touch. Her scream set me off, and I came so hard colors ripped across my vision as I roared my release. Her body clamped around my cock and contracted with the aftershocks of an orgasm that almost killed both of us for real dead.

As I floated back to Earth, I heard happy sigh. I was finally home.

"Best day of my life," I muttered as I pulled her close and my cock hardened with desire for her again.

"I want more," she whispered against my chest. "I still want more."

"Nothing would give me greater pleasure," I said as I took her lips in a kiss that made us both moan with need. "I can go all day."

"Me too." She giggled and she nipped at my bottom lip.

And we did.

And it was insane.

***

"Are we still alive?" she asked tiredly as she stretched her sore body in such a way that my extremely overused cock hardened again.

"Not sure. Don't care," I said with a chuckle as I traced the smooth contours of her hip with my finger.

"How many times did we do it?" she asked.

"Twenty? Thirty?" I answered as I pressed my hardness against her.

"Oh my God," she moaned with a grin as she took me in her hand and stroked me. "You're an animal."

"A very happy animal."

Her hand left my cock and travelled lightly up my body. She ran her finger across my bottom lip and she worried her own with her teeth.

"Don't think," I whispered. I pulled her swollen lip from her teeth and kissed her.

"I can't help it. It's almost sundown," she said as she shuddered and cuddled closer to me. "Aren't you scared?"

I thought for a moment, and realized I wasn't—not at all. I was complete and whatever the night held in store for us, I would embrace it gratefully. I finally had the love of my life at my side as my mate. Nothing had made more sense than what we had shared today. Nothing.

"No, I'm not," I told her. "Whatever happens, we'll be together. It's all I've ever wanted."

"I don't deserve you," she said softly.

"Actually you do," I said. "And I deserve you."

"I'm still going to throw stuff," she mumbled.

"God, I hope so." I laughed. "I'd miss that."

"You're truly crazy." She snickered and nipped my lip. "And I love you. Always."

"Back at you, sexy ass."

She rolled her eyes and shook her head. Her wild red curls fell into her face. "What should we do?"

"We'll hold each other close and simply wait to see what fate has in store for us," I said, wrapping her in my embrace and tucking her hair gently behind her ear.

"Fate can be a bitch," Raquel murmured as she held me tight.

"True, but she usually has a plan. Tonight I choose to trust her."

As the sun dipped lower onto the horizon I held the love of my life close to my chest. She trembled and I felt the dampness of her tears, but also the magnitude of her love. Tomorrow would be a new day. I had no clue where we would be, but as long as we were together it was good for me.

"I love you," I whispered with my lips against her forehead.

"I love you too," she whispered. "I'm afraid to close my eyes."

"I'm right here. Whatever is going to happen will happen whether we get some rest or not."

"Will you close your eyes?" she asked as she gripped my body tightly.

"Maybe."

Finally her eyes fluttered shut and she rested in my arms. She didn't fall into death, but it was still twilight outside. Trying to figure out what was going to happen was futile so I closed my eyes and let my mind wander into oblivion. My mate's Heavenly scent was in my nose and on my skin. Her body was wrapped around mine. It was absolute perfection. There was no place else I'd rather be.

***

An ominous darkness surrounded me and a feeling of unease skittered up my spine. I reached out quickly and felt Raquel, soft and alive, still by my side. We'd made it through the night and neither of us had died. The curse was broken and we would live to tell the story—or so I hoped.

The sense of relief was overwhelming, but my body stayed tense and alert. Where in the Hell were we? We were no longer lying on my bed, but instead on the cold, hard ground of some place unfamiliar. I grabbed my mate and pulled her close.

As my eyes adjusted to the dim surroundings, I felt Raquel grasp my arm.

"We're alive?" she questioned frantically.

We'd gone to bed naked and now we were naked in a dark cavern. Raquel waved her hand and dressed us in black fatigues and combat boots. Balls flapping in the wind was not the optimal choice in an unknown situation. I grinned at her color choice. We matched our surroundings—we blended right in to the darkness. Her magic constantly surprised me.

"Feels like we're alive," I answered quietly. "We're together at least, so it works for me."

"Oh my God," she whimpered softly. "I didn't hurt you. We're alive and we didn't die last night. You're still here with me."

She ran her delicate hands over my face and body, making sure I was real. Tracing my lips with her fingers and cupping my cheeks in her hands, Raquel murmured and wept silently. I did the same and thanked every deity I could think of for sparing us.

"We're both here and as alive and well as two undead people can be," I teased, trying to lighten the mood. However, I held her tight to my body. "The question of the hour is, where is *here*?"

"I don't know. What is this place?" she asked as she looked around the stark, dank area we had some how ended up in.

"I have no fucking idea," I told her truthfully. "I suppose there's only one way to find out. You ready to rumble?" I stood and held my hand out to her.

She took my hand and gave it a squeeze. "Yes, my mate. I believe I am ready for just about anything."

"That's good," I told her with a grin, "because our story starts now. Let's go kick its ass."

A soft giggle escaped her lips. With a light punch to my arm, Raquel took my hand in hers and we started our journey.

With careful steps, watchful eyes, and faith in each other, we walked slowly into the darkness—together.

Just the way fate had intended. Problem was… fate could be a bitch.

Chapter 12

.As we made our way out of the small cavern we awoke in, I took in the morbid atmosphere of our unknown location. The walls were covered in bones and skulls. It was pitch black, but being a Vampyre I could see the macabre décor clearly. The dead were stacked atop each other rather artistically —not full bodies, but pieces. They were meticulously piled from floor to ceiling. It was as strangely beautiful as it was disturbing. The scent of death permeated the air, but it was not recent. These bones had resided in their grim museum for centuries. Raquel held tight to my hand and pulled me along.

"Slow down," I urged as she began to pick up speed.

We were treading on a burial ground of epic proportions. I was sure someone or something might not be pleased.

"I know where we are," she whispered with excitement as she increased her pace.

"Would you like to let me in on the secret?" I inquired as I lengthened my stride and moved next to her.

"Under Paris. In the Catacombs," she told me as we took a right into a narrow passage.

How did we end up in Paris when only hours ago we were in Kentucky?

I shook my head. At least we weren't in the bowels of Hell. However, Hell might have been a bit more pleasant than the megatomb we were in.

"Well, this is certainly a surprise. I thought this was a tourist attraction of sorts," I said.

I cautiously moved my large frame along the corridor wall careful not to topple the morbid pyramids of the dead.

"Not this part," Raquel explained as she quickly made her way past several ornate monuments dedicated to the thousands of deceased piled up down here. "The humans don't know of this part. It got cut off from the other tunnels hundreds of years ago and basically forgotten."

Raquel took a sharp left into an even smaller hallway. My girl was fast and clearly on a mission. Ducking my head to avoid a hanging femur, I followed her wondering what exactly we were going to find at the end of our sprint through the enormous grave.

"Is it bad luck to touch anything down here?" I asked as I realized how many lifeless body parts I'd come into contact with.

"Only if you're an empath," she informed me as she swiftly breezed through the passages touching nothing.

"Nope, not an emapth, thank God," I muttered as I came face to face with a skull that had clearly been killed by a blow to the head. "That must have hurt."

"You're hurt?" Raquel asked, alarmed as she stopped mid-stride and looked back.

"Um, no. I was just chatting with a… never mind. Where are we going?"

"To Gareth."

"Your brother?" I asked.

What the Hell was Gareth doing in the Catacombs and why were we going to meet him?

"It has to be him," she insisted as she began to move again.

It was a lovely view, watching my mate's ass sway in her tight black pants as I followed, but this whole situation wasn't working for me. I needed a little more info before I plunged head first into Satan only knew what. I just got my mate. I had no plans of losing her because I wasn't prepared.

"Raquel. Stop," I said as I grabbed her arm and halted her forward progress. "A little more information would be handy."

"Oh crap," she mumbled and blushed. "You're right. I'm sorry."

She bit down on her bottom lip and shook her head causing her curls to bounce. My instinct was to tangle my fingers in her hair and bite that lip myself. However, with all the hollow dead eyes watching, I figured I'd wait for a less dismal backdrop to ravage my mate.

"This isn't exactly the place I'd have taken you on a honeymoon," I said with a wry grin.

"God, I certainly hope not," Raquel said with a shudder and a giggle.

"Explain."

"Gareth and I found this place shortly after we were turned. It was a safe haven to talk and not be heard."

"Heard by whom?" I asked curious.

All eleven of the royal children had been turned into Vampyres over five hundred years ago. It was by their choice and they'd been turned by their father—the King of the Vampyres. After a disastrous and deadly experiment of trying to turn his favorite and most beloved wife, the King discovered that a woman could not be turned after childbirth. Sadly, this information wasn't widely known amongst Vampyres and my mother died in the same process.

The King had many wives as was common and expected of royalty in that time. Heirs were imperative and the King was and is a good man. The practice of royal polygamy was abolished soon thereafter as Vampyres had true mates and couldn't breed.

Each of the royal children ruled a territory except for Juliet. She had been thought dead for centuries and wasn't awarded a territory. Unfortunately, she had been alive and well and wreaking havoc all over the place. Thankfully, she was now chained and locked in the interrogation room at The Cressida House in Kentucky.

"Demons," Raquel clarified. "They were everywhere for about fifty years after we were turned. Gareth and I found this place. We can always call each other here. Actually, Gareth can call all of us. It's his gift."

"All of you?" I asked trying to follow her train of thought.

"All of my siblings. Gareth can call us and bring us to him."

As if that answer sufficiently answered my question, Raquel turned to resume her trek.

"Whoa," I said as I caught up and took her delicate hand in mine. "I'll keep moving as long as you keep talking."

"Right," she said as we stopped short in front of a cavernous hole. "Do you want to fly down or jump?"

"What do you suggest?" I asked with raised brows and a smirk.

"Ummm… maybe we should float down. Can you do that? You're awfully young," she reminded me of our age difference with a grin.

My beautiful mate had about three hundred years on me. I took her face in my hands and chuckled. "I always forget you're older. I suppose that makes you a Vampyre cougar."

"I suppose it does," she replied coyly. "But back to my original inquiry… can you float, little mister?"

"First of all, *nothing* about me is little and does the Pope wear red shoes?" I asked insulted that she'd doubt my skills.

"Well, the old one did," she muttered, trying not to giggle.

"Damn it." I ran my hands through my hair and chuckled. "I have to keep up on my religious pop culture. Fine. Does he still wear a pointy hat?"

"On special occasions," she informed me with an eye roll.

"I like it when you're my friend," I said, tracing her full lips with my thumb.

"I'm much more than your friend." She smiled and nipped at my finger.

"Yes. You are. And you always will be. As to the preposterous question concerning my ability to float, I shall ignore it and pretend you think I am capable of anything. Clear?"

"Yep."

She gave me a sexy little salute that made my pants tighten. Holy Hell, not even the gruesome surroundings quelled my desire for the crazy gorgeous woman who was finally my mate.

"What's at the bottom of this pit we're about to drift into?" I asked as I glanced down.

The bottom was undetectable. Surely, not a good sign.

"Hopefully my brother," she answered gravely.

"Could it be someone else?" I asked as I scanned the area.

"Gareth and I are the only ones who come here and he's the only one with the power to call me to him," she said as she, too cased the room surrounding us.

"And he does this for fun?" I queried.

"Nope, he's only done it once in the last hundred years. The Demons were wreaking havoc in his territory in Asia and he needed a hand in getting rid of them," she explained with a cocky little shrug.

"Let's hope it's something as easy as that," I replied, taking her hand and began our descent into the gaping black hole.

"You know, it's probably going to be something shitty."

"With our track record, I'd have to agree," I concurred. "However, I'm good with just about anything as long as we're together."

"Anything?" She gazed at me with disbelief.

"Anything," I assured her.

Raquel squeezed my hand and my stomach tightened with a sick dread I couldn't name. I hoped to Hell and back I wouldn't have to eat my last statement.

But somehow I knew I would.

I just didn't know how yet.

Chapter 13

We dropped slowly about three hundred feet into the bowels of the earth, but the ambience was much the same as the nightmare above. With as much death as I'd dealt with in my centuries as a Vampyre, the massive crypt we were traipsing through made me uneasy.

"Where is he?" I asked as I watched Raquel pause and glance around with uncertainty.

"It's odd." She frowned and sniffed the air. "I can't find his scent."

I'd had the pleasure of meeting Gareth on many occasions over the years. He was an arrogant ass and I enjoyed his irreverence tremendously. He was also an outstanding warrior and I'd had the good fortune of sparring with him. I too tried to find his scent to no avail. Was he even here?

"Would he call you as a joke?" I asked tightly as my anger began to rise.

Raquel and I should have been locked in a room having mind blowing sex, not answering a Vampyre sibling prank call in a vault of death.

"No, definitely not. He values his body parts too much to be that stupid," she answered. She closed her eyes and concentrated. "He's here. I know he's here."

I opened my mind and let it wander. One of my gifts was reading minds. If Gareth was close by, maybe I could pick up his thoughts. He was, I did… and it wasn't pretty.

"To the right," I said tersely.

Raquel opened her eyes and stared at me. "You found him?"

"I found *someone*," I told her cautiously. It was possibly Gareth, but if it was him he'd changed dramatically.

"What the Hell do you mean?" she asked nervously.

"I'm not sure. Follow me and stay behind me," I instructed.

With a huff and a hiss, Raquel punched me in the shoulder. "I'm as powerful as you are," she insisted. "We walk side-by-side."

"While that may be true," I conceded. "I'm still a macho cavedude. I just mated with the love of my life, whom I've chased for hundreds of years. It would do wonders for my peace of mind if you would walk behind me."

She glared at me and I grinned. Even pissed off she was hotter than Hell. I could literally see her brain working as she tried to win our impasse. Then her eyes lit up and it was all I could do not to slam her against the wall and take her.

"What do I get if I do?" she asked as a smile pulled at her beautiful lips.

"What do you want?" I asked curious at what she would choose.

There was very little if anything I wouldn't do for her and I wondered if she was aware of that fact.

"I want to be on top," she informed me with a sexy glint in her eyes and her hands on her shapely hips. "And I get to boss you in the bedroom for an entire evening."

"How about this," I countered. "You can boss me in the bedroom for a week straight and every Tuesday for the rest of eternity if you walk behind me."

"Really?" She clapped her hands together with delight and danced in a circle.

It was a no brainer and a win—win. Watching her naked and atop me was a fantasy of mine. As long as I ended up buried to the hilt inside her body I didn't give a shit who was in charge.

"Really," I promised. "Now get that hot little ass behind me before you force me to spank it and let's find your brother."

"Yes, sir," she purred suggestively and dramatically lowered her gaze with a snort.

"What was that?" I asked as she continued to giggle.

"I was being submissive." She burst into full blown laughter. "Don't you want me to go all Fifty Shades of Mated Vampyre for you?"

"Sweet Jesus, did you read that book too?" I asked as I pinched the bridge of my nose and groaned. My gal was anything but submissive, and I liked it just fine—actually I loved it. She was a freaking animal in bed.

"You read it?" she demanded shocked.

"I most certainly did not," I huffed.

"But you said *too*," she accused. "As in you *read* it."

"Astrid read it and unfortunately, I got a play-by-play synopsis of the damned thing," I said with a sad shake of my head. "Those are hours of my life I will never be able to get back."

She laughed and threw her arms around me.

"So I take it you read it?" I inquired.

She nodded and winked. "I did. It reminded me of *Twilight* except they screwed all the time."

"You know it was based on *Twilight* fan fiction," I told her.

She gaped at me.

"What?"

"You read *Twilight*?"

"Absolutely not," I snapped. "Astrid did."

"I'm starting to think Astrid is a convenient excuse for you to hide your metrosexual reading tendencies."

"My metrosexual reading tendencies strictly pertain to the classics, not fiction where Vampyres sparkle in the sun," I informed her flatly.

"Come on. I thought that part was really funny," she said. "I especially liked that they drank animal blood and hated werewolves."

"Have you ever tried animal blood?" I asked her.

"Hell no. Have you?"

"On a dare from Astrid after she read the damn book. We both did," I replied sheepishly.

"And?"

"It was bland and quite gross. However, Astrid heaved for several hours after our stunt, which made the entire unsavory business worth it."

Raquel's laughter made my heart sing. The thought of making her happy for eternity made me feel ten feet tall.

"I love you," I told her.

Her laughter disappeared and her eyes glowed green with desire.

"I've loved you for so long I don't remember what it was like not to love you," she admitted and pressed her body to mine.

The feelings that rushed through me were so much more than sexual. I was whole with her in my arms. Never had I let myself imagine how perfect it would be to have her truly be mine.

"Has Astrid ever watched *Love at First Bite* or *Buffy*?" she asked with an evil snort.

"No and please don't suggest either," I begged.

I'd seen *Love at First Bite* and *Buffy the Vampire Slayer*. My sister, Cathy thought they were hilarious. We drank shots of vodka for every time a set of fangs popped out. Those were some of the very few times I'd tied one on as a Vampyre.

"How about once we find my brother and kick his ass for bringing us here, we watch every cheesy Vampyre movie ever made," she suggested with wide and excited eyes.

She looked like a child on Christmas morning. I wanted to laugh and kiss her senseless. "What do I get if I take part in this mind numbing activity with you?"

"Ummm… what do you want?" she asked with a lopsided grin.

"Actually, I have everything I've ever wanted, but… "

"But what?"

She stood up on her toes and tried to go nose to nose with me. This of course was impossible due to our height difference so I lifted her up to aid her in her quest. With her breasts mashed against my chest and my erection making me slightly dizzy, I forgot what we were talking about. The only thought in my brain was to get her naked.

"But what?" she repeated, enjoying my lust addled confusion.

"What was the question again?"

"You are such a guy." She groaned and nipped at my lips.

"And that's a problem?" I asked as I ground the evidence of my guy-ness into her girl-ness.

"Not a problem at all. When the blood returns to your brain you can set your terms. But right now we need to find Gareth," she said as she pressed her lips to mine and slid back to the ground.

She was correct and for the life of me I still couldn't figure out what the question had been. Honestly, I didn't give a fuck. Holding her and knowing she was mine trumped pretty much anything at the moment.

"I'll get back to you on terms and you will get behind me," I told her as I adjusted my pants and started moving toward where I sensed Gareth.

"Yes, sir... *master*," she quipped with another snort and a quick grab of my ass.

"Hands to yourself, Red... or we're going to have hot monkey sex in a tomb," I warned.

"Promises, promises," she muttered as she pushed me along.

I silently willed my dick to behave. It wouldn't endear me to her brother if I was jack-knifed over because of a raging erection for his sister.

No. Wouldn't do at all.

Chapter 14

I was correct. I'd sensed Gareth.

But he wasn't the same man I remembered—not by a long shot.

"Well, well, well, it's about time, sister o'mine. It was getting quite boring down here with only the rats to converse with," Gareth quipped weakly with a confidence that belied his haggard appearance. His accent was unique—British tinged with a bit of Russian.

He was heavily chained with silver and trapped in a filthy cage warded by very dark magic. The enchantment held Raquel and me about a foot back from the bars and sizzled with menace.

I hadn't seen Gareth in approximately a decade—mere minutes in Vampyre time, but I didn't remember him looking anything like he did now. He'd been a striking man and stood at least six foot four. However, he appeared to have shrunk… and aged.

How was that possible? We were immortal for God's sake. We stopped aging around thirty.

He looked at least forty-five. His jet black hair was laced with grey. His blue eyes were dull with a world weariness and his face was gaunt. This was not the vibrant, arrogant asshole I'd spent many violently pleasurable hours with, but at least his personality still seemed intact.

I stared at Gareth in shock. His pained laugh knocked me back into stark reality.

"Raquel dear, I haven't been laid in a month. I think my balls may have shrunk back up into my stomach which is not helpful to my reputation. Heathcliff my man, good to see you. As you can see, I'm in a bit of a bind here and was hoping you could help me out. All bad puns intended."

Raquel paled as she took in the horrific sight of her brother. Her slim hand covered her mouth and tears ran down her cheeks. "What happened to you?" she whispered in a strangled voice.

"Good question. I may have fucked the wrong gal," he mused with a smile on his lips that didn't come close to reaching his eyes.

"Stop it," she hissed and tried to approach the bars of the cage.

Her attempt to get closer was in vain. The magic hissed and turned a vicious and sparkling blood red. It curled into the shape of large hands and threw her back. I caught her in my arms and held her firmly. There was no way in Hell she was doing that again. Whoever had warded the cell was determined to keep Gareth inside and all others away. The magic was powerful and as black as they came.

"Who put you here?" I asked as I kept a solid hold on Raquel in case she tried again.

Gareth observed my grip on his sister with great interest. With a raised eyebrow and a smirk, he chuckled. "As to your question—I have no fucking idea who put me here. But I have a question for you... Is there something the two of you would like to share?"

"Heathcliff and I are mated," Raquel said as she stared at her brother.

He was silent and watched her strangely. "You're serious?" he asked as he attempted to stand.

His chains weighed him down and he fell to the floor with a sickening thud. I felt Raquel's gasp in the pit of my stomach. My instinct was to lash out at him. Did he too think I wasn't good enough for his sister? The simple fact that his pride was suffering blows more painful than any words I could throw at him was the only thing that held me back.

He crawled to the edge of the cage and tried to reach for his sister. The spell zapped him and his weak form was blasted back to the corner of his prison.

"Gareth," Raquel screamed.

Blood poured from a wound above his eyebrow and he quickly put up a hand to halt any idea she had of trying to approach him.

"Stay," he commanded. "Don't come near me."

"You're dying," she whispered brokenly. "You're aging and dying."

"Yes, well that sucks for me, doesn't it?" he replied wearily. "I am happy for you, beloved sister of mine—and for you, Heathcliff. I am forever in your debt for saving her and loving her."

"I've always loved her," I told the man whose intentions I'd misunderstood.

"Yes, well, you didn't give up. You broke the curse. My sister is something of a conundrum with a conscience. Quite frustrating if you ask me."

"No one asked you," she snapped.

"Touché," he shot back with a smile.

"I didn't kill him," she told her brother. "And he didn't care if I did. He loves me."

"Then he's just as crazy as you are little sister. You two should be very happy together," Gareth said as he mopped at the blood pouring down his face.

"How long have you been down here?" I asked as I assessed the area for cameras or any other recording equipment. It was clean.

"A month—a day. I don't know. Somehow I lost track of time. My brain is muddled," he said and then shook his head in confusion.

A Vampyre of his age could go a long time without drinking blood, but in his compromised state this was clearly not the case—even a day was too long in his condition. The silver chains alone had stolen much of his power and strength.

Gareth needed to feed, but getting it to him was an issue.

"You need blood," I said tersely.

"And a hooker if you happen to have one of those in your pocket," he added.

"The manwhore game is unattractive and beneath you," Raquel informed him angrily. "You're dying and aging. Someone did this to you and I highly doubt it was a flighty paramour."

"You are both correct on all of your observations," he said staring off into space. "I've tried to put the puzzle of my latest predicament together yet I've come up empty."

"Enemies?" I scanned the cage for any weakness and found none.

"Too many to count," he replied with a hollow laugh.

"Where were you right before this happened?" I asked as I rolled up my sleeve and searched for the largest artery in my wrist.

"I was at a gathering with an excessively large amount of pompous undead assholes—I'm almost sure it was yesterday. Maybe I was at the Summit."

He frowned as he observed me and pulled himself to a sitting position.

"Pot, kettle, black on the asshole part," Raquel muttered as she watched my actions with curiosity. "What are you doing?"

"He needs blood and I'm going to feed him," I explained as my fangs dropped and I bit into my wrist.

"You can't go near him," she said frantically.

Her concern for my wellbeing moved me. I turned and winked at the woman who had invaded my every thought for centuries. "That is astute, my love. However, let's see if a stream of my blood can make it past the wards."

"You're hot *and* brilliant." She quickly hugged me and promptly rolled up her own sleeve.

"Certifiable is more like it," Gareth mumbled as he crawled as close as he dared to the edge of the cage.

"Been called worse, motherfucker," I replied with a grin. "Open up."

Gareth opened his chapped and torn mouth and waited. I aimed and fired. I had to work quickly. I healed as quickly as I could open my vein.

The blood made it past the enchantment but fell short of passing through the bars. Gareth stared numbly at the pool of blood just beyond his reach.

"Damn it," I hissed. "I need a better artery."

"Your neck," Raquel insisted urgently. "If I nick it instead of piercing it, it will spray longer and farther."

"And you know this, how?" I asked amused by the gory knowledge my mate possessed.

"For a while I fancied being a doctor—even went to medical school. The non-aging thing became a problem, so now I just stick to reading medical journals for fun," she explained.

"Smart *and* sexy. Damn, but I lucked out," I stated proudly.

"Dying over here," Gareth reminded us in a tone dripping with sarcasm.

"Right. I can't really see to aim well if we use my neck. How much strength do you have to move?" I asked as I hoisted Raquel up to bite me.

"Enough," he said flatly.

"I can help with the aim," Raquel said. "Get on your knees, Heathcliff. It's closer to Gareth's mouth. If I knick your artery correctly the blood should spurt about eighteen inches. On a human it would only last about thirty seconds, but we're not even remotely human."

"Medical journals?" I asked her with raised brows.

"Medical journals," she confirmed with a giggle.

"Isn't it amazing we bleed yet have no heart?" Gareth said absently as he forced himself to his knees.

"We have hearts. They just don't beat," Raquel corrected him.

"Speak for yourself," he mumbled.

"So cynical," she snapped as she let her fangs drop and prepared to bite me.

"Not all of us have been lucky enough to find our true mates," he countered softly.

"Well if you'd quit sticking your thing into everything without a pulse, you might have better luck at finding her," she accused.

"Now where's the fun in that?" Gareth parried with a smirk. "I hate to disappoint the ladies."

Raquel's laugh was muffled in my neck. I even had to chuckle at that one. Gareth's reputation with the *ladies* would be a difficult one to live down. If he ever was blessed with finding his true mate, there would be Hell to pay.

Raquel peeked over at her brother with an evil little grin. "You'll find her, Gareth. And when you do, I hope

I'm there to see it. Whoever the *lucky lady* is… she's going to kick your sorry ass."

"Would you care to lay a bet on that, sweet sister?" he challenged.

Her pause was thoughtful and her indecision was short. "Yes. Yes, I would."

"And your wager?"

"The Renoir," she stated without hesitation.

"The one hanging in the Musée d'Orsay?" he asked with a wince.

"Yep."

"That seems a little steep." He laughed and shook his head. "You drive a hard bargain."

"It's yours, isn't it?" she asked.

"Of course it is," he huffed indignantly. "Auguste gave it to me himself. It's simply on loan to the museum."

"Well, you can un-loan it when you lose," she announced grandly. "It will look wonderful in my bedroom."

"You do know I offered to turn him," Gareth let us in on a little known fact.

"And he declined?" I surmised.

"Maybe and maybe not," Gareth said evasively. He grinned at me. "Go to the Musée d'Orsay on a Tuesday and you might find your answer."

"All right, enough bragging, Gareth," Raquel chastised. "Auguste is most definitely alive and quite charming. I'll have him to tea once we deal with the shit show we've obviously fallen into."

"That's it," I said loudly.

"That's what?" she asked confused.

"I remember my terms."

Raquel grinned and Gareth looked perplexed.

"You promised Astrid you would take up swearing. I don't believe you're holding up your end of that creative and alarming bet," I announced with a sly smile.

"And how would you have this information, my mate?" she inquired suspiciously. Her sparkling eyes narrowed to slits. It reminded me of our more destructive times...

Shit. Busted.

"I may have been present during that conversation," I admitted sheepishly yet wildly turned on by her ire.

She glared in silence—clearly displeased.

"Fine," I muttered. "It wasn't my most noble moment. I was cloaked and hid my scent. I was a desperate man, my beautiful girl—anything to be near you."

"Stalker much?" Her eyes flashed and she slapped my shoulder.

God, that was hot.

"I think it was quite brilliant," Gareth chimed in. "I'll have to remember that one—very underhanded. So darling sister, let's hear a little sample."

"You're serious?" She wrinkled her nose and groaned. "It's not me. I feel silly."

"You've always been a smidge uptight. I think some inventive profanities might do you good, and God knows I could use a laugh," Gareth commented.

"I will have your head and Astrid's very soon," she muttered as she closed her eyes and searched for something rude and offensive.

She could have my *head* whenever she wanted it. Holding her and watching her squirm as she tried to fulfill her end of the obscenity dare was delightful.

"Shall I start?" Gareth offered mildly with raised brows and a half smile.

"Go ahead." Raquel threw down the gauntlet with a snort.

"Pecker jockey," he announced with pride.

"Creative swearing only—not self description," she told him.

"Good one!" he said with a pained grunt of laughter. "Your turn."

"Forgive me," she muttered to the sky.

With her eyes scrunched shut and an endearing blush high on her cheekbones she let it rip. It was as if we were ridiculous and naughty pre-pubescent teens. I was entranced by her—everything about this woman delighted me.

"Bitch sniffer, ho gobbler, ball wad, asswaffle," she shouted and then buried her head in my shoulder. "Are you idiots happy now?"

"*Ball wad?*" Gareth questioned gleefully.

"*Asswaffle?*" I added as my body shook with mirth.

"You're both *rectum buckets* and I'm done. We have more important business than to enjoy my lack of four letter word prowess," she snapped and quickly nicked my neck. "Open your damn mouth, Gareth. Incoming."

My mate was correct on all accounts. The nicked artery spurted the blood approximately eighteen to twenty inches and Gareth was adept at moving enough to catch all of it. We repeated the process several times with my neck artery and then several times with Raquel's. Gareth's color came back and he looked less haggard. However, the aging process didn't reverse—at all.

"How do you feel?" I asked him as I licked the open wound on Raquel's neck to close it.

"Stronger. My power is coming back, but my body feels strange," he revealed as he stood without a problem.

He tested the strength of the chains. Unfortunately they held him fast. The spell that trapped him screamed of

Demon origin to me. We would need a Demon to break it—or possibly a half Demon-half Vampyre.

"There was a debate," he said as he remembered more from what had happened before he ended up bound and chained. Gareth absently touched at the wounds quickly closing on his head. "The Old Guard is quite unhappy about relinquishing their funds to charity."

It had been my cousin Astrid's idea for all of the undead to share their massive fortunes with the humans and their plights. Being that she was a True Immortal of unnatural strength and basically almost impossible to kill, the Vampyres of the world had grudgingly agreed.

"Are they trying to stop it?" Raquel asked.

"You might say that," Gareth replied as he paced his cage.

"How?" I asked. "Did you go against the Old Guard?"

"I don't know how… and yes I did," he claimed. "Although I've not yet met the infamous mate of my brother, I happen to agree with Astrid's edict."

"Do you think that is why you were put here?" Raquel asked as she paced, unconsciously mimicking her brothers moves.

"Possibly," he surmised. "But removing me from the picture does very little to end the ordinance."

"He's right," I agreed. "However, we need to start somewhere. Getting you out is paramount. Something else is going on. The blood should have reversed the aging—it didn't, which leads me to believe the cage has something to do with that part of your problem. Only a Demonic spell could do something so vile."

"And your plan?" Gareth stopped his pacing and stared at me.

"Hang on for a damned second," I ground out. "I'm developing it as I pull it out of my ass."

"Well there's something to look forward to," Gareth mumbled as he ran his hands through his hair in agitation.

"Shut up," Raquel hissed at him. "Unless you have something productive to add... *zip it.*"

"We need Astrid here," I stated. "She can most likely break the spell and possibly deal with the old bastards who are having problems with the new law."

Both Gareth and Raquel stared at me like I'd grown two heads.

"What?"

"As much as I'm looking forward to meeting Ethan's foul-mouthed and charitable mate, I think your plan has many deadly holes," Gareth replied. "The Old Guard wants her head. I would assume that's why Ethan has kept her away from the Angel Summit."

"Because she's making them tithe... they want her dead?" I was surprised.

We were a selfish race, but money was something that could be replaced.

"That's only part of it," Raquel added. "Her blood relation to Satan and her very young Vampyre age has many distrustful and furious. It's one of the points I relayed to Ethan when I came to tutor Samuel. Astrid's safer staying away from the Old Guard and the Summit. The Angels take issue with her too."

"The Summit with the Angels is not going to be a peaceful little get together like you might assume given those in attendance," Gareth added.

"Do you have any other facts to back that theory up?" I inquired.

"No, it's a gut feeling," he replied. "I do think Astrid will be a major source of consternation there."

"Holy Hell, does she know any of this?" I asked already knowing the answer. If Astrid knew they were gunning for her, she would step into the fray both with gusto and engulfed in an inferno of sparkling flames.

"Ummm... no," Raquel said slowly.

"Well, she needs to know," I said as I imagined Ethan's reaction to my telling her. It would not be pretty. However, Astrid finding out after the fact could be catastrophic, which would be far worse.

"There's too much going on here to add flame to that particular fire," Gareth cut in. "I have a few Demons that owe me favors. If you can go above and get word to one, I can get out of this Hell hole and help figure out what's going down."

"Who's running the Old Guard at the moment?" I asked as a plan hatched in my head that was sure to end badly. I was fairly certain I knew who was in charge of the old sons of bitches, but it wouldn't do to be wrong. Power tended to change hands often with our race. Aside from the royal family, the factions and allegiances of the undead were in constant motion.

"Vlad," Gareth said as Raquel audibly gasped and then paled.

Watching my mate carefully I continued to question Gareth. "How'd that happen?"

Vlad had been out of favor for decades. His over-the-top violent tendencies were becoming tiresome and dangerous to the secrecy of our existence.

"Oh you know," Gareth hissed with disgust. "He impaled a few hundred of the undead and gained a following. Your mating will be a problem for him."

"What does my mating have to do with him?" I demanded.

"Shall I tell Heathcliff or will you?" Gareth asked his sister.

Raquel glanced at the floor and refused to make eye contact with me.

"Tell me what?" I asked as I took her chin in my hand and forced her gaze to meet mine.

"He wants me as his mate," she whispered. "He's knows I'm not his true mate, but he doesn't care."

"Why? For your power?" I asked as I tried to contain my irrational fury at any man thinking my mate could be his.

"And for her body. He's wanted her for centuries," Gareth supplied.

"Not gonna happen," I ground out through clenched teeth. "If he so much as looks at you, I'll behead him and then tear the rest of his body to shreds before he turns to dust."

"Remind me never to get on your bad side," Gareth shouted with a laugh. "But... in all seriousness, if you want to find out what's really happening, I'd hide the fact that you're mated. Let Vlad think he might finally have a chance... he might be useful."

"No," Raquel insisted vehemently. "I won't pretend that."

Hatred didn't quite describe the feeling I had for Gareth at the moment. The simple fact that he'd made a good point was enough to make me want to go insane. Vampyres were tricky. Fooling one as old as Vlad would be risky. I paced and tried to work off the need to peel the skin from my body or shout and obliterate the Catacombs with a blast of magic. Gareth was right. The bile that rose to my mouth prevented me from agreeing immediately, but I knew I would consent to the horrific suggestion.

"Gareth's correct," I said so softly Raquel had to lean toward me to hear.

"Oh God," she muttered, crossing her arms in rebellion against the idea. "Are we even sure it's Vlad behind everything?"

"No. We're not sure of anything," I said tightly, trying to divorce my emotional needs from the battle ahead. "All we know is that we need to be as neutral as Switzerland and proceed with caution. I'll be your… bodyguard."

The words came out of my mouth like sludge. They disgusted me. However, I refused to let her go in alone.

Raquel blanched, but then nodded unhappily. She was as aware as I was that duty came before anything else. Never had it been this difficult.

"I'll be alerting Ethan and Astrid to the developments. I would expect them to arrive shortly thereafter… I'll also be calling on Satan."

"No fucking way," Gareth choked out and gaped at me. "You'll owe him a favor."

"That will be the least of my problems," I snapped. "I plan to protect what I love and if I have to pay for it… so be it."

"Sweet Hell on Earth, pun intended—this is going to be ugly." Gareth chuckled and shook his head, but I caught the admiration for me in his gaze.

I didn't need his approval or even want it. I wanted to punch a wall with my head, but that would be somewhat counterproductive at the moment. I just wanted to get the party started and get it the Hell over with. Watching my woman pretend she wasn't mine was going to tear at my soul, but I knew the truth.

She was mine.

I was hers and she was mine for all eternity.

I just prayed it would be enough to keep me sane.

Chapter 15

Let the fireworks begin…

"You have got to be fucking kidding me," Astrid shouted. Her four inch high Prada stiletto heels clicked on the highly polished hard wood floor as she stomped around. Sparks covered the upper half of her body and shot around the room like small fiery bullets.

We had transported from the Catacombs to Raquel's main residence—an enormous villa on the outskirts of Paris. It was difficult for Raquel to leave her brother chained and caged, but in order to free him, we had to leave him. The Summit was taking place several hours from her estate. The location of the meeting was near Mont Saint-Michel in a chateau owned by the Angels.

I'd alerted Ethan and Astrid of the potential problems and they'd transported from the states immediately. They'd left Samuel behind in Kentucky with Venus and a bevy of highly trained guards. However, Venus was probably enough. She was as vicious as she was loyal. Even I was wary of pissing off Venus and I was as deadly as they came. I'd also slipped away and privately contacted Satan. I feared that the call was a tremendous mistake, but I had to start somewhere.

"We don't have all the facts," I said as I tried to calm my volatile cousin.

I was certain Raquel liked her home and Astrid was famous for blowing out walls of buildings. Ethan paced in frustrated agitation as Raquel pushed a button on her bracelet. The grand bookcase at the far side of her great room opened silently and revealed an arsenal fit for an army.

I must be all kinds of fucked in the head. The only thought in my brain when I saw it was how sexy it was my girl owned enough weapons to obliterate a small country.

"We don't have many facts at all," Ethan corrected my assessment. "Gareth is locked in the Catacombs—aging and possibly dying—and Vlad the bastard is back in charge of the Old Guard. Not a whole lot to go on."

"And don't forget they want my ass on a platter," Astrid added as she honed in on a particularly beautiful sword. "Dude, can I use this?" she asked Raquel.

"Of course you can," Raquel told her as she removed it from the wall and handed it to her. "But if we walk into the Summit so obviously armed, it might not look good."

"True," Astrid agreed as she admired the weapon with child-like glee. "But everyone knows I'm a walking fucking time bomb even without a weapon. I may as well have a little fun with the old assbags."

"God help us all," Ethan muttered as his cell phone rang.

Unworried, I watched him answer it. All of our electronics were secure. We'd developed our own networking system long ago and we guarded it closely. We waited as we heard one side of a very terse conversation. When Ethan hung up, he was frowning.

"Who was that?" Astrid demand of her mate as he ran his hands over his face and gnashed his fangs.

"My Father. Apparently Leila, Alexander and Nathan have gone missing now."

Raquel hissed her displeasure and perused the weapons with deadly intent.

"Well fuck a duck," Astrid yelled and burned a hole in a priceless rug with her wrath. "What the Hell is going on here? Wait... I know Leila is your sister. Who are Alexander and Nathan?"

"Two of our brothers," Raquel stated with steel in her voice. "If they're trapped like Gareth, then they're also aging and dying."

"Motive?" Ethan asked his sister.

"Don't know," Raquel spat and began to arm herself with smaller guns and knives that were more easily concealed. "Not really caring at the moment. I just want to find who's behind it and destroy them—permanently."

And then my dick got hard. I needed to bed my mate soon or I was going to explode.

The unending erection Raquel always caused was now killing me. If she pulled out any more weapons, I was going to jump her in public. Decency be damned.

"The timing is curious," I said as I chose a few daggers for myself. I turned my back to the group. No need to embarrass myself with my teenage dick. "I don't believe the disappearances coinciding with the Summit are a coincidence."

"Neither do I," Ethan said flatly as Raquel nodded her agreement. "I'm just unsure about what they're after... and who's after it."

"I'd say we start with the Old Guard and figure it out from there," Raquel said decisively. "Are we paying anyone for intel within the group?"

"Yes," I confirmed. "We have three or four that will talk if the price is right."

"I'll put my father on it," Ethan said as he quickly typed out a text.

"Put Pam on the Angels," I instructed. "She's one of them and they're all terrified of her."

Pam was the King's mate and Astrid's foul mouthed Guardian Angel. She was one in a million. She'd been the favorite of the King's wives all those many years ago and had been the one who'd lost her life when he'd tried to turn her. The King was devastated for centuries until she came back to him as an Angel. Of course no one would use the word *angelic* to describe Pam. She was more like an exquisitely beautiful steamroller, with the mouth of a sailor and a heart of gold.

"We have about fifty Vamps from the American Dominion here for the Summit," I said thinking out loud. "I'm going to contact our control room at the Cressida House to relay the situation and to stay alert. It's safer and more secure if we have all the intel feeding from one source," I added. "However, we still have no solid motive."

Ethan nodded and resumed texting Pam and his father.

"Ahhh, but I think we do have a motive," Astrid disagreed as she put a few grenades in her pockets. "You all just aren't paying attention to the right clues."

"Please enlighten me then, my beautiful mate," Ethan said as he tucked his phone in his pocket and waited for whatever outlandish reasoning Astrid would alarm us with.

"I read romance novels," she stated as if that was all we needed to know.

"I know. Heathcliff told me," Raquel chimed in with a giggle as she slid a particularly evil looking katana into a harness on her back. "I heard animal blood was rank."

"Tasted like butt," Astrid confirmed with a wince. "Not that I've ever tasted butt or ever will," she assured us.

Ethan was simply confused.

"What does *butt* have to do with a motive?" he asked, hanging on to his composure by a thin thread.

"Well, aside from the fact the Old Guards sound like a bunch of gaping assholes... very little," she informed him with an innocent grin.

I shook my head and grinned. My cousin loved driving her besotted mate to the brink.

"Astrid," Ethan began tightly.

"Fine," Astrid huffed. "This is like the stories with awesome ruling families in them—could be the mob or a motorcycle gang or ranchers or sexy billionaires or even Vampyres. You know, all the dudes in the stories are hotter than my Uncle Satan's underpants and all the gals are totally smokin' and brilliant."

"Does this story about your reading preferences have a point?" Ethan asked with more patience than I could have mustered up.

"Yes. Yes it does," Astrid replied.

"And were you planning on getting to the point, my love?" Ethan inquired.

My wicked cousin laughed joyfully. "Yep. I just wanted to make sure I annoyed you enough first so you would want to spank me later."

"You have succeeded beyond your hopes," he replied with a gleam in his eye that made me roll my own.

However, Raquel just laughed and gave me a sly look—which made my damn dick even harder.

"Okay, so there are bad guys and good guys," Astrid explained. "The bad guys always are coming up with stupid, douchey plans to destroy the good guys. Bad fuckers like to monologue and wear all black. Often times they have very bad breath. Occasionally they have lots of scars and tattoos, but in the motorcycle romances the good guys are all tatted up too. In fact, sometimes it's hard to tell who's good and who's bad."

"That pretty much sums up real life," Raquel muttered.

I turned to my mate. She was correct. None of us were completely good—not even close. But… when good was weighed against bad, we definitely fell on the *less* evil side.

"Make your point please," Ethan ground out.

"The bad guys wait for a chink in the good guy's armor and then they attack."

"What's our chink, my love?" Ethan queried.

"Me," she said flatly. "I'm a liability. I'm not even a full Vamp and I'm running the show to a certain degree because I'm un-killable. In their shoes, I'd want my ass on a platter too."

"Astrid has a point." Raquel nodded. My mate pulled out a laptop computer and began typing quickly.

"The old fuckers are set in their ways and don't want change. Right?" Astrid asked as she slid a few daggers into the inside of her boot.

"Correct," I affirmed. "But as you said, they can't eliminate you."

"No, but they could weaken me by destroying what's mine," Astrid countered.

"And that would be?" Ethan prompted.

"Oh my Hell," she groused. "Has anyone been listening to my romance novel analogy?"

"Um… yes?" I said trying to follow her confusing logic because I sensed there was a gem of genius coming. The painful ass-zapping session about being kind to Raquel had taught me that lesson.

"Okay *old* people, it's simple. It looks like they're eliminating the Royal Family," she announced. "If they herald me as the problem and I'm supported by the family… the family must go. Gareth is already aging and dying. Correct?"

"Yes," Raquel replied, looking up from her computer.

"Lelia, Alexander and Nathan are missing?" Astrid continued.

"Yes," I confirmed.

"Bingo," Astrid yelled and high-fived herself.

"It's possible," Ethan said thoughtfully in regard to his mate's assessment.

"Yep," Astrid said as she did a little victory dance. "It's either that or unrequited love or a love triangle or even a hidden baby that the heroine had, but the guy left and didn't know she had his baby... and then he comes back and realizes that he loves her, but she's hiding this huge fucking secret. You know, then there are all these stupid misunderstandings and they break up, but the sex is usually so hot that they end up back together."

Again we were silent.

"Did I lose you guys?" Astrid asked with a grin.

"Yes. Yes, you did," I said hoping she was done. Alarmingly, I kind of followed her bizarre logic due to her penchant of making me listen to the plots of her damn books... not that I would admit it aloud.

"Sooooo, back to the matter at hand. Were we *all* invited to the Summit?" Astrid asked as she gave Ethan an evil eyeball.

"Yes, we were," Ethan replied with a shrug. "They're gunning for you. There was no reason to bring you here." He defended his omission. "If you kill the entire Old Guard, we could have bigger problems on our hands."

"Hmmm... so little faith in me... In the future, if you like BJ's, I'd suggest you let me know when a bunch of blood sucking fart wankers want me eliminated. Clear?" Astrid smiled sweetly, but her eyes narrowed dangerously.

"Clear." He laughed and planted a kiss on her head. "Are you planning a mass elimination?"

My eyebrows shot up. It wasn't really a bad idea...

146

"Only if they force my hand. So to avoid a bloodbath, I say we show up at the Summit and prove that I'm sane and able to lead with Ethan," Astrid said. "Easy peasy."

We all went mute.

I'm fairly sure Ethan gulped. I knew I paled.

Raquel stared at the floor and I was certain I detected a snicker.

"I'm going to take your silence as a yessssssss," Astrid snapped and began to glow.

"So now we pay Gareth a visit?" Raquel suggested abruptly, changing the subject before there was an explosion.

"Yep," I said as I flashed a shiny bejeweled dagger in Astrid's face to distract her.

It worked.

"Whoever is behind this is stirring the pot," Raquel hissed. "Look at this."

She gestured in a jerky movement to her laptop.

Amazingly, Vampyres used social media—more specifically, Facebook. Hiding in plain sight had become de rigueur. Plastered on a page that any sane human would take as a joke was a headline reading, *Where is the Leader of the European Territory? What Are the Royals Hiding From Us?*

"When was that posted?" Ethan asked as he looked over his sister's shoulder.

"Today," I said as I sat down next to Raquel and scrolled for more information.

"My people know Gareth is temporarily leading in my absence. Who ever is inciting this knows Gareth has been taken," Raquel guessed with an angry hiss.

"Or they took him," Astrid cut in.

"Do your people know of your curse?" Ethan asked.

"Former curse," I reminded him.

There was no more cryptic information on Facebook. However, what was there was enough to cause problems. ·

"No, they don't know of my curse," Raquel replied with a grateful glance at me. "Only Jean Paul and our Royal family. Of course it's all moot since the curse is gone."

"That it is, my sister," Ethan said fondly.

"Alrightyroo," Astrid said with bright eyes as she clapped her hands together. "Let's go free Gareth and the rest of your family and go kick some stanky, old, fucktard, bad breathed, Vampyre ass."

"Is that how you intend to prove you're sane?" I asked with a shake of my head and a grimace.

"Yep." She grinned and flipped me the middle finger.

I grinned right back and reciprocated. Astrid was insanity personified in the best way possible—she was violent, but only when backed into a corner. She had a conscience and she cared. One would be very shortsighted not to see the whole picture of my cousin. Compassion was very powerful—far more powerful than hatred or evil.

"We ready?" Ethan asked as he strapped on a few knives.

"Yes," Raquel answered. "I believe the saying is *we were born ready*... butt munchers."

"Fucking outstanding," Astrid shouted as Ethan stood beside her looking confused and alarmed.

I simply grinned and took my girl's hand.

"You do realize you're going to have to sit through a marathon of cheesy Vampyre movies," she threatened me with a blush of embarrassment still flaming on her cheeks.

"I do," I told her. "And I'm looking forward to it."

"You're crazy," she whispered as I placed a quick kiss on her lips.

"Crazy for you."

Her eye roll and groan made me smile. Even though I was sure we were about to walk into a shit show, my heart felt light.

Love could do that to a person.

***

"Sweet baby cousin Jesus in a banana hammock, this place is fucking creepy and I've been to Hell," Astrid announced in her outdoor voice as we carefully made our way through the narrow hallways leading back to Gareth.

"Speaking of Hell, did you contact Satan?" Raquel asked me.

Ethan groaned as he stopped walking and stared at me with horror. "Please do not tell me you invited Satan to the Summit with the Angels."

My bad plan was beginning to look worse by the second. "I did," I confirmed. "However, I've asked him to bring someone who might be able to throw the Old Guard off—especially Vlad."

"Would you like to share?" he asked as he ran his hands through his hair in frustration.

"Do you trust me?" I challenged.

"With my life," Ethan said without hesitation.

"Then let it be a surprise," I shot back.

He considered me for a long moment and then curtly nodded his head.

"God," Astrid groused as she ducked to miss a dangling skull. "All you Vampyres are so fucking cryptic and secretive. Drives me nuts."

"Darling, you're a Vampyre too," Ethan reminded her.

"Yes, but lucky for you I'm also a Demon who can hopefully bust through a nasty ass spell," Astrid declared as she marched ahead ready to save the day.

"Damn, she's hot when she does that," Ethan muttered as he quickened his pace and followed his mate.

"Are *we* that obnoxious?" Raquel asked as we watched Ethan grab Astrid's rear end.

Astrid's squeal was loud and Ethan's chuckle reverberated through the tunnels.

I paused and stared at the beautiful woman I planned to spend eternity with and I grinned.

"I sure as Hell hope so," I told her.

She giggled and pulled me along. "I sure as Hell hope so too," she said.

There was nowhere else I'd rather be. Even in the dank eerie caves filled with the deceased beneath Paris, I was happy.

As long as I was with Raquel, I would always be happy.

Chapter 16

"Ethan, good to see you," Gareth boomed as he stood and smiled. "You're looking well."

"You're not," Ethan replied as he took his brother's circumstances in with a wince.

"Well, yes. I see you are still as astute as ever, jackass. I'll have you know, my balls have not retreated into my stomach and my dick hasn't shriveled up, so I consider this a win."

Astrid watched the conversation with delight. "You really are a total alpha-hole," she said with appreciation.

"Why, thank you," Gareth replied with a small bow and a smirk. "And you must be the infamous Astrid. You're a delectable sight for sore eyes."

"And she's very taken," Ethan growled as he stepped toward the cage. "Your dick better stand down if you want to keep it."

"Stop," Raquel hissed at Ethan. "The cage is warded. Don't go near him. And Gareth don't flirt with Astrid if you value your man jewels."

"*Astrid* can handle herself," Astrid informed us as she examined the enchantment surrounding Gareth's cell. "Wow, somebody hates your guts. This is one mother humpin' doozy of a spell."

"Can you break it?" I asked as I watched her size up the situation. As flighty as my cousin could be, it would be very unwise to second-guess her power.

"Shitballs," she muttered as she gently waved her hands only inches from the ward.

It jiggled and jumped as sparks of blood red crystals poured fourth and pooled on the ground. Astrid stared with dismay.

"These shitballs you speak of... are they a good thing, or a bad thing?" Gareth asked with his tongue firmly in his cheek.

Astrid considered him for a long moment and then grinned. "I think I like you," she said with a laugh. "And because I like you, and everyone else in this little Hell-hole we're calling a room—for lack of a better word—I'm not going to break this spell."

"That sounds distinctly like you don't *like* me," Gareth shot back.

Astrid shook her head and stepped back.

"You really can't help him?" Raquel asked with disappointment.

"If you guys want the entire Catacombs and possibly a good portion of Paris to cave in, then I'm your girl. This is a job for someone—and I hate to admit this—but someone with a little more finesse than I possess at present."

"You're talking Satan, aren't you?" Ethan inquired with a grimace.

"Yep," Astrid confirmed slowly. "We'll owe him though."

"Only I will owe him," I cut in. "I've already called him. He can simply add it to my tab."

"You've clearly got it very bad for my sister or you're simply insane," Gareth said. "If anyone will owe the bastard, it will be me."

"No," Raquel insisted. "I can take the brunt of responsibility."

"Absolutely not," Ethan ground out. "You're far too attractive to owe the unscrupulous son of a bitch a favor. And you're my sister, damn it."

I agreed wholeheartedly with Ethan.

"Oh for God's sake," Raquel snapped. "I'm not a helpless damsel in distress. I'm a Master fucking Vampyre."

"Good use of the word fucking," Astrid said, congratulating her. "Master *mother*fucking Vampyre would have been stronger though."

"Astrid's correct," Gareth chimed in. "Although Master motherfucking cocksucking crotch-less panty wearing Vampyre would have been more unsettling... and therefore more powerful."

We all took a brief moment to digest that one. I glared at the aging Vampyre who still had nothing but sex on his mind.

"You really need to get laid," I told Gareth with a grimace.

"Is it that obvious?" he inquired sheepishly.

"Yep, it is. And none of you will owe my dear Uncle Fucker anything. He owes me several favors and I shall call one in. Back up. This could get messy," Astrid warned.

We gave her room. An eerie silence fell over the cave as she closed her eyes and raised her hands high. A gentle breeze whipped up from out of nowhere. Raquel moved to me and I wrapped her in my arms.

Astrid chanted in a long dead language as she sparkled like a beacon. We watched in awe as my cousin swayed to an ancient rhythm that only she could hear. Ethan's tension was palpable and I understood. My memory burned with watching Raquel summon, then dispatch the wraiths. It was horrific. However, Satan adored his niece. The ramifications of Astrid summoning the Devil were far less dangerous. It wasn't without risk, but Astrid was one of the few that had Beelzebub by the balls.

"This had better be good," a familiar and ominous voice purred from the darkness. "And Astrid darling, if you insist on calling me Uncle Fucker, I'll renege on letting you hold your wedding in Hell."

"Wait. What?" Ethan shouted.

"Quiet," Astrid hissed under her breath. "I'll explain later."

That announcement was a total shocker and I held my laughter with difficulty. Raquel gave me a *what the Hell?* look and I shrugged.

Who knew what Astrid was cooking up for her nuptials? As a rule Vampyres didn't marry. Marriage was a breakable bond and mating was not. Astrid, being a very new Vampyre, still held on to human traditions and Ethan happily granted her every whim. Honestly at first I thought it foolish, but promising to love and honor the one you loved in front of family and friends didn't seem so witless to me anymore...

"So what have we here?" Satan asked as he examined the ward with distaste.

He traced small symbols in the air that materialized and shuddered as they tried to pierce the invisible wall. Satan was a huge and imposing man. His very presence changed the atmosphere in the cave from eerie to menacing.

"Well?" Astrid asked as she stepped up next to her Uncle.

"Very sloppy," he said with narrowed eyes and thin lips. "However, it's laced with something other than Demon magic. This will require three favors from you, Astrid."

"But I only have two *as you know*," Astrid informed him as she crossed her arms over her chest and glared at the King of the Underworld.

"Oh my goodness, you're correct," he said with wide innocent eyes and an evil little chuckle. "I suppose an early invitation to Christmas next year would wipe the slate clean."

"Fuck," Ethan muttered

Astrid immediately turned and punched her mate in the arm.

Satan had almost single handedly taken down Christmas at the Cressida House a few months prior. Of course, he'd had help from Mother Nature and his daughters, the Seven Deadly Sins. The kidnapping of Steve Perry, aka Journey's front man, would forever go down in history.

"If, and I mean *if*, I say yes, you are strictly forbidden to *enhance* even one decoration," she bargained.

"Not even one?" He pouted and stamped his Armani clad foot. "Where's the fun in that?"

"Not even one. There will be no kidnapping of rock stars and you can't spend the night," she ground out.

Satan considered the offer with pursed lips and a look of displeasure.

"Take it or leave it," Astrid threatened. "And just so you know, I have a little video you might be interested in… "

"Are you blackmailing me?" he shouted with delight.

"Oh my Hell," she gasped out and paled. "I think I am."

"Apples do not fall far from their trees. You're more Demon than you want to believe," Satan told her with a lopsided grin. "And I accept your kind invitation to Christmas next year."

"I'm sure I'll live to regret it," she told him with a smile and a snort.

"I'm sure you will," he agreed and turned his attention back to the cage.

"Can you do it?" Astrid asked her uncle in a hushed tone.

Satan's sigh was large and put upon. "I am going to pretend you didn't say that," he snapped. "I really don't want to have to smite your ass when I'm done here."

"Right. Sorry, Uncle Fucker... I mean, Satan," she mumbled with an evil little grin and backed away.

"Oh and Heathcliff," he added as he turned and smirked. "Astrid's payment does not negate the request you have asked of me—or your favor."

"I didn't think it did," I replied evenly. "Can you find who I requested?"

"For the love of everything evil," Satan yelled and threw his hands in the air. "What's this crap about everyone doubting me? This is not good for my ego. I'm the fucking Devil—the King on the Underworld—the most evil one of all, for shit's sake."

The walls shook and I put my hands up in defense. "I was simply assuming that this individual might not reside in Hell," I quickly explained trying to avoid a satanic tantrum.

"Oh... okay," Satan said magnanimously accepting my justification. "He doesn't normally, but he was on a field trip to see all the Nazis being water boarded in the basement of Hell. He might have accidentally missed the bus back to Heaven."

"Holy crap, you kidnapped someone else?" Astrid hissed as she marched up to the Devil and smacked him upside the head.

Everyone in the room blanched. Who in their right mind walloped Satan?

"Let's get something straight here," Satan growled. "I did *not* abduct my hero, Steve Perry. My daughters kidnapped him for me for Christmas."

"He does have a point," Ethan added cautiously.

"See?" Satan whined like a five year old. "Not everything bad is my fault. However, if I'd thought of it I would have done it before they did."

He mumbled the second half of his sentence as he backed away from Astrid.

"Whatever," she huffed. "You cannot keep people against their will."

"But I did," Satan replied.

"It's still wrong," Astrid declared, chastising him.

"And your point?" Satan asked, truly baffled.

"Never mind." Astrid rolled her eyes and pressed the bridge of her nose. "Who did you detain anyway?"

"That is for me and Heathcliff to know and you to find out. Is this the only ward I have to break?" Satan asked as he flicked his fingers and the magic that bound Gareth oozed to the floor with a wicked hiss.

"I'm not sure," Astrid replied truthfully. "Three of Ethan's other siblings have gone missing and I'm not certain of their circumstances."

Raquel and Ethan rushed forward to their brother. Hugs, backslaps and a few tears were shed. As the spell continued to fizzle and dissolve, the silver chains that bound Gareth disintegrated to a fine powdery dust. He was free—almost.

"Why hasn't his aging reversed?" Raquel turned to Satan and asked. "He's still aging."

"Unfortunately my dear, that part of the curse cannot be reversed by me," the Devil winked at my mate and gave Raquel what I assumed was his panty melting smile.

My hands fisted at my sides and the need to take him down boiled in my veins. Ethan shot me a look that would have made most cringe. However, we were dealing with my mate here.

No one except for me was allowed to even *think* of her in a suggestive way without dying violently. Thankfully the Devil's advances clearly didn't tempt Raquel in the slightest. It would have been incredibly bad form to take on Satan—especially when I'd asked him to come.

However, he was treading on paper thin ice at the moment.

"You can do nothing?" Gareth asked diffusing the tension. "You're the goddamned Devil."

"For the love of torture," Satan roared. "I just freed your sorry ass. Does that amount to *nothing*?"

"Calm down and pull your panties out of your crack," Astrid snapped. "It's a reasonable fucking question. If you can't do it, who can?"

"That information will cost you," Satan said with a sulk.

"Mother humpin' cowballs on a pointy stick covered in poop," Astrid mumbled with disgust. "What do you want?"

"Can I get back to you on that?" Satan asked.

"No," Ethan grumbled as Astrid snapped, "Yes."

"Wonderful," Satan bellowed completely ignoring the Vampyre Prince of the North American Dominion. "I'll let you know my price. Soon."

Ethan closed his eyes and stared at the ceiling. I was certain he was praying for patience. Satan was tough to swallow under any circumstance—let alone one where he clearly had the upper hand.

"Gareth will continue to age until he finds his true mate. Whomever placed this shoddy ass spell also cursed him," the Devil informed us.

"Is it a Demonic curse?" I asked.

Satan made a huge show of rolling his eyes and silently counting to ten as his lips moved wordlessly. Watching the Devil pout like a toddler would have been humorous if the stakes weren't so high.

"If it were Demonic, I could remove it," he ground out. He looked at Gareth. "It's not Demonic. This was obviously a two or more asshole job. I removed the Demon spell part. The curse is your problem."

Gareth nodded. What else could he do?

"My curse was removed by finding my mate," Raquel said thoughtfully.

"Then it stands to reason that the same person who cursed you, cursed your brother," Satan said as he pulled out his cell phone and began tapping away.

"What are you doing?" Astrid demanded.

"I'm playing Soda Candy Crush. I'm on level 660 and I found a way to cheat to get more lives. Besides, it's getting boring here," Satan replied.

"Wait. You know how to get more lives without paying for them?" Raquel asked, intrigued.

"I do," he purred suggestively and approached her. "Would you like me to show you how?"

"No," I said cutting off his advance. "She would not."

There was no way in Hell we were going to owe the Devil a favor to find out how to cheat at Soda Candy Crush.

"Hello," Gareth cut it. "Still aging over here."

"Why do you think it's the same person who cursed both Raquel and Gareth?" Astrid asked her uncle.

"Cursing is a gift," Ethan explained before the Devil could exact another favor for an answer. "Very few immortals have the unfortunate gift of laying curses on other immortals."

"Do you know anyone who has this gift?" I asked.

"No. I don't," Ethan answered and then glanced at the Devil with narrowed eyes. "But I would guess he does."

"Holy Hell, this outing is turning out far to be more interesting than I thought it would." Satan clapped his hands and grinned. "How about this? We can work out a deal while we find your other siblings. Do you happen to know where they are?"

I want to punch the man, but didn't dare. Satan forgot about his game as he added up new favors in his head.

"I can find them," Gareth said stepping forward. "Who's missing?"

Nathan, Alexander and Lelia," Ethan informed him tersely. "You can call them here?"

"Not sure that would work if they're in the same situation I was in. However, I can go to them," he replied.

"Your gift?" Astrid asked Gareth.

"Yes. And I can take you with me. It won't be pleasant, but it will work."

"Please," Astrid laughed. "I was yanked to Hell by Demons. Nothing can top that."

"Are you trying to hurt my feelings?" Satan inquired silkily.

"You have feelings?" she countered.

"Well no, but it sounded good. Didn't it?" Satan replied with a smirk and a shrug.

Ignoring the Devil, Gareth took charge. "Ethan, Astrid, Satan and I will find the others and meet you at the Summit. I'd highly suggest you two hide your mating. Vlad may be very valuable to us. And as you know... he wants Raquel."

I growled my displeasure at the shitty plan resuming and nodded curtly. Vlad had better be fucking valuable or he would die—slowly.

"I hate that tally whacker," Satan announced gleefully. "I can't wait until the bastard ends up in my neck of the woods. But I was under the impression that Napoleon was in charge of the Old Guard at the moment."

"Napoleon is a fucking Vampyre?" Astrid asked, shocked. "Who made that little turd a Vamp?"

"Don't know," Satan answered. "But when you meet him please call him a little turd. I'll owe you three favors if you do."

Astrid contemplated his request thoughtfully as Ethan firmly shook his head no. Napoleon was a hateful bastard and evil to the core. Even though Astrid could take him, it would be foolish to have him as an enemy.

"Five favors and I'll call him an assbucket turd knockin' little shit for brains," she offered ignoring Ethan's very audible groan.

"Deal," Satan shouted and rubbed his hands together in anticipation of a smackdown or more likely a bloodbath. "Oh and if you tell Vlad *'you vant to suck his blood'* I'll let you call me Uncle Fucker for two weeks."

"But I don't *vant* to suck his blood." Astrid giggled.

"Trust me on this one. Just tell him," Satan said with a covert wink to me.

The Devil had the information on Vlad despising the way he'd been portrayed in film from me. Part of my favor was directly related to this little tidbit. Vlad was known to go ballistic when mocked.

"Are we ready?" I asked, ignoring Satan as I glanced at our motley crew.

"No, but we're going anyway," Raquel sued as she quickly hugged her brothers and Astrid. "Let's get this twerk-wanking shit show on the road."

"Wow. Good one," Astrid said, congratulating her again.

"Thanks," my mate replied with a blush. "Did it make sense?"

"No, but what the Hell does making sense even mean?" Astrid said. "Think about it—we're dead, we can fly, my uncle is Beelzebub, and I'm un-killable. Sense left this train station a long fucking time ago."

"We make sense out of the chaos," I corrected Astrid as I took Raquel's hand in mine. "I'm as alive as when I still had breath. We're survivors and we have reasons to go on. Today is a mere blip in the eternity that we've been given. I plan to take it by the balls and twist till it screams for mercy."

"Again," Satan added, grinning at all of us. "I'm am starting to seriously enjoy this day."

I chuckled and shrugged.

"I like your positive attitude too," Astrid said with a thoughtful nod. "I'm ready to grab some hairy balls and twist till they explode. I shall then yank them till they're detached and shove them down the bad guy's throat."

All of the men—*including me*—groaned and covered our balls with our hands in a visceral reaction to her plan. Astrid and Raquel high fived and tried without success to bite back their laughter.

"Not exactly what I meant, Astrid," I muttered with a wince.

"I know," my cousin assured me with an evil little smirk. "I just like to see you all bent over in phantom pain."

"That's just mean, Astrid," Satan gasped, but gave her an approving thumbs up.

"If we're done here, we have to go," Raquel advised. "Time is beginning to be of the essence. We'll see you shortly."

"This is serious. Do not doubt it for an instant," Ethan advised as touched his sister's cheek. "The Old Guard is powerful and may have many allies that we're unaware of.

Stay as neutral as you can and wait for backup. Hopefully, we'll be there soon."

"You don't think I can handle a bunch of old-as-dirt dead people?" Raquel asked her brother with narrowed eyes as her fangs descended.

It was all kinds of sexy. The uncontrollable monster on my pants agreed.

"Oh I *know* you can, especially with the killing machine you mated with at your side. I just don't want to miss out on any of the fun," Ethan replied with a wink.

"Death, destruction, and dinner in Paris. I couldn't have asked for a nicer damned day," Satan declared as he took his place on the far side of the room with Gareth, Astrid and Ethan. "Okay. Let's get this party started."

"Yes, let's," I agreed with a salute to my friends.

And with that we all transported away in spectacular blasts of glittering magic.

Chapter 17

Everything was stark white—the walls, the furniture, the drapes and the marble flooring. Not a spec of color as far as the eye could see. It was cold and foreboding. If Heaven was decorated like this, I might actually consider Hell.

"Damn, the Angels have unimaginative taste," Raquel whispered as we cautiously made our way across a grand but strangely empty foyer. "Where is everyone?"

"Security is definitely lacking," I muttered as I glanced around.

We stood out like evil beacons in our formalwear—all black against the backdrop of blinding white. Astrid had the forethought to bring me a tux and Raquel had changed into a black sheath that hugged her curves sinfully. The thought of peeling it off of her with my teeth consumed my brain.

With a shake of my head to clear the lascivious intentions from it, I closed my eyes and reached out to the minds of our people who were in attendance at the Summit. The thoughts of our warriors were tense and guarded. With a text on my secure line, I communicated with Henry, one of my top generals.

Where are you? I asked him.

Ballroom. Are you here? Henry asked in return.

Yes. Status?

Strange… boring. Not a word uttered against the Royal Family. Just business about territory rights and upholding the treaties. Henry informed me.

Nothing seems amiss? I queried.

No, nothing.

We'll be in shortly.

Odd. If the Old Guard wanted to embarrass or implicate the Royal Family, the Summit was the perfect place to do it. What else could be going on?

"They're at a meeting in the ballroom. Everyone is there," I told her.

"Shall we just waltz in and surprise them?" she asked with a bloodthirsty little grin.

Damn it. It was either the smile or maybe the way her eyes lit up at the thought of spilling some blood that undid me. I adjusted the bulge in my pants and carefully considered my answer. If we stole away in a parlor, we could have a quickie. However, relieving the ache in my balls wasn't necessarily a top priority. No matter what we were facing, my priorities always shifted to Raquel when we were alone.

"I do believe waltzing in is a fine plan, my love. It would be difficult for anyone to abduct you in a crowd of Angels."

"The only person I want to be abducted by is you." Raquel batted her long lashes and my pants got tighter. "Could you arrange that?"

"God, Raquel." I groaned. It took everything I had not to say the Hell with the Summit and whisk her away to a secluded place—anywhere. I'd even go back to the damn Catacombs if it meant we could be alone. "You're killing me here."

"Darling, you're already dead." She laughed with delight and kissed me. "Do you want me to help you out with your problem?" she asked, referring to the painfully obvious erection in my pants.

"Now?" I asked.

"Yes. Now," she whispered with glee.

"Can we do it fast?" I asked liking the direction we were going.

"So fast it will make your head spin," she purred. "Both of them."

I placed my hand on the wall to keep the dizziness at bay. Raquel could probably make me come with her voice alone. The thought of taking her in the Palace of the Angels made my balls so tight I had to lean forward. I was the luckiest bastard in the world.

"Do it," I ground out and moved to unzip my pants.

"Stay still," she instructed. "I'll do all the work."

And the day got even better…

"Close your eyes," she whispered in my ear. "Concentrate on my voice. Hear and visualize everything I'm saying and your *big* problem will go away. I promise."

"Are you that good?" I teasingly challenged.

"I'm that good plus ten," she guaranteed.

Her breath feathered warm and sweet on my cheek. The scent of her was my addiction. My need for my mate was almost debilitating. At this point if we didn't take care of my *problem*, I'd be useless in a battle or whatever was about to go down.

"I'm ready," I said gruffly.

"You're alone in a beautiful room on a big bed—the lights are low and there's a gentle breeze blowing through the open window. Your sexy body is completely bare and you're so hard it hurts," she said softly.

"That's fairly accurate," I choked out.

"Shhhhhh," she admonished. "Just listen… you hear a noise outside your room. A laugh and a moan of desire," she continued, pulling me into her spell.

Her tone was hypnotizing and I pictured her entering the room gloriously naked and falling atop me. The thought of her bare breasts made my fangs drop.

"There's a soft knock at the door. Someone wants to join you. Someone needs you more than life itself. Someone wants to pleasure you. Someone wants to fuck you so badly you can feel the need through the closed door. Do you want this?" she asked in a barely audible whisper.

"Yes," I hissed. "I want it."

Her light giggle caused me to clamp my hands to my sides. The desire to grab her was enormous along with my dick at this point. However, the game was sexy so I fought to still myself.

"You tell the person to come in… "

She paused and I thought I would fucking burst. Why the Hell did she pause?

"And?" I urged her on waiting impatiently for her description of me burying myself to the hilt inside her willing body.

"And in run Martha and Jane naked as jaybirds except for an image of your face waxed out of their private areas. They grunt with glee and their sagging bosoms smack them in their heads as they sprint for your naked body. They jump you and hump you like Samuel's baboon, Blobbityflonk, humped the couch last week when we were tutoring him. They lick you from head to… "

"Stop! Sweet Jesus in Hell," I grunted as my eyes flew open and my erection deflated instantly. "I'm going to be ill."

"Do you still have your problem?" she inquired with a shit-eating grin and a very un-ladylike cackle.

"No. No I don't, but I now have an image that's goddamned un-erasable living in my frontal lobe," I griped.

"You're welcome." She shrugged unapologetically and smirked.

"For scarring me for eternity?" I shot back.

"Yep, and for getting you to think with the right head," she added with a wink. "Better to use the one on your shoulders when dealing with the Old Guard and the Angels."

"You could have been a bit more gentle," I complained. "I feel defiled."

"I thought you liked it a little rough."

"Stop," I insisted and raised both hands in surrender. "Just leave me with alone with my flaccid dick. I don't think I can take another visualization if you make me hard again."

"No problem. Happy to have helped."

"Remind me never to ask for help like that again," I told her with a grimace.

"Will do. You ready to enter the shit show?"

I glanced down at my now un-tented pants and chuckled. She really was that good plus ten.

"Yes. I'm ready."

***

It was just as Henry had reported—staid and monotonous. The Angels, about a hundred, sat on the left side of the room. They were clearly one unit, all dressed in flowing white robes that blended into the décor splendidly. Pam was the only celestial creature who stood out in her purple robe and floral headpiece. I smiled at her audacity. She could have sat on either side as she was an Angel mated to the King of the Vampyres, but she loved stirring it up.

The hundred Vampyres were a different story. They were dressed to impress in Prada, Gucci, and everything in between. Clustered on the far right sat the Old Guard. Just as expected, Vlad was clearly in charge of the faction. Raquel's father, the King, and a contingency of younger Vamps from all over the world were separated from Vlad and his cronies by a few feet.

To the untrained eye it was minimal, but to me it was a clear line drawn in the sand. Raquel's almost inaudible hiss led me to believe we were in agreement on that point. The loyalists for our King outnumbered the Old Guard, but the sheer age of the elders meant the power division was equal.

We slipped in quietly. It gave us a brief moment to assess the situation. Initially our entrance went unnoticed as the head Angel droned on about punishments for breaking treaties. It was old news—beheadings, banishments to Hell and other unsavory forms of justice. For the times we lived in, our tenets were still quite medieval. However, we were both violent races and brutal consequences were what most of us understood.

"Greetings everyone," Raquel called out when the Angel took a brief pause to check his notes. She moved to the center of the room with the confidence of a deadly Vampyre Princess—exactly what she was. "I'm delighted you chose to hold the Summit in my European Dominion. I sincerely apologize for my tardiness. I've had a few issues to deal with."

"Apologies accepted," the Angel with the notes said as he took Raquel in with shocked surprise. "And thank you for agreeing to host. We were informed you would not be in attendance."

"Whomever relayed that message to you was gravely mistaken," Raquel replied in a steely tone juxtaposed with the gracious smile.

I walked several steps behind my mate assuming the position of her guard. I noticed the King's raised brow, but he very wisely stayed silent. We'd chat later.

"It's almost *sundown* Princess," Vlad stated calmly as he stood and gave her a perfunctory bow. His dark eyes perused her from head to toe with undisguised lust. "I would assume you would like to resume the meeting in the morning."

The air in the room changed from bland to electrically charged with his words. The simple fact that he knew of her curse meant one of two things—we had a traitor in our midst who had given him the information or he'd placed the curse.

Vlad's demeanor was benign, but his eyes told a different story. I was reminded immediately and viscerally that this was no game. The rules were wildly unclear at the moment, but the match had begun.

"Never assume, Vlad," Raquel replied evenly as she stared him down. "Makes an ass out of you and me... but mostly you in this case."

The laughter was somewhat restrained, but it came from both sides. However, the Old Guard was not amused.

"Well, hot damn," Pam yelled and clapped her hands like she was at a concert. "This is more

like it. I've fallen asleep over here at least eighteen fucking times listening to Roberto yack on about how to kill a naughty immortal. You're looking lovely, Raquel."

"Thank you, Pam. Purple suits you," Raquel replied.

A smattering of Angels chuckled at the veiled insult on their hue-less attire, but most just appeared bored.

"We shall adjourn," the head Angel, Roberto, told the King. "Please feel free to join us back here for an informal gathering."

"We'd be delighted." The King nodded as he took Pam's arm and politely shook hands with Roberto.

"After a brief recess to freshen up, please join us in the great room," Roberto announced to the crowd who began to disperse.

Surrounded by Old Guard, Vlad approached Raquel and brusquely took her arm. My instinct was to kill, but that would make me wildly unpopular and most likely get me removed from the Summit and sent straight to Hell. Literally.

He was just as I remembered—long black hair with eyes to match. His cheekbones were sharp and his perpetually downturned lips were thin. He stood about an inch shorter than me and fancied himself a ladies' man. Although any lady who chose to be wooed by *Dracula*—a name he despised—would have to be mighty forgiving to overlook his penchant for *impaling* people… no pun intended.

With colossal difficulty, I reined in my inclination and behaved like a proper guard was expected to—for the most part.

One could argue I was slightly too close, but on the off chance Vlad tried to abduct her I was staying near enough to grab her. Of course, Raquel could give Vlad a violent run for his money, but my caveman tendencies would not be denied.

Fuck. This was harder than fighting the Trolls and Wraiths. I tilted my head down to hide my fangs. A sign of aggression wouldn't do.

"Raquel my sweetling, it's so good to see you. You're as ravishing as ever," Vlad complimented her.

"And you're as inappropriate as I remembered," she replied as she expertly extricated herself from his grip.

"Don't be mean, Raquel," he said with a pout on his lips. "I was so hoping our paths would cross."

"Why?" she asked.

"To reminisce about *old* times and make some beautiful *new* memories together," Vlad said, implying a past where he'd seen my mate naked.

Not working for me.

At all.

I was very aware it was hypocritical to judge Raquel's past. I had quite a past of my own. We were centuries old and a very sexual race. However, I was a newly mated man. I was seconds away from coming apart at the seams and going medieval on Dracula's ass—right or wrong. The tension in my body was impossible to overlook.

"Your guard's a bit over zealous, isn't he?" Vlad inquired in a condescending tone. "Is that you, Heathcliff? Interesting... I see you've been demoted."

His laugh made me grind my fangs and the casual and bored smile that I gave him deserved an Oscar.

"Correct, Drac... I mean Vlad. I owed my Prince a favor and he asked me to protect his sister. Far be it from me to go against orders," I replied easily. "Speaking of orders, I believe it's time for you to retire, Raquel."

Her glance was surprised, but she nodded curtly. "Yes. I think I will. It's been a long day. Vlad, please excuse us."

"I'd like some time with you tomorrow," he insisted as his eyes bored holes in me. "Alone."

"No can do, old man," I told him with a grin and a small bow. "You know... orders and all."

With that, I took a shocked Raquel by the arm and led her quickly away. Five more seconds and I would have destroyed him. This guard thing was not working out very well for me. Hiding the fact she was mine was eating me alive.

"He doesn't know the curse is broken," I told her tightly as I led her from the room. "Let's keep it that way."

"Are you sure that's why you're manhandling me out of the reception?" she demanded.

"Yes. No. Just walk before I throw you over my shoulder and carry you out."

"You're being an alpha-hole," Raquel hissed as she smiled politely and waved at attendees.

172

Ignoring her accurate assessment, I marched her past them as quickly as decorum would allow. I knew I was being very un-guard like, but I was losing it fast.

"We should convene," the King whispered as he stepped in front of me halting our exit.

"At my home outside of Paris, father," Raquel told him as she gave him a quick hug. "Heathcliff is having a few boundary issues with our game of pretend. We should probably go."

"Yes, I can see that," the King replied biting back his mirth. "We'll go to the reception and meet you in an hour."

"Yes, Your Majesty. We'll be waiting," I said with as much respect as I could muster.

I was loyal to and adored my King. However, he was in my way at the moment and very little could stop me from leaving the room with his daughter. My frustration was clearly evident as the King stepped aside and let us pass.

"Rude much?" Raquel snapped as I guided her back to the foyer.

"Losing it here," I admitted tersely as I pulled her into an alcove and wrapped my arms tightly around her. "You ready to leave?"

"We're transporting?" she asked. Her brows were raised and she tried unsuccessfully to wiggle from my grasp. "I thought maybe we could fly and you could work off a little of your macho caveman bullshit."

"Nope. Flying takes too long and I'm fond of my macho caveman bullshit," I shot back flatly. "Again. Are you ready?"

The look she threw my way would have withered a lesser man. I was not a lesser man and unfortunately it just made my dick hard. This did not go unnoticed by my mate.

"You realize you're crazy, don't you?" she accused.

"Tell me something I don't know," I hissed. "You're the one who makes me crazy."

"Back at you," she bit out.

"We can have this conversation where we can be heard or we can go back to your palace. Your call, Princess," I said.

"This is going to be a very long eternity," she muttered. "You're a pain in my ass."

"And thank God you have a very nice one," I complimented her and grinned at her disgusted snort of laughter.

"Leave," she instructed. "Now."

We did just that in a blast of multicolored sparkling glitter.

Raquel was correct in her prediction. It would be a long wonderful, aggravating, challenging, somewhat violent, loving, and sex filled eternity.

I couldn't wait.

Chapter 18

"You have some nerve getting pissed off about my past," Raquel shouted as she picked up a priceless antique and prepared to hurl it at my head. She eyed the crystal figurine critically and at the last minute thought better of it.

My weight was distributed evenly between both feet. I was ready to dodge either left or right depending on what breakable object might be hurled my way.

"I know it's not reasonable," I ground out. "It's hypocritical. However, it might have been helpful to know you'd slept with the fucker."

"How, pray tell, would that have been helpful to you? Because I will tell you now, I *do not* want lists of the women you've bedded over the last few hundred years," she snapped and casually eased herself over to a collection of brass statues.

Her eyes blazed green and her fangs dropped. She was ready for a smackdown and all I wanted to do was strip her naked and bend her over the couch. It was hotter than Hell, but her obvious jealousy is what made the problem in my pants exquisitely painful.

I kept my eyes trained on her hands. She was fast and had outstanding aim. I was no one's fool.

"Fine," I growled. "I'll admit my behavior isn't rational. But if he lays a hand on you again, he'll have to regrow a new one."

"You cannot be my guard," she said wearily and flopped down on a sleek leather couch. "If we have to *pretend* not to be mated, I'll need Jean Paul to be my keeper. You can't handle this. Vlad clearly has more information than we thought. He knows of the curse."

"Speaking of Jean Paul," I said slowly knowing my popularity was about to take another nosedive. "He has to be the one who revealed the secret. No one in your family would ever do such a thing."

It did occur to me that there was one family member that could be a potential loose cannon, but I was fixated on the image of her sleeping with Jean Paul. Rational thinking had left my repertoire for the moment.

"Never," she insisted vehemently. "He would *never* do that."

"I'm going to ask this next question once," I said, absolutely sure she would throw something. "You will answer it and I will do my best to block said answer from my brain."

Her silence was stony and her stare was furious. It was wrong of me to ask, but I had to know.

"Have you slept with Jean Paul?"

The brass candelabra narrowly missed my head. It whistled as it flew by and smashed a priceless lamp on a side table.

"I will not grace that with an answer," she yelled as she picked up something shiny and cocked her arm back.

"You already did," I retorted angrily.

"I most certainly did not."

The shiny piece exploded into a million little shards it hit the wall mere inches from my face. Even though I was ready to go ballistic at the thought of Raquel and Jean

Paul, I realized how much I was enjoying our exchange of old. At least we weren't destroying someone else's home this time.

"Just tell me it's over," I said in what I thought was a reasonable tone.

"Do you really think I would have mated with you if I was involved with someone else?" she asked in a tone so quiet I got scared for my undead life.

"Well… I didn't say you were sleeping with him *now*. I meant… like ever."

"Your regard for my morals is sadly lacking and makes me wonder about yours," she hissed.

"You still haven't answered the question," I challenged, fairly sure I should stop while I was still alive. However, my inner alpha-hole had a mind of his own and wouldn't be denied. My damn mouth kept moving as if I was possessed by the Devil. If only I had that as my excuse.

"Get this through your thick and stupid skull before I break it in half," she stated, incensed. "My sexual past is not your concern. You will never ask me that question again."

"It's a legit question," Jean Paul commented calmly from the doorway. "I'm fine if you want to tell him the truth."

"He doesn't deserve the truth," Raquel spat and pulled a short dagger from her inner thigh.

Seeing him standing so comfortably in her home was almost my undoing. I knew this impasse was my fault entirely. Goddamn it, messy was going to be a way of life for us if I made it through the next few minutes. My mate and a sharp dagger didn't bode well for me.

"No," I said with a decisiveness that belied how I actually felt. "Raquel is right. It's not my business. Not now—not *ever*. Although if you ever even think about her like that again, I'll kill you."

It was the best I could do under the circumstances. I was possessive and greedy and wanted every part of Raquel to myself, but if I didn't cave a little it would be a brutal uphill battle to build a future together. I was smart enough to know that. The last two hundred years I'd been only half-alive without her. I would not fuck it up by being jealous over something in her past. I probably had more conquests than she did anyway.

Their laughter caught me off guard. I watched with my fists balled at my sides. Jean Paul took his place on the couch beside my mate as if he belonged there. Raquel's giggle floated across the room like music and simply infuriated me.

It dawned on me that I was being played, but for the life of me I couldn't figure out how.

"It's really not nice to toy with him like this," Jean Paul told her in his fucking debonair French accent. "He will find a way to repay you."

"Ugggghhhh," Raquel grunted as she watched me warily. "I don't like his tone or his insinuations."

"Hmmm…" Jean Paul stroked his chin and feigned deep thought.

I seriously wanted to rip his head off.

"His tone is that of a newly mated Vampyre," he assured Raquel. "And I would surmise if the tables were turned, you would have been a Hell of a lot more unpleasant."

"That's not true," she snapped and punched his arm. "Take that back right now."

His laughter and way with her held a familiar ring to it. I couldn't put my finger on it, but my fists slowly unclenched.

"Raquel, the poor man is suffering and so close to removing my head I'm getting a bit nervous. If you don't tell him, I will."

"Fine," she groused. "I'll tell him. But Heathcliff, you've lost your panty privileges for a month."

"That's just mean," Jean Paul muttered under his breath.

I couldn't have agreed more.

"There is no way Jean Paul would have revealed my secret to Vlad or anyone else," Raquel started and then paused to make my Hell last a bit longer.

"Raquel," Jean Paul prodded her on with an eye roll. "Put the poor man out of his misery."

She huffed and placed a kiss on Jean Paul's head. The very same head I was going to remove in five seconds if someone didn't enlighten me.

"I raised him basically from birth and turned him when he came of age," she told me, staring me down and daring me to say something.

"Holy Hell, Raquel. You are so mean," Jean Paul coughed out on a laugh.

"Well, it's true," she shot back gleefully.

"Yes, but..." he said hesitantly.

"Wait. That sounds a little, ummm…" I stuttered.

"Sounds a little what?" she demanded as she crossed her arms over her chest and waited.

Goddamn it, if her position didn't give me a better shot of her cleavage. I closed my eyes and willed my dick to stay calm.

"Ummm… weird?" I said unable to come up with something eloquent or literal that wouldn't end my life.

"Well, it would be weird, gross, disgusting and fucking illegal if I'd *slept* with him," she shouted. "But I have never and will never have sex with Jean Paul."

"Illegal?" I asked.

It was the only word, other than the phrase *sex with Jean Paul*, that jumped out at me. I mean, I knew I was younger than her, but how young did she like them before me?

"Do not tell me what you are thinking," she said in a voice that could give one nightmares. "And I have slept with him—many times over the years, but not the way you and your pea sized brain think."

"Raquel, I am so close to being beheaded by your mate, that I'm putting the poor bastard out of his pain. I'm her brother," Jean Paul volunteered with a grin.

The tension in my body left and shame took its place. "Explain," I ordered. This was certainly a mortifying lesson about trust... and what a pig I could be.

"Although you don't deserve it, I will," Raquel said as she stared angrily at me, her eyes narrowed dangerously.

"Fine point, well made," I agreed.

She paused in surprise and took me in. It was rare for a Vampyre to be humble, but I was being an untrusting ass to the one woman I would die for. I was going to need a few lessons.

"After royal polygamy was abolished, my mother left my father and married a human man. She gave birth to Jean Paul shortly after I'd chosen to be turned. My mother and Jean Paul's father both died in a plague when he was still a baby... so I took him in."

"She raised me and spoiled me rotten." Jean Paul reminisced fondly. "When I became of age, she gave me the choice to live out my life as a human or become a Vampyre and spend eternity with her making my life a living Hell. I chose the later because I love her. Completely. She is my blood and I will die for her," Jean Paul vowed.

I now felt lower than a slug.

"So yes, I have slept in the same bed with my sister. When I was a child, I was terrified of the dark. Raquel, who by the way is tone deaf, would cuddle me and sing to me for hours. The agony of listening to her massacre tunes kept the imaginary monsters away," he announced with a chuckle and a wicked glint in his eye.

"Now that's just rude," she admonished him as she blushed in embarrassment.

"Does the King know?" I asked as I tentatively approached Raquel and Jean Paul. I wasn't sure if I was welcome yet—or ever.

"Of course he does. My father loves Jean Paul like a son," she stated. "Jean Paul is the one who likes it to be kept a secret. If our enemies knew he was my brother, they would try and use him as collateral against me."

"So brother-in-law, there you have it," Jean Paul said as he stood and put his hand out to me.

I took it in mine and lowered my head in respect. "I'm sorry."

"If you hadn't been such a dick, I wouldn't have made you suffer like that," Raquel said still keeping her distance. "I was excited to tell you about Jean Paul. He lives here in my home with me."

"I am her brother. However, very soon you will come to realize she treats me like a child," Jean Paul added with a chuckle.

Raquel's eye roll and snort pulled a small smile from my lips. God, my jealously had certainly fucked up this little family get together.

I now recognized what I couldn't put my finger on. Their relationship was similar to mine and my sister Cathy's. His cockiness with me in Kentucky and his anger at my mule headed ways where Raquel was concerned now made perfect sense. Also now that I knew, I could see the resemblance.

"Again, I'm sorry. It seems I have little self-control when Raquel is part of the equation," I apologized once more to Jean Paul.

"Well, chasing a stubborn gal for several hundred years would no doubt do that to a man," he added letting me off the hook with a lopsided grin. "I overheard that the King and Pam are coming. I'll get things ready."

"How did you hear that?" I asked, positive we hadn't spoken of it since we'd been back.

"I was at the Summit of course," he replied with a satisfied smirk. "I'm never far from my sister."

"That's slightly disconcerting," I muttered thinking about some of the more pornographic interludes she and I had shared.

Jean Paul's belly laugh brought a smile to Raquel's face and my own wasn't far behind.

"Dear God." He groaned and shuddered. "No worries, my friend. Only in public venues do I track my sister."

"He can morph," Raquel informed me with pride.

"He can what?" I asked, confused.

"My baby brother can take the human forms of others and walk undetected among us. Of course I know it's him, but I'm quite sure you wouldn't be able to tell," she bragged.

This was new to me. I was aware Demons could take other forms. I'd seen Satan do it myself, but a Vampyre? I stared at Jean Paul with a new respect.

"I beg to differ," I challenged with an offended raised brow. "I'll be able to tell. Morph into your sister. I will tell you who is who."

I turned my back and waited. Raquel's giggle of delight made me hopeful that the panty privileges threat had been a bad joke.

"If I'm right, you will remove the ban on me getting into your panties," I informed her with my back still turned.

"And if you lose, you are going to get very friendly with your hand for the next two months," she pronounced grandly.

Shit. I was going to get this correct. I *had* to get this correct.

I heard some shuffling around and some laughing. My gut tightened. Me and my big mouth could potentially land me in whack-off Hell.

"Are you ready?" I inquired. If I was capable of sweating, I'd be in a pool of water at the moment. My pride and my sex life were on the line.

"Yes," two identical voices answered in unison.

Again. Shit.

Slowly I turned around and stared at them. The resemblance was uncanny and alarming. They were completely identical—almost. My grin of relief came with an audible grunt of satisfaction. I pointed at the real Raquel. Not even for a moment did I not know who she was. I'd recognize her till the end of time.

"How did you know?" she squealed in disbelief. "You didn't even have to think about it."

"He knew because you've shared blood," Jean Paul said as he took back his own form.

It was stunning in its simplicity. In the blink of an eye he was a different person—no fan fare or magical glitter. Truly a chameleon.

Amazing.

"Plus, my guess is that Heathcliff would know you anywhere, my sister," Jean Paul added as he strode across the room to make his exit.

"You knew he would guess correctly?" she asked her brother incredulously.

"Yep," he said as he picked up his pace to leave.

"You threw me under the bus," she accused with a laugh.

"This is true, but I felt sorry for the poor sap after the fun we've had with him. Giving him back his panty privileges was the very least I could do," he called over his shoulder as he sprinted the rest of the way out of the room and down the hall.

"I like your brother."

"You would," she said as she eyed me warily.

I circled her like a lion stalks its prey. She stood her ground and watched me with undisguised interest.

"We have a half an hour before your father and Pam arrive. I won the bet. Hand over your panties," I instructed.

"I can't," she replied with a smirk and a shrug.

"Welching on a bet, Red?"

"No, Heathcliff. I'm not wearing any panties. Therefore, it stands to reason I can't give them to you."

Faster than a human eye could follow, I pinned her body to the couch with my own. Her sexy ass was pressed against the very hard evidence of my desire for her. I was in the gateway of Heaven. Now it was time to cross the threshold.

"I'm afraid I'm going to have to pat you down to verify the veracity of your statement, ma'am," I whispered in her ear as I tamped back the need to tear her dress from her body.

"Is that legal, *officer*?" Raquel giggled and let her head fall back on my chest giving me better access to her slender neck.

"Absolutely not. However, I enjoy living dangerously."

"This is inappropriate behavior. I have a very jealous mate who will happily tear you from limb to limb for even looking at me," she informed me trying not to laugh.

"He sounds like a brilliant man. However, he's not here and I plan take what I want," I told her as I slid my hands purposely down her body.

Her nipples pebbled beneath my palms and her soft moan was music to my ears. "Raise your hands and put them behind your head," I instructed gruffly.

"Is this normal police procedure?" she inquired as she slowly raised her arms and seductively placed them behind her head.

"Yes. Yes it is," I told her as my fingers skimmed her flat stomach and toyed with the hem of her dress.

The material was silky, but nowhere near as soft as her skin. Raquel's low hiss of desire made all thoughts of the game disappear. I was not a policeman, I was a deadly Vampyre who had just mated with the love of my life and being inside her was my only mission—or to put it more accurately, my obsession.

"We don't have much time," she insisted as she helped me along by raising her dress up over her hips, proving without a doubt that she was definitely panty-less.

"Holy Hell," I muttered harshly as I took the perfect round globes of her ass in my greedy hands and squeezed.

My right hand snaked around to the front of her body and I pressed my fingers into her tight wetness. So fucking hot. So fucking beautiful.

"I'd like to make love to you after I've made you come at least four times," I ground out through clenched teeth as I tried to rein in my inner caveman.

"I already came once while you were talking," she said frantically.

She rocked against my hand with wild abandon and I made sure to send her over the edge once more. Her muffled scream against the pillows was so damn hot I almost came myself.

"We don't have that much time. Are you willing to take a rain check on the other two pre-sex orgasms?" I was desperate to be inside her.

"Are you willing to fuck me over the couch until I can't see straight?" Raquel challenged as she yanked her dress over her head.

"I can make that happen," I told her as I undid my belt and jerked my pants down in a shaky movement.

At the moment I was lucky I could do anything seeing as all the blood from my brain had traveled to my dick. She was so goddamned gorgeous and so goddamned mine. Raquel leaned over the arm of the couch, turned her head over her shoulder and gave me a smile that went straight to my balls. Her wild red curls framed her face and her eyes sparkled green with desire.

All bets were off as far as controlling myself. Taking her hips in my hands, I spread her legs apart as far as they would go with my knee. The need to make her mine made coherent thought and polite behavior impossible.

Taking myself in hand, I put my dick right where we both wanted it to be and I plunged in so fast and deep I was certain I would pass out. Her cries of ecstasy matched my own. I sheathed myself completely and stilled.

Time held its breath and the feeling of being merged together into one entity stole my voice. It was magical. It was perfection. It was how we were meant to be.

"I love you," she whispered and reached back to grab my hand.

She was so delicate, yet the strongest, most deadly and brilliant woman I knew. Maybe I was still getting used to the fact that it was no longer a chase. The pursuit was over and I had finally won... we had won.

"You will never be able to understand how much I love you," I whispered as I leaned over her body and placed kisses along her shoulder. "I can't describe it with words."

"Then show me with your body," she urged as she moved seductively beneath me.

She didn't have to ask twice.

Nipping at her ear I felt her body shudder in response. With great purpose, I slowly eased out of her and watched how beautifully our bodies joined together in love and passion.

Then she tightened her inner muscles and trapped my cock like a vise inside her. The time for slow and easy was over. My brain became useless and the need between us escalated to animal like proportions. Establishing a punishing rhythm, I showed her with my body what my words couldn't convey.

Raquel rocked back and forth meeting me thrust for thrust. Words and moans tangled together as they fell from our tongues. I felt the tingling in the base of my spine and I knew I was close.

I needed to see her.

I had to see her face.

Pulling out, I heard her gasp in dismay. The chuckle that came from deep in my chest was full of cocky male satisfaction. My woman wanted me as much as I wanted her. I flipped her to her back and laid her on the couch gently.

"I've got you baby," I promised as I slid back into her welcoming body. "I have to see you come."

"Fuck me," she begged as she grabbed at my hair and pulled my lips to hers.

The kiss was as wild and out of control as we were. Our tongues clashed and the overwhelming craving to taste her consumed me.

"Bite me," I demanded as I scraped my fangs along the silky skin of her neck.

Her eyes sparkled and her sultry laugh went all through me.

"On three," she gasped out as the speed of our lovemaking reached a frenzied pace.

Magical glitter flew everywhere as I roared my release. Raquel's body clamped around me and held me fast as our simultaneous orgasms ripped through us. Color blurred my vision and I held her like I would never let her go.

As the aftershocks of her orgasm shook her body, I placed kisses on her trembling lips.

"I am so in love with you it hurts," I said softly.

Her eyelids fluttered open and I pressed my forehead to hers.

"If it keeps getting better, we've not going to survive this mating," she said in horse voice punctuated with a small giggle.

"If this is the way I have to die, I'll die a happy man," I teased, tucking her wild sex mussed hair behind her ear.

"You're extremely good at this," she purred contentedly.

"I know," I replied, unsuccessfully trying to bite back my very self-satisfied grin.

"Oh my God." Raquel rolled her eyes and pulled my hair. "You are such a big dick."

"Thank you," I said with a smirk.

"I didn't say you had a big dick. I said you were a big dick."

"This is true," I agreed.

"Wait. What's true? That you're a big dick or you have a big dick?"

"Both," I stated and planted a kiss on her lips before she reached behind her and popped me in the head with something breakable. "Relax your trigger finger, Red. I'm just kidding."

"Uh… huh," she said as she lovingly traced my lips with her finger. "Right."

"We should probably get dressed," I told her at loathe to separate my body from hers. "It might be slightly inappropriate for my ass to be on display when your father arrives."

"Too fucking late! Pun intended," Pam yelled gleefully from the doorway. "You two are just like rabbits. And that's a mighty cute ass you have there, Heathcliff."

"Now darling," the King said with a chuckle. "They've just mated. You remember how it was when we joined together."

"Ummm… Dad?" Raquel squeaked out as she blushed from head to toe.

Being a gentleman, I covered my mate's naked body with mine giving my in-laws an even clearer picture of my bare ass.

"Yes, dear?" the King inquired kindly.

"Would you guys mind giving us a minute here?" Raquel asked as she put her hands over her eyes in mortification.

"No worries. We'll meet you in the kitchen in five," the King offered as he pulled a still cackling Pam from the room.

We were silent for a long moment as we stared at each other and tried not to laugh. It felt as if we were in high school and had been busted having sex in the basement of her father's home. Of course we were hundreds of years old and we were in Raquel's house… but it felt the same.

"Well, that was certainly embarrassing," Raquel said with a snort as I rolled off of her and handed her back her dress which had ended up draped over a lamp.

"Correct. However, if they'd arrived a few minutes earlier, it would have been hellacious," I said with a grin.

"Sweet Jesus," Raquel groaned. "You're right. Let's just be happy for small favors today."

"I can do that," I said as I offered my now fully clothed mate my hand. "Next time what do you say we lock the door?"

"Works for me."

She grabbed my hand and slapped my ass. We walked out of the room with our heads held high.

I was the luckiest bastard in the world.

The whole wide world.

Chapter 19

Politely ignoring the pornographic scene they'd walked in on, Pam and the King greeted us warmly— although it was very obviously killing Pam not to tease us mercilessly. She kept giving us the evil eye coupled with an enormous grin. Jean Paul was clearly up to speed on the latest gossip. His smile was large and he gave me a covert thumbs up.

The family I'd mated into was nuts... and I was fine with that. Very fine.

"Are we ready to get down to business?" the King asked as he made himself comfortable at the large solid oak kitchen table.

"Looks to me that Heathcliff and Raquel have already been there and done that," Pam muttered under her breath with glee.

Thankfully, everyone chose to pretend we didn't hear the reference to the X-rated movie Raquel and I had just starred in.

"Yes," Raquel said as she seated herself next to me and shot Pam a look that made her simmer down.

"Well my dear, it appears that the Angels were not only told you were not attending the Summit, it was implied that you were ash," the King said with a disgusted shake of his head.

"They were told I was *dead*?" Raquel asked shocked.

"Yep," Pam confirmed. "I wanted to set the doucheheads straight, but amazingly I held my tongue. I decided finding out who spouted such bullshit was more important than shocking my brethren Angels with my creative use of language."

"Very wise of you dear," the King said lovingly.

"Damn right," she agreed. "It was all from that twatwaffle, Vlad."

Pam confirmed what we had suspected—far more descriptively than any of us would have.

"Vlad is aware of the curse," Raquel said as she absently stroked my hand. "Someone told him about it."

"This is true," the King said tightly. "Or perhaps he placed the curse."

"But what about Gareth?" Raquel questioned. "And Leila, Nathan and Alexander?"

"We only know for sure that Gareth was cursed. Has Ethan checked in?" Jean Paul asked as he set a platter of chips and a variety of salsa in front of Pam.

She dug in with gusto as we all looked on with amusement and a bit of envy. Angels could eat. Vampyres could not. For a brief moment, I felt Astrid's pain of not being able to consume food.

"Haven't heard from Assjacket, Ethan or Gareth yet," Pam mumbled through a mouthful of food. "We've tried to contact them, but we haven't been successful."

Pam loved to mess with Astrid's name. I'd heard everything from Asshead to Assbutt to Asswipe from the Angel's foul mouth. Astrid didn't seem to mind. She had many profane endearments for her Guardian Angel as well. To an outsider they seemed contentious with each other, but that was as far from the truth as one could get. Both would kill and die for each other.

"That doesn't bode well," I muttered as I tapped out a private code on my cell to Ethan that he should answer immediately.

Nothing. *Shit.*

"Satan's with them," Raquel volunteered hesitantly. "They should be safe."

The groans of dismay from the King, Pam and Jean Paul were loud and guttural. Again my original plan seemed less appealing by the second. However, it was happening for better or worse. The Devil never failed to deliver.

"Who got Satan involved?" the King asked with a shudder.

"I did," I replied evenly and waited to be lambasted. "He's bringing someone who should be able to throw Vlad off his game."

"Astrid needed the Devil too," Raquel added quickly, trying to lessen the ire directed at me from her father. "She couldn't break the Demon spell holding Gareth without caving in Paris."

"My girl is growing up," Pam said with pride and nudged her unhappy mate. "Couple of months ago that child would have taken out the entire fucking United States without meaning to. So who owes the sneaky little bastard favors?"

"Obviously Heathcliff does," Raquel confirmed with a sour expression. "However, Astrid plans to have the Devil owe *her* by calling Napoleon an assbucket turd knockin' little shit for brains when she gets to the Summit."

"That's certainly going to go over well," Jean Paul snorted as dropped his head to the table with a thud.

"Napoleon isn't there," the King informed us with a slight wince. "I hear he's hung up at the moment."

"Hung up?" I repeated, confused.

"Hung up." Pam nodded and visibly gagged. "Pole shoved up his mean, undead ass. Hanging high at Dracula's pad. Ass harpooned. Butt spiked. Impaled," she tacked on at the end of her colorful diatribe just in case all her other references had flown over our heads.

They hadn't.

"Well, that's certainly some piercing news—heinous pun intended," Raquel said with a half giggle-half groan. "Will he live?"

"People *that* mean never die." Pam shook her head and went to the refrigerator. "Damn," she bellowed happily. "You undead people sure keep a nicely stocked fridge for people who can't drink anything but blood."

"I knew you were coming," Jean Paul told her.

"Did you bake a cake?" she sang with a smirk.

"Ummm… no," Jean Paul laughed. "You would want nothing I cooked seeing as I can't taste it."

"No worries, child. I'll be fine with what's here."

Pam grabbed some fancy French cheese, crackers, potato chips, cheesecake, a cooked chicken, whipped cream, a jar of pickles and Ranch dressing and settled back in.

"So Vlad informed the Angels of my demise?" Raquel questioned as she gaped in horror at Pam's buffet.

"Yes," the King said tersely, oblivious to his mate's line up of mismatched of edibles—or possibly used to it. "It was before we'd arrived and we decided not to set anyone straight. More of a chance to find out what's going on if we played as if we were uninformed."

"He means we acted like dumbasses," Pam added with a wink as she dipped her chips in the salad dressing

The visual of the breathtakingly beautiful Angel slathering grease covered paper-thin fried potatoes in white goop was all kinds of wrong, but Pam was Pam…

"And you found out what?" I asked as I placed my fingers under Raquel's chin and closed her mouth before she commented on Pam frightening array of food and questionable table manners.

"Strangely, not much," the King said as he lovingly rubbed his mate's back while she ate. "I want to know if Vlad cursed you, Raquel. I want proof so I can tear him apart with my bare hands."

"Get in line," I snapped. "However, I do believe we're overlooking the obvious. At this point, there's no way to determine if Vlad placed the curse on Raquel, or Gareth or the others if they've been cursed. Only he can tell us that."

"Well, that certainly isn't gonna fucking happen," Pam said with a mouthful of cheese and crackers. "That bastard would rather shove a pole up someone's ass than deal with his own shit."

"He wouldn't tell us… but he *might* tell someone else," I said cryptically.

"Who? Raquel?" Jean Paul asked, clearly unhappy at the thought of his sister going one on one with the bastard.

"Nope," I replied.

"All right, I'll bite. Who in Jesus-in-a-thong's-name are we overlooking?" Pam said as she offered a squirt of whipped cream to her mate, the King.

He politely declined and gave her a kiss on her nose.

"The missing puzzle piece," I said enjoying the perplexed expression everyone's face. "The only one who would reveal Raquel's secret and the one who tried to kill her. The lovely gal I have in mind had to have informed Dracula as he shall be known henceforth, that Raquel was slated for death."

"Holy shit… *Juliet*," Raquel said as her fangs dropped and her eyes turned green with fury.

"Well Hell fire and damnation, why on earth do we always forget about that canker sore?" Pam bellowed and punctuated her disgust with a table slam that sent all the food flying.

"Wishful thinking?" Raquel suggested as she deftly ducked a flying cheesecake.

"It breaks my heart to agree with your summation, but I fear it's correct," the King said quietly.

Juliet had been missing for hundreds of years and the King had searched tirelessly for his renegade daughter. His hopes of a joyous reunion had been dashed tragically in the last year. Not only had Juliet tried to kill Raquel, she'd also tried to kill Astrid and help some unsavory Demons take over the world. Thankfully, her skills were lacking and her insanity made her stabs at power a joke.

But innocent people had died because of Juliet. Being locked up in the Cressida House was just the beginning of the Hell she was going to have to pay for all she'd done— especially if she was involved in this mess as well.

"I want to avoid a war with the Angels," the King stated firmly. "We can't afford to fight them. Untold numbers of our people and theirs would die needlessly if this is all the brainchild of Vlad."

"Then we simply need to trick him into admitting his guilt in front of us and the Angels," I stated logically.

All at the table stared at me as if I'd lost my mind.

"And I want to be a unicorn that poops rainbow glitter," Pam said in her outdoor voice. "That shishkabobbing fool ain't gonna come clean on anything. And I guarantee you that spear-happy motherfucker will never tell the Angels shit about anything."

"Ahhhhh, but I think he will," I disagreed. "He just needs the right person to ask. Possibly our own certifiable Juliet would do the trick in persuading him."

The chorus of *no's* and a loud *you're fucked in the head* from Pam rang out in the kitchen. I just smiled and waited. I was far from crazy. I was fucking brilliant.

"You are not bringing Juliet to Europe," Raquel said vehemently. "She won't help us anyway—especially if she's involved in all this with Vlad."

"Raquel's correct," the King added. "Juliet's a loose cannon and it would be a very unwise move to bring her here."

"If he admits it to her, we avoid a war. We steer clear of senseless death. We stay on good terms with the Angels and they get to punish Vlad. It's a win—win," I said cockily knowing I was only revealing part of my plan.

I knew I was being an ass, but I was enjoying myself tremendously

"If she wasn't so damned unbalanced it would be a solid plan," Raquel insisted, still in protest mode. "She'll do anything to destroy us. You can't possibly be thinking about relying on her with something so large and potentially deadly for our race."

"Yep, I am," I admitted with a casual shrug.

"You're an idiot," Raquel snapped and ran her hands through her hair in frustration. "A total idiot."

"Let him finish," the King said watching me, his curiosity piqued. "You're only revealing part of this plan. Finish."

"We need Juliet, but does it actually have to be *the real Juliet*?" I asked as I glanced over at Jean Paul.

Jean Paul had stayed quiet for the last few minutes and watched the scene play out with a small smile on his lips. He knew exactly where I was going with my line of thinking and he was as entertained by the confusion as much as I was.

"You know what?" Raquel huffed as she slapped my shoulder hard. She'd caught on, but wasn't pleased to have been played. "You are a dick. Brilliant, but still a dick."

"Thank you." I gave her a small bow and blew her a kiss.

"I still as confused as shit here," Pam shouted. "Anyone want to clue me in?"

"Well," Jean Paul started, and was cut short by Pam slapping her hand over his mouth.

"No! Don't tell me. I hate it when I know how a movie or book ends. I want to be surprised," she announced with an evil little grin. "How does Satan play into this? No! Wait. Don't tell me."

Satan… damn it. I'd almost forgotten about him. Pam had a fine point. My original plan was to piss Dracula off. Not going to be helpful with a better plan in place. I needed to get hold of the Devil and tell him to abort plan A. The problem was I couldn't get through to any of them at the moment.

Fuck.

"I'll let Satan know to drop the original plan," I muttered as I tried to reach Ethan with our secret code.

Again, nothing.

"Still no answer?" Raquel asked as she glanced at my phone with concern.

"No," I replied tightly.

"I'm sure they're fine," she said firmly. "We'll just stop Satan from doing whatever he was going to do when they get there."

"Sounds like a plan," I said as I stood and prepared to go back to the Summit.

The only problem with that scenario was that the Devil did whatever he wanted whenever he wanted. He'd been enormously amused at the thought of Vlad going ballistic when he showed up with the famous and dead actor who'd immortalized *Dracula* in film. It was common knowledge that Vlad violently despised the depictions of himself in literature and film. Normally my ideas were faultless. This one… not so much.

I vant to drink your blood might be the line that ends the human, Angel and Vampyre races…

Fuck. Fuck. Fuck.

"We need to get back to the Summit now," I snapped.

"What about Raquel?" the King asked. "I don't think it wise to reveal the curse is broken yet."

"He's right," Jean Paul said. "We don't want Vlad suspecting anything is amiss."

"While all this may be true, what we really don't want is Satan showing up with Bela Lugosi and having him tell Vlad he wants to drink his blood," I said, revealing my shitty plan to all.

"Holy shitknockers," Pam screeched and jumped up and down like a bouncing ball. "That is so fucking awesome! I wish I'd come up with it myself. He'll split in half like Rumplefuckingstein."

Raquel just stared at me in disbelief and tried desperately to bite back her laughter. "Was that really plan A?" she asked on a burst of giggles.

"Yes. Yes, that was plan fucking A," I hissed as everyone in the room let their laughter rip. "I didn't have much to go on, so I figured I'd start by pissing the bastard off."

"You shall certainly succeed at that, my friend," the King said, still chuckling.

I grinned and shook my head ruefully. "It was not my finest, but as I said, I had to start somewhere."

"I think you should still use plan A," Jean Paul said thoughtfully. "It will definitely get him to leave the room and then I can go to work."

"Or Dracula will blow up the room and everyone in it," Raquel added and sobered us all quickly.

"Nah, Roberto will zap his ass so hard and so fast, Vlad won't even know what hit him. I'll let Roberto in on

199

the secret," Pam said with her eyes as wide and excited as a child's on its birthday.

I smiled at Pam's willingness to help my cause. "Actually, I need to have a word with Roberto as well. Can you get me a private meeting?"

"Does Davis Hasselhoff like his hamburgers?" she demanded with her hands on her hips and brows arched high.

I was silent because I had no fucking clue if her answer meant yes or no.

"She'll get you the meeting," the King said as he watched his nutbag of a mate with fondness. "She just has an unusual way of imparting the information."

"That she does," I agreed and took Raquel by the hand. "Can you stay cloaked if we go back now?"

"Does the Pope wear red shoes?" she asked me with a wicked twinkle in her eyes.

"The old one did," I shot back with a grin.

She giggled and gave me a kiss. "Of course I can stay cloaked. I'm a Master fucking Vampyre," she whispered.

"That you are, my love. Everyone ready?" I asked.

The chorus of yeses were strong and confident.

It was time to go kick some Vamp ass—well one Vamp's ass. I just hoped it didn't result in a war.

Chapter 20

It was a shit show of epic proportions...

Never, ever again would I ask Satan for help.

"Oh my God," Jean Paul shouted over the din of Angels and Vampyres arguing at ear splitting levels. "This is not what I was expecting."

"Fucking awesome," Pam bellowed as she took in the scene.

Satan stood calmly smiling in the middle of the pristine white great room while accusations flew. He was clearly not a welcome visitor. I glanced around looking for Astrid, Ethan and Gareth, but they were nowhere to be found, Neither was the guest I requested the Devil bring.

I glanced up to the Heavens and thanked God for small favors. Clearly Satan hadn't retrieved Bela Lugosi... yet. I needed to call off my request or at least save it until we needed it for a distraction. However, getting to the Devil was an issue. Not only were loud disagreements going on, there was an inordinate amount of pushing and shoving—fangs and wings were clashing.

Son of a bitch...

"Good evening everyone. So sorry to be late to the clusterfuck. I was busy taking a shit on the stock market. It's so delightful to play with such greedy fuckers," Satan bellowed joyously as the crowd—both Angels and Vampyres—froze in horror. "I must say, I did some outstanding damage to the tech sector."

The silence was loaded. The grumbling started slowly and rose steadily. It was a very well known fact that Vampyres and Angels were heavily invested in technology—especially the Old Guard Vamps. The rabid displeasure and the nervous tapping of phones sounding like frantic tap dancing. Clearly they were checking their stocks. The shocked grunts and hisses of fury confirmed that Satan had indeed taken a shit on the stock market.

"Yes," the Devil purred as his eyes turned red with glee. "I do believe I leveled a few *big* ones."

His laugh was positively maniacal and it was difficult not to join him. The expressions of rage on the faces of the Old Guard were tremendously enjoyable. Of course, I probably suffered some losses due to Satan's screwing with the market, but I didn't give a shit. Money came and money went. The need for endless riches had never defined me.

"This Summit did not include any invitations for *Demons*," Vlad sneered as he stepped forward out of the crowd and went toe to toe with the irreverent King of the Underworld.

Holy Hell, Vlad was as stupid as he was arrogant—but mostly stupid. Satan was *not* someone to fuck with.

"Now that's just rude," Satan pouted and made himself comfortable on a nearby couch.

"You must leave. *Now*," Vlad continued cockily as he puffed out his chest and postured.

"But I brought some of your friends, *Dracula*," Satan informed Vlad in a silky tone that made everyone in the room uncomfortable.

A few snickers escaped at Satan's use of the despised moniker, but they were quickly muffled as Vlad snapped his head around to find the perpetrators. The arrogant Vampyre literally seethed with anger at the name he so hated, but the feral look on Satan's face stopped him from writing his own death warrant by attacking him.

Wait. What the Hell did Satan mean by *friends*? I'd only requested Bella Lugosi.

"Yes, it was tiresome to gather such an illustrious group together, but I'm quite sure it shall be well worth it," Satan said breezily as he stood and took a few steps toward Vlad.

The Vampyre took several steps back, but then stood his ground. Vlad's power couldn't be discounted and Satan was very aware of this fact. He watched Vlad through a narrowed gaze and an evil little grin on his lips.

"I'm sure I have no clue what you're speaking of," Vlad spat. "But you are not welcome here, Beelzebub. You are neither Angel nor Vampyre."

"Ahhhhh....," Satan shot back smoothly with an undercurrent of menace that made me yet again regret asking for his assistance. "That's where you're wrong, *Dracula*."

Vlad's body shook with outrage at Satan's repeated use of the detested title, but he held himself at bay. "I don't believe I am wrong, *Demon*."

"If you weren't such an infuriating blowhard asshole, I might actually like you. I usually adore cretins like you, but there's something wildly unappealing about you," Satan told him as he conjured a glass of wine out of thin air and took a calculated sip. "I'm a *Fallen Angel*, you imbecile. I have every right to be here," he hissed venomously as Vlad took another few discreet steps back.

"He's correct," Roberto, the Angel in charge said as he closed his eyes and expelled an enormous put upon sigh. "We may not want him here, but he does have the right to be present."

"Thank you, Roberto." Satan winked at the annoyed Angel. "I'd say it's lovely to see you again, but it's not."

"And the same to you, Lucifer," Roberto replied dryly. "How long are you planning to stay?"

"Not long," Satan assured a somewhat relieved Roberto. "Just long enough to stir the pot a bit—so to speak."

"I see," said Roberto as sparks of displeasure began to float around his body. "Satan?"

"Yes?"

"Please do whatever you need to do and be on your way. However, if it includes anyone dying I will smite your sorry ass to Hell and make sure it stays there for a few centuries," the Angel promised with a benign smile on his angelic face.

"It's no wonder I fell, you Angels are utterly boring, with no fucking sense of adventure or humor," Satan said flippantly. "You used to be sssssssssssssooooooo much fun, Roberto."

Roberto snarled. Satan grinned and blew him a kiss.

When had the Devil developed a lisp? Out of habit, I turned to ask Raquel and realized although she was next to me no one could see her. I lightly touched the air and felt her. Her presence kept me centered instead of distracted.

"Do it now, Satan. Have your fun and be gone," Roberto snapped.

"So be it. I'll be right back. I need to get Dracula's buddies. I locked them in the trunk of my Aston Martin so they wouldn't get away. It's so difficult these days to get kidnap victims to play nice. Do you feel me, Roberto?" he asked the now fuming Angel.

"Lucifer," Roberto growled.

"Don't get your panties in a wad, Bert," Satan purred, undeterred as he strolled out of the room. "Stick around. I think you'll enjoy this. And please don't any of you think about leaving... I'd hate to have to drag you back in for the show."

As he left the room, impenetrable iron bars instantly appeared on all the windows and doors essentially trapping everyone in the large ballroom. The shouts of fury came fast and magic flew around the room like bullets. I had a very limited amount of time to put plan B into action, but that didn't stop me for a second. I felt Raquel's cloaked hand touch my shoulder and I sprang into action. The melee was actually to our benefit.

"Roberto," I said as I took the powerful Angel's arm and steered him to the outside edges of the room that were far less populated. "We believe Vlad is the catalyst in trying to eliminate the Royal Family."

"Very serious accusation, Heathcliff," he replied flatly as he glanced down at my hand that held his arm in a vise like grip. "What proof do you have?"

Slowly removing my hand, I gave him a tight smile and a shrug. "Not much at the moment, but if you follow my lead I believe you'll be able to take the bastard into custody within the hour."

His gaze narrowed and a small smile played at his lips. "This interests me," he allowed cautiously. "However, if you're wrong it will be both you and the Royal Family that will suffer."

"If I'm wrong, the entire immortal world will suffer," I shot back.

The Angel stared long and hard as he considered my request. His posture was relaxed, but his eyes revealed his rabid fascination. The Vampyres were not the only ones who wanted to be rid of Dracula…

"Does your King believe this to be true?" he asked.

"I speak for myself, but… " I started.

"I do believe it to be true," the King said as he, Pam and Jean Paul quietly approached. "My children have been cursed and disappearing. Vlad is aware of the curse which leads me to suspect his involvement."

"He has the power to place curses?" Roberto hissed as silver and white glittering sparks flew from his fingertips about his head.

"Calm your fucking jets, Roberto," Pam advised sharply as she doused his flames with a wave of her hand. "If you blow up the room, we all lose."

"Pam," he said through clenched teeth. "Your alliances are spread thin. You are an Angel mated to a *Vampyre*. Why should I believe any of this? The undead are not the most trustworthy race."

"And neither are the Angels," Pam added cryptically as she stared Roberto down. "I seem to have a few recollections that might interest a couple of higher ups."

"Are you threatening me?" he inquired with a raised brow.

"Do I need to?" Pam asked innocently.

The tension was fucking palpable. The standoff was intense and if we weren't under a time constraint it would have been interesting to watch the deadlock play out. However, time was of the essence. Forcing the hand of an Angel was risky, but the consequences of letting Vlad get away with what he was doing were far more risky.

"Can you cloak and hide you scent?" I asked Roberto, interrupting the silent face off between him and Pam.

The Angel snorted derisively. "Do you have any more ridiculous questions?" he huffed in exasperation as his eyes narrowed dangerously. "I am three thousand years old. What do you think the answer to that ludicrous request is?"

"I'm going to go with a yes on that one," I replied as I catalogued a reminder to myself to have Pam share what she had on Roberto.

He was an uppity son of a bitch, but I already knew that. Most Angels were. But the truth was I needed him and his self-righteous ass at the moment. Unless we had a witness that wasn't a Vampyre, we'd have information and accusations coming from only one side. His unwillingness to participate was not working for me—at all.

Wait the fuck a minute… I didn't need Pam to *tell* me anything. I opened my mind and let it flow to Pam's. She was ready for me. Roberto's indiscretion was forefront in her head. Her covert wink let me know she was expecting me. Holy shit, this was good. Roberto was a bad boy.

"Garden of Eden," I said flatly. "That damn snake was a pesky little bastard wasn't he?"

Satan's elongated sssss now made sense. He didn't have a lisp, he was reminding Roberto of the role he'd played in Eden. I'd always thought the snake was Satan, but I also thought the Pope still wore red shoes.

The Angel's hiss of rage momentarily made me doubt using the information, but winning was never easy. It would be quite boring if it were simple.

"I can cloak. I can hide my scent, and I can also kill you. Permanently," he ground out with lips barely moving.

"Perhaps," I agreed as I felt Raquel squeeze my arm tightly. "But I'd put up a Hell of a fight. It would stand to reason if I have this knowledge others might too. Killing me might open a can of wormssssssssss that would have you spending more time with your comrade in Hell."

"Enough," Roberto snapped. "I will do as you ask… *this time.* I will not be blackmailed into anything in the future. Are we clear?"

"Very," I replied in a clipped tone. "After Satan brings in his guests… "

"You mean his kidnap victims?" Roberto corrected.

"Semantics," I replied smoothly, ignoring his sharp intake of breath at my insolence. "After Vlad sees the guests, I'm quite sure he'll leave the room. Cloak yourself and follow him. I'll be with you."

The Angel stared at me through hooded eyes. His lips thinned and he made a low whistling sound through his clenched teeth. "You have large balls for a Vampyre," Roberto commented.

"Thank you," I replied trying not to wince at the pinch my mate delivered to my ass.

"Wasn't a compliment," he shot back. "You have a plan?"

"I have a plan," I confirmed as he looked at me doubtfully.

"I will do this more out of curiosity than any allegiance to your Royal Family."

"I beg to differ," Pam hissed under her breath.

"What was that?" Roberto inquired.

"I said I feel like a heifer," Pam lied with a serene smile. "Ate my own weight in whipped cream about a half hour ago."

Before Roberto could reply a hush fell over the two hundred Vamps and Angels in the great room.

Satan was back and all fucking Hell was about to break loose.

Chapter 21

"No fucking way," I muttered as I watched Satan stroll back into the room with a terrified entourage—two of them weren't even dead yet.

"No one will believe this," Pam said as she yanked out her cell phone and hit record.

This was not what I'd requested and my stomach clenched. I was torn between laughing at the Devil's selection and roaring that the use of humans, *no matter how amusing,* was unacceptable.

Bela Lugosi was dead and understood the Underworld, immortals and all the rest of the shit that went on under the human's noses. He apparently enjoyed visiting Hell on a regular basis. There was even a rumor he'd once beat Mr. Rogers at poker—a difficult feat at best. I could only assume Leslie Nielson was also up to speed on the bizarre goings on in the afterlife. His somewhat calm demeanor led me to hope this was accurate.

However, Gary Oldman and George Hamilton appeared to be on the verge of a mental breakdown or pissing themselves. Not good. Not good at all.

All of the men were clad in Dracula costumes from their respective films. The unfortunate atrocious bun—for lack of a better word—on Oldman's head was at least twice the size I'd remembered from watching the movie.

Satan was positively giddy as he lined the four men up on a raised platform at the far end of the large room.

"On three boys," he directed.

The crowd surged forward toward the evening's unusual entertainment, but all eyes were on Vlad. He had gone utterly still and red flames began to shoot out around him. It was highly doubtful he would incinerate the Angel's great room, but the expression on his face didn't bode well for a damage free evening.

"What is going on?" Roberto demanded as he waved his hands and turned all the bars covering the windows and doors in the room to ash. "What is that idiot thinking?"

I decided to keep the information that Bela Lugosi had been my idea to myself. I figured since Satan had taken it upon himself to bring four Draculas, not just one. I was off the hook.

"It's a ploy to piss Vlad off and separate him from the Old Guard," I explained quickly as I took his arm and pulled him to a position closer to Vlad. Losing him would be disastrous. Raquel was next to me. I could feel her even though I couldn't see her. I made sure Jean Paul stayed close as well.

Roberto's chuckle took me by surprise. "Fucking brilliant," he muttered.

Damn it, if I'd known he would approve, I would have taken credit.

"Your Majesty and Pam," I instructed in a whisper. "Find Ethan, Astrid and the rest. If Satan's back they should be here too. Get them up to speed and have them ready to fight."

"But I need to film this shit," Pam said.

"Trust me. It's being filmed," I told her.

Cell phones were out and aimed at both the stage and Vlad. There would have to be major damage control after this one.

"Come," the King said as he took Pam's hand and quickly slipped from the room.

And the show continued…

"One, two, three," Satan bellowed, barely able to contain himself.

"I vant to drink your blood," the four men choked out in a strangled whisper.

"Louder boys!" Satan insisted. "No one could hear you."

"I vant to drink your blood," they said with a bit more volume.

"Better," the Devil congratulated the frightened foursome. "Now do the thing I showed you. And Leslie, do that thing with your eyes like you did in Airplane. That just slays me," he said as he clapped his hands together in delight.

It had the makings of a horrific reality show. Bela Lugosi, Leslie Nielson, Gary Oldman and George Hamilton spread out and became something akin to an air guitar rock band as they chanted, *I vant to drink your blood* over and over. Bela was the lead singer. Gary was on drums with his vamp-bun bouncing dangerously to the left. Leslie was on air guitar making googly eyes and I was fairly sure George was on an invisible keyboard. Fucking unbelievable.

"This is for you, Dracula," Satan yelled as the crowd began to laugh.

Even the Old Guard was shocked enough to chuckle at the mortifying spectacle. However, Vlad was quaking— literally.

For a brief second, I was certain he was going to blow up the room. The flames engulfing his body burned so bright I had to shield my eyes. Clearly Roberto and Satan were on the same page. As Vlad raised his hands above his head in a psychotic rage, he was zapped on two sides from both the Devil and the Angel standing next to me. They weren't killing blows. They were warning blows.

"Enough," Vlad screamed as he quickly recovered from the cautionary zaps. "This will end immediately."

"But wait," Satan said, goading the unstable Vampyre past his limit. "We've rehearsed more. Tell everyone your name boys."

"I. Am. *Dracula*," Bela Lugosi announced grandly as he whipped his shiny black cape around him and gave the crowd his patented evil eye.

The applause was loud and Bela took a deep and heartfelt bow.

"No," Leslie Nielson shouted, shoving Bela out of the way and waggled his brows so high I thought they would hit his hairline. "I am *Dracula*."

Clearly the actors were now relishing their roles thanks to the laughter from their audience. They were unaware of the deadly Vampyre seconds away from losing his shit.

"I am tan *Dracula*," George Hamilton proclaimed in his best Transylvanian accent.

Satan's spit take and loud guffaw were more amusing than the shit show on the stage. Not to be outdone by his competition, Gary Oldman jumped out in front, removed the pins from his bun, tore his shirt open as his hair tumbled around his face and revealed a pair of fake fangs.

"I am the real *Dracula*," he grunted as he gnashed his plastic teeth at the now shrieking crowd.

"Is it time to break dance or do we fake fight and bite each other now?" George Hamilton called out to a doubled over Satan.

"Fucking improvise," Satan commanded through tears of mirth.

And they did.

And it was brilliantly horrific.

And it did exactly what I wanted and expected it to do.

As Vlad fled the room in a furious huff, I grabbed Roberto and Jean Paul and tailed him.

"Cloak," I hissed as we picked up our pace. "We can't lose the bastard."

"I can find a needle in a haystack," Roberto bragged as he disengaged his arm and cloaked himself.

At this point I lost the ability to know if he was still with us, but I simply had to hope he'd keep his word. Jean Paul and I stayed in corporeal form and I led the way. We stayed close to the walls and followed him through several long hallways. I felt Raquel's presence and halted as Vlad turned right into a room and slammed the door violently behind him.

"Raquel, you need to stay away unless you can hide your scent. It will destroy the entire plan if he knows you're there," I whispered. "Plus he wants you and there's no telling what he'll do in this state."

"I know," she grumbled. Her disembodied vice floated through the air. "I'll go search for Ethan, Astrid and the gang and bring them here. Do not, under any circumstances, die. I will find you and kill you dead myself if something happens to you. Do you understand me?"

"That's true love," Jean Paul said with a chuckle.

"A little violent if you ask my opinion," Roberto's body-less voice chimed in.

"No one asked," I said, relieved that he had kept his promise and followed. "I'm not sure exactly what will happen once we're in," I admitted carefully, "but stay cloaked until I drop mine and we'll improvise."

"Like the *Draculas* on stage?" Roberto inquired tightly.

"Yep," I told him with a grin. "We can break dance and bite each other."

"You undead people are highly unorganized," he said in a tone laced with disgust.

"Yes well, we're also highly motivated killing machines," I replied flatly. "Most of us have consciences and can control our violent tendencies, however those like Vlad can't. I say we go in and have a good time."

"Because killing others is so delightful," he spat.

"No, but eliminating bad fuckers is wildly enjoyable," I shot back.

"I suppose when you put it that way… " Roberto conceded. "But I'd prefer to take him alive if he's committed these transgressions you accuse him of. Far more fun to torture the bastard."

"I thought you weren't into that," I said with an eye roll.

"I'm *into* justice. I adhere to an eye for an eye philosophy," he replied.

"Then I'd suggest you have a long stake ready. Vlad seems to be quite fond of them."

Roberto took back his corporeal form for a moment and his feral smile chilled me to the bone. The Angel literally glowed with vicious energy. He was a sick fuck and I never wanted to end up on his bad side. Angels were as unpredictable as Demons. Knowing his dirty secret would either save me at some point or make me a target.

"Are we going to just float in and wait for the idiot to talk to himself and admit his guilt?" Roberto asked, exasperated.

I was tempted to say yes just to piss the Angel off, but this was not the time to have fun at the expense of the uppity bastard.

"While I find that idea intriguing, I have a better plan in mind," I said. "Jean Paul, morph now."

"Wait, this Vampyre can morph?" Roberto asked, completely shocked.

214

"*Mais oui*," Jean Paul answered the question with a shrug and a lopsided grin. "Watch and learn," he added cockily.

The Angel's sharp intake of breath at the insult had me biting back my own grin. I liked my new brother-in-law a lot. He was arrogant, talented, and deadly—a fine combination.

Without fanfare or sound, Jean Paul morphed into an identical version of Juliet. It was eerie and somewhat alarming as I had wanted to kill the woman with my bare hands only days ago. His voice was hers too. His mannerisms were a little off though.

"Damn it," I said aloud as I tried to think of a solve.

I was unsure how well Vlad was acquainted with Juliet. Would he notice the differences? In his heightened state of distress, would he even notice she was there?

"Jean Paul, keep your movement to a minimum and your sentences short."

"I will," he said in her voice. "I've not been around her enough to know her ways. I'll only do and say what I think is essential."

"She's vain," Raquel cut in sheepishly.

"You're supposed to be gone," I told her.

"Correct," she replied. "But since I'm still here, let me help."

I nodded tersely. I wanted her safe and away from whatever was about to happen. It was also true that Vlad may be able to sense her and that would blow our cover. But my ulterior motive for her wellbeing was my main motivator.

"Juliet pulls on her hair when she's unhappy and gestures with her hands often when she's speaking. Her answers to questions are usually curt and she interrupts constantly," Raquel offered in a hushed voice.

"Got it," Jean Paul said.

"She also hates her family—especially me and Astrid."

"Well, she certainly sound like a lovely gal. She's one of the Royal children?" Roberto asked snidely. "Why are we trying to save them if this is the way they behave?"

Ignoring him was far better than flattening him.

"I want you to knock at the door and go in. We'll be right behind you," I instructed Jean Paul. "Are we ready?"

Everyone nodded and I felt Raquel slip away. It did wonders for my peace of mind that she wasn't going to be present during what I was certain would turn deadly for someone—hopefully not one of us.

Roberto and I cloaked and covered our scent. Jean Paul did a few jumping jacks and practiced pulling on his long blond hair. He looked so much like the evil bitch that it was difficult to remember that it was Jean Paul in the form of Juliet.

With a final nod and a bit more hopping around, Jean Paul knocked on the door.

And the second act started.

216

Chapter 22

The room Vlad had escaped to wasn't large. It was as white and luxurious as the rest of the Angel's compound, but this one had some color. The walls were lined from floor to ceiling with icy white marble bookshelves, but the volumes housed in the heavy shelving at least lent some life to the room.

Vlad paced the short expanse as red flames shot erratically around the room.

"Hello, Vlad," Juliet aka Jean Paul said as she stood in the open doorway.

I had moved into the room and positioned myself close to Vlad and prayed Roberto had done the same. On a good day, I could probably take Vlad down. I hoped today was one of those days. He had several thousand years on me and had tricks up his sleeve that I was unaware of, but he wasn't gunning for me at the moment. I was counting on his fury to make him sloppy. However, a confession of what the fuck he was up to was necessary first.

"What are *you* doing here?" Vlad hissed as he approached her, yanked her into the room by the arm and slammed the door shut.

"I heard there was a party I wasn't invited to—*yet again*. So I decided to crash it," she snapped and shoved him away from her.

"Of course you did," he replied and watched her through hooded eyes.

He still sparked dangerously, but there was a new energy in the room. Juliet walked the perimeter of the room and casually knocked books and trinkets from the shelves. My eyes stayed glued to Vlad as he took her actions in with interest.

"You failed your mission," he said tightly. "Raquel is here at the Summit and I don't see you holding the child."

Juliet ignored him and continued on her destructive mission.

"Did you hear me?" he ground out as he grabbed her by the hair and forced her to make eye contact.

His fangs were out and his eyes blazed green. Juliet's lips thinned to a displeased line and she spat in his face.

"Remove your hands or I'll do it for you," she threatened as her fangs descended and her eyes went green with fury.

Fuck, Jean Paul was good.

Vlad's guttural laugh rumbled through the room as he pushed her roughly away. "You're a foul piece of work, Juliet," he growled.

"Thank you," she replied with a sneer. "I'm a product of my upbringing and the company I keep."

"That you are, my mate—that you are."

What the fuck? They were *mated*?

Jean Paul froze inside his disguise and was clearly speechless. Vlad didn't seem thrown by Juliet's silence.

"Still playing hard to get I see. As soon as I've done your dirty work you'll have no more excuses and you'll finally mate with me," he said in a bored tone. "I'm holding up my end of the bargain. You simply keep failing yours."

"I have no idea what you're talking about," Juliet told him with a shrug and a brilliant deranged laugh that demonstrated her instability.

She turned back to her destruction of the library and began to hum a disjointed melody to herself. Juliet pulled at her hair and tossed book after book to the floor.

"I've told you I'll make good on my promises. I've had several of your siblings cursed. They'll age and die within the year."

"You cursed them?" she inquired with an arched brow as she turned to Vlad.

His chuckle was chilling and his actions were an abomination. With a blast of magic that set the pile of books on the floor aflame, he struck Juliet in the face with his fist. Her body flew across the room and she landed in a heap on the floor. Every instinct I had was to kill him, but I knew Jean Paul would not fare well if he was revealed. I cursed myself for not knowing if Jean Paul retained his power when he took on someone else's body.

"What is wrong with you?" Vlad bellowed and gut kicked her. "I had to give up hundreds of millions of dollars and part of my power to make that deal with the Angels. If I could have cursed them myself, don't you think I would have?"

Juliet spit blood out of her mouth and several teeth as she crawled to her feet.

"You stupid fuck," she hissed. "I never told you to give up anything."

"Well that's *new*," he said in a deadly quiet voice that made my stomach roil.

Was the jig up? Did he suspect Jean Paul wasn't Juliet? That would definitely end badly. However, the most alarming part was that an Angel had placed the curses.

I was fairly sure I felt fury emanating from Roberto, but thankfully Vlad was too focused on Juliet to notice.

"What's *new*?" she demanded as she wiped the blood from her face with the back of her hand.

"You told me to give up my immortal life if necessary," he said slowly pronouncing each word with care. "Everything I've done I've done for you, my love."

And I thought Roberto was a sick fuck…

Juliet shrugged and smiled. It was frightening. She was missing teeth and bleeding from her mouth and nose. Her blonde hair was matted with blood and the front of her dress was torn.

"I'm surprised you're not fighting back," he said as he approached her and gently dabbed at the blood running from her lip.

"I'm tired," she replied stonily and slapped his hand away. "Anyway, if Raquel is here why don't you just kill her?"

"You know why." Vlad abruptly turned away and began to pace.

"Remind me," she prompted in a shrewish tone. "Tell me again about *Raquel*."

"I will just to watch you squirm, but I will beat you for your insolence later, Juliet," he said with a smile.

"This isn't a beating?" she hissed as she smeared her blood on her hand and pushed it at his face.

"No, it's not. You should know that by now, my sweet. As to your sister, she's mine. She's denied me too long and I've grown weary of waiting. I gave you a chance to destroy her and you failed… so I get to have her."

"Raquel hates you," Juliet informed him with an ugly laugh. "She'll never have you. You'll be lucky if I mate with you."

"You'll be lucky if you *survive* to mate with me," he informed her with a depraved wink. "However, if you can behave long enough for me to ruin the rest of your family, you will be mine."

"Just ruin? Tell me again all the promises you've failed to keep so far. I want to be sure you remember."

"You're becoming tiresome," he said shaking his head. "I shall spell it out this one last time for you since you seem to be daft this evening. You have asked me to prove my devotion to you by killing your family. I find the idea appealing since they're worthless and have held power for far too long. It's time for a *change*. However, I lust after Raquel and I want her for a toy. You may have a toy of your own choosing. How many fucking times do I have to explain this to you?" he roared as he backhanded her again.

Clearly Jean Paul aka Juliet had had enough. Kicking Vlad's feet out from under him, Juliet straddled him and brought her elbow down on his nose with force and fury. The crunch was sickeningly satisfying. Although Vlad's death would have been more welcome.

"There's my girl," Vlad choked out in triumph as he took her by the neck and squeezed. "I wasn't sure she was still in there. Now will you calm down or do I need to help you along? Because it would give me great pleasure to beat you into unconsciousness."

"I'll behave," Juliet gagged out and grasped at his hands. "But you can't have Raquel as a toy. If you want me, you will leave her alone."

Vlad observed her coldly and then a vicious smile spread slowly across his lips. It was macabre as his nose was still gushing blood from Juliette's hit. "Fine, you win."

"I win what?" Juliet asked watching him warily as she got up and backed away.

"Raquel is here at the Summit. You will kill her and I shall watch. If you won't let me have her, I'll at least get the pleasure of watching you destroy her."

"She's strong," Juliet hissed.

"Not at night she's not," Vlad shot back with a chuckle. "You'll kill her in her death sleep."

"That's cowardly," Juliet spat.

"Since when have you grown a conscience, my darling? My plan is sensible and we're far more likely to get away with it."

"What about my father and Pam?" Juliet inquired as she mopped away the rest of the blood on her face with a pristine white pillow from a chair.

We were going to get a Hell of a bill from the Angels.

"No worries," Vlad said silkily. "Several of the Old Guard are prepared to burn them to ash tonight."

"That's lovely." Juliet's laugh was laced with sarcasm.

"Yes," Vlad agreed, oblivious to her cynicism. "Fires are such tragedies. Now shall we go and kill your sister? The night is wasting away."

There were many reasons I wanted to rip Vlad apart with my bare hands, but he just signed his death warrant with this one. He would never lay a finger on Raquel. I'd die first.

"Where is she staying?" Juliet asked as she pulled wildly at her hair.

"I would assume at her palace outside Paris," he surmised. "If we can't find her, I know a few Angels that will be happy to help."

"Silly me, I thought the Angels were angelic," Juliet quipped dryly.

"Everyone has a price."

I hesitated to open my mind to the thoughts in the room as it pulled on my energy and focus, but I needed to check in with Jean Paul. As I reached out to Jean Paul, I was halted by the turbulence blasting through Roberto's head. The chaotic images that assaulted my brain belonged to the Angel. His fury consumed his thoughts. They were mostly a tornado of color and ire. Faces of Angels flashed through his mind at warp speed. I was aware that he was trying to identify the celestial traitor. His outrage at the thought an Angel had placed the curses ate viciously him. I was fairly sure that, although he might be physically present, Roberto wasn't mentally here in the room with me anymore. I debated if Jean Paul, in his beaten down state, and I could take Vlad down without Roberto's help. I gave us 50/50 odds.

Ripping my mind from Roberto's, I mentally floated to Jean Paul but was stopped again, I was halted by someone's thoughts that should definitely not be in this room. I ground my fangs together and zoned in on my mate. If I'd had my way, she wouldn't be in this country. She would be safely thousands of miles away and heavily guarded, waiting for me to return to her. Alas, that wasn't what fate had intended. Raquel was a powerful force of nature and deadly in her own right. I should have known she wouldn't leave—backing away wasn't in her nature.

God damn it, what in the Hell was she thinking? And if she was *here*, where were Ethan, Astrid, the King and Pam?

In my cloaked state, I moved swiftly across the room and found her. Even invisible I could feel her. I took her in my arms and headed for the door. She was leaving. I was unsure how much she'd heard, but I refused to let her near Vlad.

I reached out to Ethan to speak to him telepathically. If he were close enough, he would hear me as our Prince was gifted with communicating with his people.

"Ethan are you here?" I asked.

"Yes, damn it. Where in the Hell are you?" he answered tightly.

"With Vlad and Juliet," I reported.

"What the fuck?" he shouted. *"She escaped?"*

"No. Hell no," I assured him quickly as I rerouted and pulled Raquel away from the door as Vlad and Juliet were headed right toward our cloaked bodies. *"It's Jean Paul. He morphed and took her form."*

"*Again, what the fuck?*" Ethan shot back. "*Never mind, you can enlighten me on that one later. Is Raquel with you?*"

"*Yes, she is,*" I replied tersely wanting to throttle my mate for disobeying.

"*We found Leila, Alexander and Nathan. They've been cursed and they're in bad shape. Gareth took them back to the Cressida House in Kentucky. They'll be safe there,*" Ethan confirmed.

"*Good. Vlad and Juliet are involved, but the curses were placed by an Angel.*"

"*This is certainly a WTF kind of day,*" Ethan growled.

"*Agree. Find your father and Pam. Old Guard are going to try to burn them to ash tonight,*" I instructed.

"*You have Vlad?*" he demanded.

"*I will shortly,*" I ground out. "*That fucker is mine.*"

"*Good luck.*"

"*I don't need luck,*" I told him. "*It's far past his time.*"

As Vlad and Juliet exited the room, Roberto, Raquel and I took back our corporeal forms. I shot Raquel the evil eye, but she only grinned and winked. She would be the fucking death of me.

"The Vampyre is yours. I heard his confession and I'll back you up with the Council. Alive would be better than dead, but I don't care what you do to him. If you have no choice, kill the bastard," Roberto stated coldly. "I have some Angels to interrogate. And Heathcliff, although I'm loathe to admit this, I owe you a *very large* favor for the information I've gleaned tonight."

On that cryptic note, he vanished in a flash of bright golden light. I had no doubt he would find what he was looking for, I just hoped he would share the information when he discovered it. We might possibly need it to save Gareth and the others. The name of the Angel who placed the curses was exactly what I would use my favor on.

"How long were you in here?" I asked Raquel as I checked my watch for how much of the night was left.

"The entire time," she admitted.

"You can't cover your scent."

"Says who?" she countered.

"Ummm… me?"

"Correct," she replied with a smirk. "You assumed I couldn't and never asked me if I could."

"Color me stupid," I muttered.

"Nope," Raquel disagreed. "Color you overprotective. Sooner rather than later, you'll have to accept that I can take care of myself—been doing it for about five hundred years." She paused and gently laid her hand on my face. "I love you *and* your sexy ass, but I will put said ass in a sling if you treat me like a helpless female. You are mated to a Master Vampyre," she added with an arched brow and a giggle.

"As are you," I told her. "A Master Vampyre with macho caveman bullshit tendencies."

"I happen to like those tendencies in the bedroom, but not when you treat me as a lesser in our real life," she replied softly.

"That's truly not my intention," I argued.

Fuck. Was it?

No.

I knew how powerful my mate was. It was part of why I loved her.

Shit, shit, shit. She was right.

"I'm sorry," I apologized. "It was my inner alpha-hole talking. I will try. I will also fuck up. Bear with me."

"I accept your apology and I will bear with you till the end of time, Heathcliff. Always."

Taking her beautiful face in my hands I touched my lips to hers. "We should go," I whispered.

"Yep, we need to beat them to the Paris palace so I can pretend I'm dead," Raquel said as she placed her hand in mine.

"Since you were privy to that Hellish scene, do you have a plan in mind?" I asked trying very hard to not be autocratic. Damn it, this was going to be hard.

"Yep. Kill Vlad," she vowed.

"Works for me," I said as I pulled her close and raised her eyes to mine. "You'll be careful?"

"Of course I will. I have everything to live for," she replied. She wrapped her arms around me and we disappeared in a cloud of peach and gold glitter.

Smiling, I shook my head and laughed as we were hurtled through space and time.

She was correct. We both had everything to live for and today was not my day to die.

Chapter 23

The air in the room was thick with malice and the scent of fresh blood. We were in the great room of Raquel's home and unfortunately we weren't alone. I'd taken the lead in the transport and went to the area I was most familiar with... bad move. I should have chosen the bedroom, but as I had never been in there that was an impossibility.

"Well this is certainly *interesting*," Vlad said with a barely bridled fury as he attempted to veil his shock. He shoved Juliet away roughly and took a few measured steps forward. "Isn't it way past your bedtime, Raquel?"

Not exactly the welcome we were expecting.

They stood about twenty feet from where we'd landed. Juliet's eyes were huge and she sported a few more bloody bruises than when we'd last seen her only about twenty minutes ago. Thankfully, Vlad looked a little worse for the wear as well. That was one sick relationship and I was furious that Jean Paul had to pretend to be Juliet and bear the brunt of the psycho's violence.

"How did you break the curse?" he demanded. His sparking hands clenched and unclenched at his sides even though his voice stayed eerily calm.

"How did you know about it?" I shot back, stepping in front of Raquel.

Old habits were not dying at the moment. Raquel smacked my back and took her rightful place next to me.

"My bad," I muttered.

"I should say so," she replied with an eye roll.

Vlad's insolent stare was jarring as he took us in and a hideous smile spread across his thin lips. "I wasn't talking to you, *guard*. But since you asked so politely, my Juliet told me. However, it appears she left out the important fact that the curse is old news."

He turned on Juliet with flaming hands and hit her so hard she crumpled to the floor. Raquel's angry hiss filled the room and Vlad laughed.

"Get up. No time like the present to kill your sister. Do it quickly," he directed Juliet tonelessly, growing bored with the game.

"That Juliet won't harm me," Raquel told him as her hair began to fly about her head and her power began to fill the room.

"She most certainly will," Vlad spat the words contemptuously as he grabbed Juliet by the arm and pulled her to her feet. "She despises you and likes to keep me happy. You see, I've decided if I can't have you then no one can. Juliet shall end you while I take care of your guard."

"Good luck," I threatened softly.

"I missed that," Vlad lied with a chuckle and a disgusted shake of his head. "Bet you're regretting that favor to your Prince now, aren't you?"

"Actually, it's wasn't a favor at all." I shrugged and took Raquel's hand in mine as Vlad's eyes narrowed to slits. "*You see* as a newly mated Vampyre, I refuse to be away from my mate."

"I'm sorry," he ground out as his fangs descended and he took a few more steps forward. "I'm certain I must have misunderstood."

"Well you can't misunderstand this," I retorted as I pushed Raquel back and landed a serious punch to his throat. It should have collapsed his esophagus, but his power and age made regular incapacitating blows difficult.

Vlad grunted and gagged, but recovered in seconds. He retaliated swiftly with a crushing blow to the side of my head. He may be older and more powerful, but I was fighting for something I loved—all he had was hate. I staggered back and waited for him to make the next move.

"Hello boys," Raquel interrupted in a shout, taking both Vlad and I by surprise. Her skin glowed iridescent and her voice dripped false sweetness. "Before we get into it—which I'm sure will be delightful—I wasn't quite done insulting *Dracula*."

"Do. Not. Call. Me. That," Vlad bellowed. His entire body began to sparkle ominously.

"Whoops," Raquel apologized with a giggle. "You're *old* age must be catching up with you. I said… *that* Juliet won't kill me."

"Losing the curse and mating with someone far beneath you must have addled your brain," he replied, shaking his head in mock sorrow as he glared at her. "I heard you clearly. You simply don't make sense."

"Oh but I do," she replied as she crossed the room and took Juliet's hand in hers.

Raquel pulled her away from Vlad as he watched, growling low in his throat. They stopped inches from me. The bastard observed in confusion as Juliet wrapped her arms around Raquel and hugged her lovingly.

Jesus, I was glad I knew Jean Paul was her brother. Anyone touching my mate besides family at this point was going to die.

"Juliet, come back here immediately. You will be *very* sorry for this," Vlad warned.

"Actually, I won't," Juliet replied as she flipped him her middle finger and seamlessly morphed back into Jean Paul.

He wore the same bloody bruises that he'd acquired as Juliet. He was not in his best form and I wanted him to leave. Vlad's roar of displeasure blew out the sidewall of the room. Things were picking up and Jean Paul was in no shape to fight.

"Transport out," I ordered tersely.

"Not on your life," he snapped, his French accent heavier in his fury. "I get a piece of that fucker."

"Heathcliff's right," Raquel implored her brother. "Go. Now."

"I'm not going anywhere," he said challenging both his sister's and my authority.

"Fine," I ground out as I pressed my wrist to his mouth. "Drink."

"Are you done over there?" Vlad asked, pulled himself back together with difficulty. "I'm getting bored with your idle chatter. I have places to go and people to kill."

"You have choices, Vlad," I said carefully.

Jean Paul drank quickly and his open wounds began to close. Sadly, I was certain he would have more open wounds shortly. We all probably would. A violence-free ending wasn't in the cards… but one could certainly try.

"You're giving me choices, guard?" he sneered. "That's rich."

"The Angels know everything. Roberto was in the room with you and our Juliet. Your days are numbered. If you cooperate now, your punishment might be swift instead of long and drawn out as the Angels are wont to do."

"Do I look like an imbecile to you?" Vlad inquired caustically. His eyes blazed green with hatred and insanity.

"Debatable," I answered honestly, with a grin.

With great effort Vlad swallowed his retort and casually took a seat on the couch. He turned on a dime and behaved as if he'd come for a civil visit. The tension in the room was palpable, but he studiously ignored it.

Smoothing out his blood spattered evening coat, he checked the sharpness of his fangs with his fingertips. Seemingly satisfied, he crossed his legs and made himself comfortable—he then made a huge show of counting us.

"One, two, three of you... and only one of me," he confirmed aloud. "I don't think that's fair."

"Seriously?" Raquel asked with a wrinkled nose and disgusted snort.

"Quite, my dear," he purred. "However, I'm far more powerful than the three of you put together. So let me tell you how this will play out."

He paused and removed several knives from his jacket pocket. Placing them on the coffee table in front of him, he pulled a handkerchief from his breast pocket and went to work cleaning his weapons.

"First I will kill your *guard*. I don't like that he has tasted what is mine. And Heathcliff, your reputation as a deadly warrior will be such a delight to disprove."

His laugh was purely to goad me, but I was far smarter than that. Timing would be everything.

"It will be your punishment, Raquel—to watch him die. Next will be the one who fooled me." He glanced over at Jean Paul and showed him his fangs. "I'm going to rip your head from your body... with my teeth. And then I will have you, Raquel. Unfortunately for you it will only be once as I will burn you to ash when I've had my fill."

"That's an ambitious list," I commented as I took the seat across from him. "My goal is far more attainable."

"Really?" he inquired not looking up from cleansing his knives. "And what's on your agenda this fine evening?"

I laughed and his eyes shot to mine in surprise. Time and space idled for a moment as I observed the madness in his gaze.

"One thing," I told him. "There is one thing on my list."

"Are you going to share?" he asked silkily as he stood and rose to his full height.

I considered him for a long moment and grinned at his posturing. Not for a moment did I discount who he was and the power he had. His age alone made him extremely deadly, but his wrath and ego gave me the upper hand.

"I'm going to destroy you."

"Well in that case, why don't we even up my odds?" he suggested.

A flash of red light splintered the room. I put my hand up to shield my eyes from the blast and quickly moved back to Raquel and Jean Paul. As the brightness receded, I realized Vlad had called for back-up. Ten Old Guard Vampyres stood in a line behind him. Their lifeless stares bored into us. This was getting more interesting and fucked up by the second. My need to tear them apart consumed me and I itched to start tearing heads from shoulders.

"Shall we do this honorably?" he snarled.

"Do you even know what that word means?" Raquel inquired sarcastically as she readied herself for battle. "The odds aren't exactly even."

"Too bad, so sad," Vlad sang with a laugh that held no mirth. "Fuck it. Kill the males, but leave Raquel. She's mine. And I've changed my mind, dear Raquel. I'm going to kill you before I take you."

"That is fucking gross," Jean Paul muttered, disgusted.

"And not going to happen," I growled as I dove head first into the fray.

And so it began.

There was no honor—none at all.

However, there was blood.

A lot of blood.

***

They came at us fast and furious. This was a far different game than I'd ever played. I was a Master Vampyre; however, these fucks were Master Vampyres with about a thousand years on the three of us combined. Fangs ripped through skin, and magic shot around the room like dozens out of control boomerangs. As I gripped the head of a particularly aggressive Vampyre, I caught Raquel out of the corner of my eye.

She was truly splendid. A fucking beautiful killing machine. My girl wasted no movement as she took on the Vamp gunning for her. Jean Paul held his own—barely—sparring with two of the ugly undead bastards.

"You're mine," a Vampyre with wild eyes and gnashing fangs screamed as he came at me like a freight train from the bowels of Hell.

Exactly where I planned to send him.

"Not today," I grunted as I met him head on.

We grappled in a match for our lives. He threw punch after punch backed up with a sorcery that flamed through my insides with sickening jolts. Flipping backward, I caught his head in my legs and crushed his trachea. It gave me the precious second I needed to overcome him. In a fluid movement, I tore the head from the son of a bitch and permanently ended the screams of agony he'd wailed seconds ago.

Where the fuck was Vlad? There was a momentary foreboding stillness in the air and I spotted him across the room watching. Such a fucking coward.

In the brief second I'd taken to find Vlad, I'd been struck. Pain shot through my body and seared like fire at the end of my left arm as I realized my hand was gone. The flying magic cast by the Old Guard tore through our bodies like knives. My stump tingled immediately as it began to regenerate, but it would take an hour that I didn't have for it to be reformed and useful. Ripping heads with one hand was difficult. Using my good hand, my fangs, magic and my legs would have to suffice. There was no other choice.

Directly in my sightline, Jean Paul struggled with two Vamps on a mission to destroy. He was bleeding profusely and his arm was attached by only a tendon, but he was still in the battle.

Removing my eyes from my next aggressor would be deadly, so I focused and fought like I'd never fought. The gory satisfaction of decapitating and destroying overwhelmed me and I attacked as if there was no tomorrow coming.

Sound was distorted and my vision was blurred by the vile magic ricocheting around the room, but I moved with precise actions and one goal. Kill the fuck in front of me and get to Vlad before he got to Raquel.

Pain was secondary as dark red blood spurted from multiple wounds on my body. I think I'd killed six. The one in trapped in my vicious chokehold roared as I snapped his neck and yanked his head from his body with my forearms. Raquel's victorious shout and Jean Paul's grunt of satisfaction as my deadly mate pierced the heart of her attacker with her stiletto heel was music to my ears. We'd made it.

They were all dead. All ten of them lay in tattered heaps in different stages of decay around us. Half had already turned to ash. Now to get to the root of all evils…

I quickly cased the room to make sure we hadn't missed anyone and searched for Vlad. Jean Paul was across the room leaning against the wall. It was holding him up. He smiled weakly and gave me a thumbs up.

Raquel was about ten feet from me. She was torn up, bleeding and weak, but she was alive and looked gorgeous to me. Her smile was wicked and I felt the stirring of lust in my lower half. There was nothing about the woman that I wasn't addicted to.

And then there was silence. Silence was always bad in movies.

It was far fucking worse in real life.

Vlad stood on a table at the end of the room cringing in disgust and swearing at the fallen Vampyres. He muttered unintelligibly as he bent down and grabbed his weapon.

It happened in slow motion—like trying to sprint under water. Raquel's eyes were on her brother and in her damaged state her stance was lax and open. The long pointed silver stake in Vlad's strong hands gleamed under the lights of the massive chandelier that had somehow survived unscathed in the battle.

It was only a split second, but it felt like an eternity.

My shout of warning to Raquel as the pole jetted toward her heart only confused her. She turned to me and left herself even more exposed and open than she was only moments ago.

Jean Paul fell to the floor and tried to scramble over to her to knock her out of the way.

Vlad's shout of triumph rang hollow in my ears as images of Raquel from the last two hundred years whirled through my brain. I would love her in this life and beyond. Nothing would change that. The last several days of my life had been the most wonderful I'd known and I wouldn't trade any of it.

I'd even take the next chapter in our love story gratefully if it meant she would live.

Autopilot was my mode as I mentally gauged the velocity and weight of the silver stake with a critical eye. In split seconds, my entire world crumbled around me. I shot from my spot and flew at Vampyre speed into the path of the stake. Raquel's scream pounded through my head as a fire like I'd never known pierced my chest.

Fuck… I'd hoped it would hit lower. Lower would have been so goddamned much better. The room spun and as my body contorted as my mouth filled with liquid. I tried to swallow. If I could drink, I'd be fine—but it just kept coming up. Nothing would go down. Why wouldn't it go down?

"Damn you, Heathcliff," Raquel shouted from a far away place. "You can't die on me. You promised you wouldn't die. I'm a Master fucking Vampyre. I don't need your macho caveman bullshit tendencies. I need you… I need you to live," she sobbed hysterically.

She shook me, but it felt like someone else's body was moving. A reddish haze covered everything in my vision and with sickening clarity, I realized I hadn't killed Vlad. Raquel was above me crying like the world was ending. Tears fell from her eyes and onto my face.

I had to tell her to run. Vlad was still here. He wanted to hurt her.

Where the fuck was Jean Paul? Words refused pass my lips as my joints sizzled agonizingly with the silver from the stake streaming through my blood.

"You will not die. You will not die," she ground out as she bit down on her wrist and pressed it to my mouth.

Her blood poured over my chin along with my own that refused to stay within the confines of my body. She was so very beautiful, even in her distress. Her shouts grew softer even though her beautiful lips continued to move frantically. Slowly she began to fade away.

I was drowning in my own blood. I couldn't thrash or even explain. The stillness of my body was not a comfort. It was a failure. The fire raging inside me was a combination of the silver winding its way through my system and fury. Fury at not having ended the life of the man that wanted to kill the most important person in the world to me.

I knew it was too late. I knew there was no way to reverse the effects of the silver, not to mention I was fairly sure the fucking stake went through my heart. The heart that was breaking slowly as I watched my mate come apart as she mumbled garbled words at me and pressed her soft lips to my face. The world was so fucking unfair…

Her scent was faint, but it was there. I needed to remember. I wanted to take it with me. I needed…

I loved her with my heart, my soul and now my life… but it was good.

She was good.

She would live.

I could close my eyes.

I'd saved her.

And then my beautiful world that held Raquel as the center of the universe faded to black.

Chapter 24

"Well this is some fucked up shit," a hushed female voice said.

"Be quiet," another snapped in frustration.

The pacing around the area was rampant and the whispering nonstop. Tension filled the air and the staccato tapping of heels on hard wood produced the rhythm of a disjointed tap dance. The rustling of papers and far off sounds of splashing water slightly muted the drumming of the feet on the floor.

"This was an enormous mistake," the loudest of the men informed the crowd. "It's against the laws of nature and we're not even sure who in the Hell is even in there now."

"I don't care," a woman said flatly. "I'll know."

"Was this selfish?" a different female asked quietly.

The woman with the flat voice replied coldly. "In the same situation you would have done exactly as I have done. *Do not* judge me until you've stood in my shoes."

The silence was long and then the movement recommenced.

"It's been a week, child. There are only hours left. If you haven't said your goodbyes... the time has come," a kindly male baritone said trying to comfort the flat voiced woman.

"If anyone so much as utters a goodbye, I will end you. If you have no faith then I'd suggest you leave," she hissed.

The raw pain in the woman's tone was heartbreaking. Her belief in a miracle was undeterred even though she seemed alone in her convictions. A soft murmuring of words jumbled together assuring the poor woman that they would stand by her floated in the air like muffled music in a somber key.

"I know you people don't want to hear anything more from my fucking trap, but there were stipulations to this deal," the woman who'd spoken first revealed.

"What are they?" the woman with the flat voice asked tonelessly. "Actually I don't care. He is owed a favor and I called it in. What's done is done."

"Well... because it wasn't technically you he owed the favor to, he tagged on some motherfucking extras," the foul mouthed one replied.

"What in the Hell else on a shit stick did that pompity ass-jacking buttknocker want?" a higher angry female voice demanded.

"That we swear on our lives this never happened and that if something goes awry we are to destroy... "

"Stop," the woman with the flat voice snarled. "I won't hear this."

"You have to," the loud man insisted. "Are you willing to end him if he's not who we want him to be—who we knew?"

"Again," she ground out. "I won't hear this."

"Fine. Did they find the other bastard yet?" the loud male asked tightly.

"No, but there isn't a corner of this earth where he'll be safe. The entire army of our race and that of the Angels are searching," came a terse reply.

"When they find him, he's mine," the woman in pain growled. "The Holy Ones have promised to mute his power and have given me permission to destroy him... slowly."

"As is your right, my child," the gentle voice of the kind male told her.

"I want everyone... to leave," the broken woman said haltingly. "I want to be alone."

"Is that safe?" came a new voice. "We don't know... "

"I *know*," she whispered in reply. "I will always be safe in this place. Go. Please."

The hesitant pattering of feet leaving faded away slowly. Whatever the woman was waiting for she clearly wanted to wait alone.

"Are you sure?" a solitary and grief-filled voice asked.

"Yes. I'm sure."

The quiet was nice and I hoped the woman would be okay. She was so broken and so sad. I wished to comfort her, but I wasn't really here. My physical and spiritual self was balanced somewhere in limbo. It was tiring, but it simply was what it was. Helping was out of the question as I was set to leave to go somewhere. I didn't know where, but I knew the time had come for me to depart this plane.

A cool hand touched my face and drops of warm water caressed my lips and chin. The flat voice of the woman wasn't as lifeless now that she was by herself.

"I'm so sorry," she whispered. "I've prayed constantly that what I've done hasn't caused you pain... but I simply couldn't let you go. I spent over two hundred years running from you because that's what I thought was best for you. But I was wrong and stupid. The Angel owed you and I made him pay. What he did was unnatural and he didn't want to do it, but Pam kept hissing like a snake and eventually he caved."

The sound of soft sobbing pulled at my heart and again I wanted to comfort this sad woman, but again… I wasn't really here.

"That's why I did what I did. Maybe it *was* selfish, but I found a loophole and I took it. You hadn't turned to ash yet. I begged on my knees and I'd do it again. The Angel told me there was a fifty percent chance it wouldn't work—that you would permanently die anyway, but I didn't care. If there was even a one percent chance of you coming back to me, I would have taken it. It's okay if you need to go—I'll let you go," she said in a choked voice. "But I'll follow you. This life means nothing to me without you in it. Nothing. I love you, Heathcliff. I will always love you and I'll be with you soon."

I heard the swish of what sounded like a wall opening and the clanking of metal. The presence of the woman drew near again and I caught a faint whiff of her scent. It was familiar and made me want to stay even though I knew it was time to go. Maybe I could delay a little while longer. She was kind and strong and smelled so damned good. This Heathcliff was a very lucky man to have her love and devotion.

I'd stayed for such a long time even though there were others that pulled for me. For some unknown reason I was still here. Maybe it was the woman.

The feather light touch of lips on mine soothed me and the thought of leaving was less appealing. Suddenly I longed to kiss the lips that pressed against mine, but I was trapped in a place that held me tight.

"I'll wait for you to turn to ash and then I'll take my own life with this sword. It's a beautiful sword. You would like it. It's not frilly or girly. It's a piece I wanted to give you as a gift. I had it made for you over a hundred years ago knowing I'd never give it to you… and sadly I was correct."

She was quiet for a few moments and then I was aware of a slim hand holding tightly to mine.

"It's only fitting that I use this sword to kill myself. It feels full circle," she explained with conviction.

It was lovely that she wanted to die for me. I wondered what I had done to inspire such loyalty.

Wait. What the fuck? She was going to kill herself?

Was I dead? I didn't feel dead. I mean I couldn't move or talk or see… but I could hear her. I could smell her. She was mine.

I couldn't remember her fucking name, but her face was clear and beautiful behind my closed lids—her red hair, her full lips, her soft skin.

Goddamn it, was I dead or not?

"I heard that shit," a different female voice huffed as I heard her march back into the room. The voice sounded vaguely like one I should know. "He would be furious if you offed your ass after he died saving your sorry butt."

"I said I wanted to be alone," the one who was mine snapped.

"And I want world peace and stiletto heels that don't crunch my fucking toes and give me blisters."

"Oh my God, Astrid," the one whose scent kept me here groused. "If he's gone, I have nothing. Nothing. I will follow him till the end of time. And there is no such thing as stilettos that don't crunch toes."

"I call bullshit on all of that except the crunched toe part. First of all, Heathcliff's not gone yet. If you pull a fucking Romeo and Juliet thing and whack yourself right before he wakes up, I will be so fucking pissed I will find you in the afterlife and beat your ass," Astrid vowed.

"There are only minutes left," my girl said harshly. "Just leave."

"Have you tried smacking him in the head or giving him titty twisters?" she suggested.

"Ummm… no."

"He hates titty twisters. All guys do. Watch and learn," Astrid said with frightening determination in her voice.

This Astrid was all kinds of crazy and I hoped she wasn't referring to me in reference to the *titty twister*. Unfortunately she *was* referring to me and she twisted with gusto.

I wanted to shove her away. I ached to make sure the one who was mine didn't hurt herself. I needed… Son of a bitch. I needed to kill Vlad.

I needed to make love to Raquel—my mate.

And I really needed to throw my titty twisting cousin across the room.

Now.

"Off," I choked out in a voice that seemed to belong to someone else. "Off of me. Now."

"Holy shitballs on fire, I can't believe that worked," Astrid squealed.

I pried open my eyes and was greeted with the gaping open-mouthed stare of my cousin.

"Mother humpin cowballs," she yelled. "Your eyes are silver."

"And my nipples are on fire," I shot back weakly. "Where is she? Did she harm herself?" I demanded as I tried and failed to sit up.

"Do you know who I am?" Astrid demanded. "Do you know who you are?"

I closed my eyes and let my heavy head fall back on what I assumed to be a bed. "I am Heathcliff. You are my certifiable cousin, Astrid. My mate Raquel is somewhere in this room and if she doesn't come to me right now, I'll explode."

"I'm here," Raquel cried out as she wrapped her arms around me and planted little kisses all over my face and neck. Her tears fell freely and she gently ran her hands over my still sluggish form. "Are you really back?" she whispered biting back her sobs.

"I'm here. I've been here, but I didn't know I was me," I told her as I tried to remember what had happened. "You made a deal with Roberto?"

"I called in your favor. He brought you back," she said and waited for my reaction.

"I was dead?"

She nodded and chewed nervously at her bottom lip.

"How in the Hell did he do that?" I asked, shocked. I knew Angels had enormous power, but bringing back the dead… or undead as it were.

"If you'd been human, he couldn't have done it," Pam volunteered as she and the King rushed back into the room.

Ethan and Jean Paul followed close behind and everyone stared at me with wonder.

"It's him?" Ethan asked cautiously.

"*Him* has a name, asshole," I said with a fatigued grin.

"Oh good. It is him," Ethan confirmed as a huge relieved smile stretched across his lips.

"I titty twisted him," Astrid volunteered with a wicked glint in her eyes.

All the men including myself grunted in phantom pain as Astrid did the motions of a robustly severe titty twist.

"It's you, but you're more now, my friend," Pam said as she examined my eyes carefully.

"Explain," I said as I gingerly pulled myself to a sitting position with help from Raquel.

"Well, now there's the conundrum," Pam said with a chuckle. "You're a prototype. This has never been done before, but your silver eyes are those of a young Angel."

"Am I still a Vampyre?" I asked, confused. I didn't feel any different than I always had other than the sluggishness of having been out cold for a week. "Am I dangerous to you?"

Astrid stepped forward, placed her hands on my face and closed her eyes. She chanted softly and I felt her massive power flow through my body. Her eyes popped open and she stared at me with a perplexed expression.

"You're not dangerous, but Pam is correct. You are much more than you were before, my cousin."

"Is this a good thing or a bad thing?" I questioned warily.

"That's up to you," she answered vaguely with a lopsided grin.

"That was awfully cryptic for a new Vampyre," I told her with an arched brow and a matching grin.

"Right?" she said gleefully. "I'm finally catching on to this undead shit."

"Do you have fangs?" Raquel asked as she gently rubbed my back and rolled her eyes at Astrid.

I reached into my mouth and promptly cut my finger on the razor sharp tips of my fangs as they descended. The relief I felt was absurd.

"I do." I laughed as I sucked on my bleeding finger.

The taste of blood and the nearness of my mate caused a raging hunger to well inside me. Dizziness overtook me and I slumped back on the bed.

"He needs to feed," the King guessed correctly.

Everyone began to pull up their sleeves and Raquel halted them with a loud and unladylike clearing of her throat. The laughter and catcalls followed my friends out of the room as they all left. Congratulations about not biting the dust were called rudely over shoulders.

And then we were alone.

Feeding could wait. I had a few things I needed to discuss with my mate...

"Vlad got away?" I asked.

She nodded. "Jean Paul went for him after you were staked, but he transported away."

I digested this information and kept my eyes glued to hers.

"We'll get him and when we do, it will be his last day on earth," she promised with vengeance in her lovely eyes.

I nodded and traced her angry frown with my fingertip.

"I want you to promise me something," I said slowly.

"Anything."

"If something happens to me, I want you to go on."

"No," she replied without hesitation and held my gaze defiantly.

"No?" I shot back.

"Let me ask you something," she said as she crawled into the bed with me and snuggled close. "What would you do if I died and there was a chance we could be together in the afterlife?"

Damn it, she had me.

"I would... " I started, trying to think of a clever way out.

"You would join me. You would come to me because that's where you're supposed to be. You can ask nothing of me that you wouldn't do yourself," she insisted quietly, but with steel in her voice.

She was correct and my love for this delicate beautiful woman grew to proportions I wasn't aware I was capable of.

"I'm sorry. It's the damn macho caveman bullshit tendencies," I muttered and pulled her closer.

"Well, we *are* in the bedroom."

Her eyes twinkled and turned a sexy shade of green.

"And I do believe you said as long as I kept the caveman in the bedroom you could live with him."

My smile grew large and my pants tightened considerably.

"But wait," she said with concern and pushed herself away. "You're too weak. Let's just take it easy for a few days. I'll feed you and we can hold each other while we sleep."

"While I appreciate your concern, and I really do—but my dick is killing me and I'm pretty sure blue balls won't help my recovery one bit."

I took her hand and placed it on the evidence of my *not* weak erection.

"Maybe we could combine dinner and a date," she purred suggestively as she pulled her dress over her head.

"I think that is an outstanding idea." I deftly unhooked her lacy bra and tore her barely there panties from her perfect body. "I'll be better in no time if all my hungers get satisfied."

She narrowed her eyes and giggled in such a carefree and joyous way it made my heart soar. I was so in love with her.

"I can work with that scenario," Raquel said as she crawled on top of me and pressed her body to mine. "I love you, Heathcliff."

"I would die for you, Raquel."

"You already did. Please don't do it again."

"Fine point. Well made," I told her as I hugged her like I would never let her go.

"Are you ready for dinner and a date?" she inquired as she ground her hips into mine, sending stars across my vision.

"I am so ready," I said as I grabbed her ass, plunged my fangs into her wantonly exposed neck and took her up on her offer.

All of the details and clutter of what had happened could wait till another day. I was where I was supposed to be with the woman I'd died for safely in my arms.

I was ready.

And so was she.

Ten times ready and it was absolutely Hotter than Hell.

The End (for now…)

Note From the Author

If you enjoyed this book, please consider leaving a positive review or rating on the site where you purchased it. Reader reviews help my books continue to be valued by distributors/resellers and help new readers make decisions about reading them. You are the reason I write these stories and I sincerely appreciate you!

Many thanks for your support,

~ Robyn Peterman

Visit me on my website at
http://www.robynpeterman.com.

Sign up for my email list to get updates.

Coming In 2016

Excerpt from SWITCHING HOUR

Chapter 1

"If you say or do anything that keeps my ass in the magic pokey, I will zap you bald and give you a cold sore that makes you look like you were born with three lips."

I tried to snatch the scissors from my cell mate's hand, but I might as well have been trying to catch a greased cat.

"Look at my hair," she hissed, holding up her bangs. "They're touching my nose—my fucking *nose*, Zelda. I can't be seen like this when I get out. I swear I'll just do it a little."

"Sandy…" I started.

"It's Sassy," she hissed.

I backed up in case she felt the need to punctuate her correction with a left hook. You can pick your friends, your nose and your bust size, but you can't pick your cell mate in the big house.

"Right. Sorry. Sassy, you have never done anything just a little. What happened the last time you cut your own bangs? Your rap sheet indicates bang cutting is somewhat unhealthy for you."

She winced and mumbled her shame into her collarbone. "That was years ago. Nobody died and that town was a dump to start with."

"Fine." I shrugged. "Cut your bangs. What do I care if you look like a dorkus? We're out of here in an hour. After today we'll never see each other again anyway."

"You know what, Miss High and Mighty?" she shouted, brandishing the shears entirely too close to my head for comfort. "You're in here for murder."

That stopped me dead in my pursuit of saving her from herself. What the hell did I care? Let her cut her bangs up to her hairline and suffer the humiliation of looking five. Maybe I wasn't completely innocent here, but I was no murderer. It was a fucking accident.

"You listen to me, Susie, I didn't murder anyone," I snapped.

"*Sassy.*"

"Whatever." She was giving me a migraine. Swoozie's selective memory was messing with my need to protect her ass. "Oh my Goddess," I yelled. "I didn't sleep with Baba Yaga's boyfriend—you did."

"First of all, we didn't sleep. And how in the hell was I supposed to know Mr. Sexy Pants was her boyfriend?"

"Um, well, let me see… did the fact that he was wearing a *Property of Baba Yaga* t-shirt not ring any fucking bells?"

I was so done. I'd been stuck in a cell with Sassy the Destructive Witch for nine months—sawing my own head off with a butter knife had become a plausible option. I was beyond ready to get the hell out.

"Well, it's not like the Council put you in here just to keep me company. You ran over your own familiar. *On purpose*," she accused.

I watched in horror as she combed her bangs forward in preparation for blast off and willed myself not to give a rat's ass.

"I did not run over that mangy bastard cat on purpose. The little shit stepped under my wheel."

253

"Three times?" she inquired politely.

"Yes."

We glared at each other until we were both biting back grins so hard it hurt. As much as I didn't like her, I was grateful to have had a roomie. It would have sucked to serve time alone. And coming up with different female names that started with the letter S had helped pass the time.

"I really need a mirror to do this right," Sassy muttered. She mimed the cutting action by lining up her fingers up on her hair before she commenced.

I walked to the iron bars of our cell and refused to watch. Our tiny living quarters were barren of all modern conveniences, especially those we could perform magic with, like mirrors. We were locked up in Salem, Massachusetts in a hotel from the early 1900s that had been converted to a jail for witches. Our home away from home was cell block D, designated for witches who abused their magic as easily as they changed their underwear.

From the outside the decrepit building was glamoured to look like a charming bed and breakfast, complete with climbing ivy and flowers growing out of every conceivable nook and cranny. Inside it was cold and ugly with barren brick walls covered with Goddess knew what kind of slime. It was warded heavily with magic, keeping all mortals and responsible magic-makers away. At the moment the lovely Sassy and I were the only two inhabitants in the charming hell-hole. Well, us and the humor-free staff of older than dirt witches and warlocks.

I dropped onto my cot and ran my hands through my mass of uncontrollable auburn curls which looked horrid with the orange prison wear. I puckered my full—and sadly lipstick-free-lips as I tried to image myself in the latest Prada. The first damn thing I was going to do when I got out was burn the jumpsuit and buy out Neiman's.

"Fine. We're both here because we messed up, but I still think nine months was harsh for killing a revolting cat and screwing an idiot," I muttered as the ugly reality of my outfit mocked me.

I held my breath and then blew it out as Sassy put the scissors down and changed her mind.

"I can't do this right now. I really need a mirror."

It was the most sane thing she'd uttered in nine months.

"In an hour you'll have one unless you do something stupid," I told her and then froze.

Without warning the magic level ramped up drastically and the stench of centuries-old voodoo drifted to my nose. Sassy latched onto me for purchase and shuddered with terror.

"Do you smell it?" I whispered. I knew her grip would leave marks, but right now that was the least of my problems.

"I do," she murmured back.

"Old lady crouch."

"*What*?" Her eyes grew wide and she bit down on her lip. Hard. "If you make me laugh, I'll smite your sorry ass when we get out. What the hell is old lady crouch?"

My own grin threatened to split my face. My fear of incarceration was clearly outweighed by my need to make crazy Sassy laugh again. "You know—the smell when you go to the bathroom at the country club...powdery old lady crouch."

"Oh my hell, Zelda." She guffawed and lovingly punched me so hard I knew it would leave a bruise. "I won't be able to let that one go."

"Only a lobotomy can erase it." I was proud of myself.

"Well, well, well," a nasally voice cooed from beyond the bars of our cell. "If it isn't the pretty-pretty problem children."

Baba Yaga had to be at least three hundred if she was a day, but witches aged slowly—so she really only looked thirty-fiveish. The more powerful the witch, the slower said witch aged. Baba was powerful, beautiful and had appalling taste in clothes. Dressed right out of the movie *Flash Dance* complete with the ripped sweatshirt, leggings and headband. It was all I could do not to alert the fashion police.

She was surrounded by the rest of her spooky posse, an angry bunch of warlocks who were clearly annoyed to be in attendance.

"Baba Yaga," Sassy said as respectfully as she could without making eye contact.

"Your Crouchness," I muttered and received a quick elbow to the gut from my cellmate.

Baba Yaga leaned against the cell bars, and her torn at the shoulder sweatshirt dripped over her creamy shoulder. "Zelda and Sassy, you have served your term. Upon release you will have limited magic."

I gasped and Sassy paled. WTF? We'd done our time. *Limited magic?* What did that mean?

"Fuck," I stuttered.

"But… um… Ms. Yaga, that's not fair," Sassy added more eloquently than I had. "We paid our dues. I had to withstand Zelda's company for nine months. I believe that is cruel and unusual punishment."

"Oh my hell," I shouted. "You have got to be kidding me. I fantasized chewing glass, swallowing it and then super gluing my ears shut so I would have to listen to anymore play by plays of *Full House* episodes."

"*Full House* is brilliant and Bob Saget is hot," she grumbled as her face turned red.

"Enough," Baba Yaga hissed as she waved a freshly painted nail at us in admonishment. "You two are on probation, and during that probation you will be strictly forbidden to see each other until you have completed your tasks."

"Not a problem. I don't want to lay eyes on Sujata ever again," I said.

"It's Sassy," she ground out. "And what in the Goddess' name do you mean by *tasks?*"

Baba Yaga smiled—it was not a nice smile.

"Tasks. *Selfless* tasks. And before you two get all uppity with that *'I can't believe you're being so harsh'* drivel, keep in mind that this is a light sentence. Most of the Council wanted you imbeciles stripped of your magic permanently."

That was news. What on earth had I done that would merit that? I conjured up fun things. Sure, they were things I used to my advantage, like shoes and sunny vacations with fruity drinks sporting festive umbrellas in them, served to me on a tropical beach by guys with fine asses...but it wasn't like I took anything from anyone in the process.

"I'm not real clear here," I said warily.

"Oh, I can help with that," Baba Yaga offered kindly. "You, Zelda—how many pairs of Jimmy Choo shoes do you own?"

I mentally counted in my head—kind of. "Um... three?"

Baba Yaga frowned and bright green sparks flew around her head. "Seventy-five and you paid for none of them. Not to mention your wardrobe and cars and the embarrassingly expensive vacations you have taken for free."

When her eyes narrowed dangerously, I swallowed my retort. Plus, I had eighty pairs...

"And you, Sassy, you've used your magic to seduce men and have incurred millions in damages from your temper tantrums. Six buildings and a town. Not to mention your *indiscretion* with my former lover. If I hadn't already been done with him you'd be in solitary confinement for eternity. Can you not see how I had to fight for you?" she demanded, her beautiful eyes fiery.

"Well, when you put it that way," I mumbled.

"There is no other way to put it," she snapped as her mystical lynch mob nodded like the bobble-headed freaks that they were. "Zelda, you have used your magic for self-serving purposes and Sassy, you have a temper that when combined with your magic could be deadly. We are White Witches. We use magic to heal and to make Mother Earth a better place, not to walk the runway and take down cities."

"So what do we have to do?" Sassy asked with a tremor in her voice. She was freaked.

Baba Yaga winked and my stomach dropped to my toes. "There are two envelopes with your tasks in them. You will not share the contents with each other. If you do, you will render yourselves powerless. *Forever*. You have till midnight on All Hallows Eve to complete your assignments and then you will come under review with the Council."

"And if we are unable to fulfill our duty?" I asked, wanting to get all the facts up front.

"You will become mortal."

Shit. My stomach dropped to my toes and I debated between hurling and getting on my knees and begging for mercy. Neither would have done a bit of good...There was no way in hell I could make it in this world as a mortal—I didn't even know how to use a microwave.

And on that alarming and potentially life ending note, Baba Yaga and her entourage disappeared in a cloud of old lady crouch smoke.

"Well, that's fucking craptastic," I said as I warily sniffed my envelope—the one that had appeared out of thin air and landed right between my fingertips.

"You took the words right out of my mouth," Sassy replied as she examined hers.

She tossed her envelope on her cot as though she were afraid to touch it and turned her back on it. I simply shoved mine in the pocket of my heinous orange jumpsuit.

"So that's it? We just do whatever the contents of the envelope tell us to do?" Sassy whined. "Okay, so we're a little self-absorbed, but I do use my magic to heal. Remember when I kind of accidentally punched the guard in the face? I totally healed his nose."

I laughed and rolled my eyes. "He was bleeding all over your one and only pokey jumpsuit."

"Immaterial. I healed him, didn't I?" she insisted.

"And then I zapped your skanky jumpsuit clean," I added, not to be outdone by her list of somewhat dubious selfless acts. "However, I get the feeling that's not the kind of healing magic Baba Yasshole means." I sat down on my own cot, still stunned by our sentence from the Council.

"You know what? Screw Baba Ganoush!" Sassy grunted as she grabbed her envelope and waved it in the air. I sighed and put my hand on her arm to prevent her from doing any damage to her task.

"Yomamma. It's Baba Yomamma, Sassy. And seriously—what choice do we have at this point except to do what she says? You don't want to stay in here, do you? I say we yank up our big girl panties and get this shit done. Deal?"

I stunned myself and Sassy with my responsible reasoning ability.

She made a face but nodded. "Baba Wha-Wha said we couldn't share the contents of our envelopes. There's no way in hell we can open these together and not share."

"Correct. Baba Yosuckmybutt is hateful."

"You want to get turned into a mortal?"

I shuddered. "Fuck no. So now what?" I asked as I played with the offending envelope in my pocket.

"See you on the flip side?" Sassy held up her fist for a bump.

I bumped. "Probably not. While it's been nice in the way a root canal or a canker sore is nice I think it's time for us to part ways."

Sassy grinned and shrugged and I answered with my own.

"So we walk out of here on three?" she asked.

"Yes, we do."

We both took a deep breath. "One, two, three…"

The door of our cell popped open the moment we approached it, clanging and creaking.

We exchanged one last smile before Sassy hung a left and headed down the winding cement path that led to freedom. She made her way down the dimly lit hallway until she was nothing but a small, curvy dot on the horizon.

I clutched the envelope in my pocket with determination and sucked in a huge breath.

And then I hung a right.

Chapter 2

Dearest Zelda,

Apparently your Aunt Hildy died. Violently. You have inherited her home. Go there and make me proud that I didn't strip you of your magic. You will know what to do when you get there.

If you ever use the term "old lady crouch" again while referring to me I will remove your tongue.

xoxo Baba Yaga

P.S. The address is on the back of the note and there is a car for you parked in the garage under the hotel. It's the green one. The purple one is mine. If you even look at it I will put all of your shoes up for sale on eBay. And yes, I am well aware you have eighty pairs.

"Motherhumper, what a bee-otch—put my shoes up for sale, my ass. And who in the hell is Aunt Hildy? I don't have a freakin' aunt named Hildy. Died violently? What exactly does 'died violently' mean?" I muttered to no one as I reread the ridiculous note. Goddess, I wondered what Sassy's note said, but we had gone our separate ways about an hour ago.

My mother was an only child and I hadn't seen her in years—so no Aunt Hildy on that side. My mom, *and I use the term loosely*, was an insanely powerful witch who had met some uber-hot, super weird Vampire ten years ago and they'd gone off to live in a remote castle in Transylvania. The end.

And my father...his identity was anyone's guess. In her day my mother had been a very popular and *active* witch. I suppose Baba *I Know Freakin' Everything* Yaga knew who my elusive daddy was and Hildy must be his sister.

Awesome.

I hustled my ass to the garage and gasped in dismay. In the far corner of the dank, dark, musty-smelling garage sat a car… a green car. A lime green car. Even better, it was a lime green Kia. Was Baba YoMamma fucking joking? Why did I have to drive anywhere? I was a witch. I could use magic to get wherever I wanted to go.

Crap.

Did I even have enough magic to transport? Could I end up wedged in a time warp and stuck for eternity?

And what, pray tell, was this? A Porsche? Baba Yoyeastinfection drove a Porsche… of course she did.

I eyed the purple Porsche with envy and for a brief moment considered keying it. The look on Boobie Yoogie's face would be worth it. Another couple of years in the magic pokey plus having to watch my fancy footwear be auctioned off on eBay was enough to curb my impulse. However, I did lick my finger and smear it on the driver's side mirror. I was told not to look at it. The cryptic note mentioned nothing about touching it.

Glancing down at my orange jumpsuit I cringed. Did they really expect me to wear this? What the hell had become of me? I was a thirty-year-old paroled witch in orange prison wear and tennis shoes. My fingers ached to clothe myself in something cute and sexy. Did I dare? How would they even know?

Wait… she knew I called her old lady crouch. She would certainly know if I magicked up some designer duds. Shitballs. Orange outfit and red hair it was.

Thankfully the car had a GPS, not that I knew how to work anything electronic. I was a witch, for god's sake. I normally flicked my fingers, chanted a spell or wiggled my nose. The address of my inheritance was in West Virginia. How freakin' far was West Virginia from Salem, Massachusetts?

Apparently eleven hours and twenty-one minutes.

It took me exactly forty-five minutes of swearing and punching the dashboard to figure that little nugget out. Bitchy Yicky was officially my least favorite person in the world. However, I was a little proud to have made the damn GPS work without using magic or blowing the car up.

***

Five hours into the trip I was itchy, bloated and had a massive stomachache. Beef jerky and Milk Duds were not my friend. Top that off with a corn dog and two sixty-four ounce caffeinated sodas and I was a clusterfuck waiting to happen.

Thank the Goddess New England was gorgeous in the fall. The colors were breathtaking, but they did little to calm my indigestion. The Kia had no radio reception, but luckily it did come with a country compilation CD that was stuck in the CD player. I was going deaf from the heartfelt warblings about pickup trucks, back roads and barefoot rednecks.

Pretending to be mortal sucked. Six more hours and twenty-one minutes to go—shit. Sadly I found myself longing for even the hideous company of Sassy. Being alone was getting old.

"I can do this. I have to do this. I will do this," I shouted at the alarmed driver of a minivan while stopped at a traffic light in Bumfuck, Idon'tknowwhere.

"I'm baaaaaaack," something hissed from behind me.

"What the fu... ?" I shrieked and jerked the wheel to the right, avoiding a bus stop and landing the piece of crap car in a shallow ditch. "Who said that?"

"I diiiiiiiid," the ominous voice whispered. "Have yoooooooou missssssssed me?"

"Um, sure," I mumbled as I quietly removed my seatbelt and prepared to dive out of the car. Maybe I could catch a lift with the woman I'd terrified in the minivan. "I've missed you a ton."

"You look like shiiiiiiit in ooooorrrrangeeeee," it informed me.

That stopped me. Whatever monster or demon was in the backseat had just gone one step too far.

Scare me? Fine.

Insult me? Fry.

"Excuse me?" I snapped and whipped around to smite the fucker. Where was he? Was he invisible? "Show yourself."

"Down heeeeere on the flooooooor," the thing said.

Peering over the seat, I gagged and threw up in my mouth just a little. This could not be happening. I pinched myself hard and yelped from the pain. It *was* happening and it was probably going to get ugly in about twelve seconds.

"Um, hi Fabio, long time no see," I choked out, wondering if I made a run for it if he would follow and kill me. Or at the very least, would he get behind the wheel of the Kia and run me over... three times. "You're looking kind of alive."

"Thank youuuuuuuu," he said as he hopped over the seat and landed with a squishy thud entirely too close to me.

I plastered myself against the door and debated my next move. Fabio looked bad. He still resembled a cat, but he was kind of flat in the middle, his head was an odd

264

shape and his tail cranked to the left. Most of his black fur still covered him except for a large patch on his face, which made him resemble a pinkish troll. He didn't seem too angry, but I did kill him. To be fair, I didn't mean to. I didn't know he was under the wheel and I kind of freaked and hit reverse and drive several times before I got out and screamed bloody murder.

"So what are you doing here?" I inquired casually, careful not to make eye contact.

"Not exxxxxxactly sure." He shook his little black semi-furred head and an ear fell off.

"Oh shit," I muttered and flicked it to the floor before he noticed. "I'm really sorry about killing you."

"No worrrrrrries. I quite enjoyed being buried in a Prrrrraaada shoeeee box."

"I thought that was a nice touch," I agreed. "Did you notice I left the shoe bags in there as a blanket and pillow?"

"Yessssssssssssss. Very comfortable." He nodded and gave me a grin that made my stomach lurch.

"Alrighty then, the question of the hour is are you still dead… or um…"

"I thiiiink I'm aliiiiive. As soon as I realliiiized I was breathing I loooooked for you."

"Wow." I was usually more eloquent, but nothing else came to mind.

"I have miiiiiiiisssed you, Zeeeeldaaaa."

Great, now I felt horrible. I killed him and he rose from the dead to find me because he missed me. I should take him in my arms and cuddle him, but I feared all the jerky and Duds would fly from my mouth if I tried. He deserved far better than me.

"Look, Fabio… I was a shitty witch for you. You should find a witch that will treat you right."

"But I loooooooovvve you," he said quietly. His little one-eared head drooped and he began to sniffle pathetically.

"You shouldn't love me," I reasoned. "I'm selfish and I killed you—albeit accidentally—and I'm wearing orange."

"I can fix that," he offered meekly. "Would that make you loooooooove meeeee?"

I felt nauseous and it wasn't from all the crap I'd shoved in my mouth while driving to meet my destiny. The little disgusting piece of fur had feelings for me. Feelings I didn't even come close to deserving or returning. And now to make matters worse, he was offering to magic me some clothes. If I said yes, it was a win-win. I'd get new clothes and he'd think I loved him. Asshats on fire, what in the hell was love anyway?

"Um...I would seem kind of shallow if I traded my love for clothes," I mumbled as I bit down on the inside of my cheek to keep from declaring my worthless love in exchange for non-orange attire.

"Well, youuuuuuu are somewhat superficial, but that's not alllllllll your fault," Fabio said as he squished a little closer and placed the furry side of his head in my lap.

"Thank you, I think."

A compliment was a compliment, no matter how insulting.

"You're most welcome," he purred. "How would you know what loooooove is? Your mother was a hoooooooker and your poor father was in the darrrrrk about your existence most of your liiiiiiiife."

"My mother was loose," I admitted, "but she did the best she could. However, my father, whoever the motherfuck he is, just took off after he knocked up my mom. And P.S.—I'm the only one allowed to call my mom a hooker. As nice as the fable was you told me about my dad... it's bullshit."

"Noooooooo, actually it's not," Fabio said as he lifted his piercing green eyes to mine.

"Do you know the bastard?" I demanded, noticing for the first time how our eyes matched. That wasn't uncommon. Most familiars took on the traits of their witches, but I wished he hadn't taken on mine. It would make it much harder to pawn the thing off on someone else if he looked too much like me.

"I knoooooow of him."

"So where the hell is he if he knows about me now?" My eyes narrowed dangerously and blue sparks began to cover my arms.

Fabio quickly backed away in fear of getting crispy. "Asssssssssss the story goes, a spell was cast on him by your moooooother when he learned of your existence. From what I've heard he's been trying to break the spelllllllllll by doing penance."

I rolled my eyes and laughed. "How's that working out for the assmonkey?"

"Apparently not veeeeeeery well if he hasn't shown himself yet."

I considered Fabio's fairytale and wished for a brief moment it was true. Maybe my father didn't know about me. I always thought he didn't want me. That's what my mom had said. Of course she was certifiable and I'd left her house the moment I'd turned eighteen. I did love her but only in the same way a dog still loves the owner who kicks it.

Fabio's story was utter crap, but it was sweet that he cared. Other than Baba Yopaininmyass, not many did.

"Where did you learn all that fiction?" I asked as I eased the lime green piece of dog poo back onto the road before the police showed up and mistook me for an escaped convict.

"Yourrrrrrrr file," he answered as he dug his claws into the strap of the seat belt and pulled it across his mangled body. "Evvvvvvery familiar gets a file on their witch."

"Here, let me," I said as I pulled the strap and clicked it into the lock. "Was there anything else interesting in my file?"

The damn cat knew more about me than I did.

"Nothing I caaaaaan share."

I pursed my lips so I wouldn't swear at him—hard but doable. I wanted info and I knew how to get it. "What if I reattached your ear? Would you tell me one thing you're not supposed to?" I bargained.

"I'mmmmm missssssssing an ear?" he shrieked, aghast.

"Yep, I flicked it under the seat so you wouldn't flip out."

His breathing became erratic. I worried he would heave a hairball or something worse. "Yessssss, reattach it, please."

I opened my senses, and let whatever magic Baba Yasshole had let me keep flow through me. Light purple healing flames covered my arms, neck and face. Fabio's ear floated up from under the passenger seat and drifted to his head. As it connected back, I had a thought. It was selfish… and not.

"Hey Fab, do you mind if I fill in the fur on your face?" It would be so much easier to look at the little bastard if I didn't see raw cat skin.

"Ohhhhhhhhhh my, I'm missing fur?" He was positively despondent. Clearly he hadn't looked in a mirror since his resurrection.

"Um, it's just a little," I lied. "I can fix it up in a jiff."

"Thhhhhhank you, that would be loooovely."

The magic swirled through me. It felt so good. The pokey had blocked me from using magic and I'd missed it terribly. The silky warm purple mist skimmed over Fabio's body and the hair reappeared. Without his permission I unflattened his midsection, reshaped his head and uncranked his tail. It was the least I could do since I'd caused it in the first place.

"There. All better," I told him and glanced over to admire my handiwork. He looked a lot less mangled. He was still a bit mangy, but that was how he'd always been. At least he no longer looked like living road kill. "Your turn."

"Your Aunt Hildy was your father's sissssssster and she wasssss freakin' crazy," he hissed with disgust.

"You knew her?"

"Ahh no, but sheeeeeee was legendary," he explained.

"Why the hell did she leave me her house?" I asked, hoping for some more info. I'd already assumed she was my deadbeat dad's sister. I wanted something new.

"I suppose you will take ooooover for her," Fabio informed me as he lifted and extended his leg so he could lick his balls.

"Get your mouth off your crotch while we're having a conversation," I snapped.

"Youuuuu would do it if youuuuuu could," he said.

"Probably," I muttered as I zoomed past six cars driving too slow for my mood. "But since I can't, you're not allowed to either."

"Can I dooooooo it in private?" he asked.

"Um, sure. Now tell me what crazy old Aunt Hildy did for a living so I know what I'm getting into here."

"No clue," Fabio said far too quickly.

"You know, I could run your feline ass over again," I threatened.

"Yeeeeeep, but I have six lives left."

I put my attention back on the road. "Great. That's just great."

Chapter 3

"What the fu... ? *Fabio, I'm naked,*" I screamed somewhere around mile marker thirtytwowhatthehell in Pennsylvania. "What are you doing?"

"Trying to give youuuu a new outfiiiiit," Fabio whined as he turned away in horror.

I was unsure if I was more pissed that I was naked in the driver's seat of a lime green Kia or about the fact that he clearly found me heinous to look at.

"You know," I ground out through clenched teeth, "most people consider me hot."

"Yesssssss, well, I'm a cat and I find yoooooour nudity allllaaaaarming."

"Then dress me," I snapped. "In something really cute and expensive to make up for insulting my exposed knockers."

"Your knockers are looooovely, but it's not appppppropriate for me to ogle your undraaaaaped body."

He was a freakin' wreck.

"Is that against some kind of witch slash familiar law?" I demanded as I looked down at myself. I looked good.

Witches had crazy fast metabolisms and all of us were stupidly pretty.

"Yesssssss," he said as he twitched uncomfortably in his seat.

"Naked here," I reminded him.

The car filled with magic so quickly I gasped and held on to the steering wheel with all my might. The little fucker was strong. Who knew he had so much magic stored up in his mangy little carcass? A heat covered my body and I swerved to miss a semi truck.

"For the love of the Goddess," I shouted. "Hurry up or we're going to die here."

"Do youuuu want paaaaants or a skirt?" he asked.

"At the moment I'm not picky. I'm panicked. Just make sure it's not orange and I'll be happy."

"Asssss youuuu wish."

The magic receded as quickly as it had begun. I was too shaken to even look down to see if I was dressed. I was getting rid of him as soon as I could. He was a fucking menace—not that I was a prize—but an imbalanced cat was more insanity than even I could handle.

"Dooooo you liiiike it?" he asked with an absurd amount of pride in his voice.

"I'll tell you in an hour when I get up the courage to look down. Where in the hell did you get so much magic? Familiars are not supposed to be stronger than their witches."

"I'm nooooot stronger," he insisted. "Youuuuu are stronger thaaaaan you know."

"Well, at the moment I'm not. Boobah Yumpa has me running on half a tank," I told him. "It's part of my punishment for killing you."

"Buuuuut I'm not deeeeead," he replied logically.

He was correct, but Butthole Yaga never changed her mind. Ever. It was actually something I liked about her, though I would never tell her. I'd grown up so horrendously, any female authority figure who had semi-sane rules was appealing to me.

"Yeah, she doesn't cave easily."

"You're wearing Maaaaax Midnight jeans and a vintage Minnie Mouuuuuse t-shirt with hot piiiink combat boots," he said.

That gave me pause. Hot pink combat boots were beyond awesome and Max Midnight jeans cost seven hundred dollars a pop. My freakin' cat had good taste. Maybe I'd keep him a little while longer.

"Are you serious?"

"Yessssss. I can change you iiiiif that diiispleases you."

"NO," I shouted. I wasn't sure if we would live through another change, plus if what he said was true I was a very happy camper. I glanced down and sighed with joy and relief. He was true to his word. I looked hot. "I like it."

His purr was cute until I looked over at him and noticed he was going for his nut sack again. "What did I tell you about that?" I glared at him in disgust.

"Soooooorrry," he whispered contritely. "Habit."

"Well, Fabio, you're going to have to break that one or I'll get you neutered."

"Youuuuuuuu wouldn't." He gasped and crossed his little kitty legs over his jewels.

"Try me."

That shut him up for about five minutes and seven seconds.

"Are weeeeeeeee there yet?"

"No."

"How much looooooonger?"

272

"I don't know."

"More thaaaaaan two hours?"

"No clue."

"More than three hooooouuuuurs?"

I bit down on my bottom lip so I didn't shout a spell at him that would permanently destroy his voice box. I was certain it wouldn't go over well with Booboo Yoogu.

"Willlllll it be sooooooon?"

"Fabio?"

"Yesssssss, Zelda?"

"Lick your balls."

"Realllllllly?" He was so excited I cringed.

"Yes really, but get in the back seat. However, if I hear any slurping or purring I will throw your furry ass out of the window and leave you there. Are we clear?"

"Duuuuuly noted."

He jumped in the back seat and we had a peaceful ride the rest of the way there.

***

Aunt Hildy's house sat high on a hill and was the most beautiful thing I'd ever seen. It was a white Victorian with a wraparound porch and turrets. Wildflowers covered the grounds and the trees blazed with color. Only a few major drawbacks kept me from screaming with joy at my good fortune.

For one, it was located in the middle of nowhere. Since we had little to no supplies we trekked to town. The closest town, if you could call it that, was a half an hour away and consisted of Main Street. The town square was dominated by a statue of a cement bear missing one side of his head. The rest of the block included a barbershop, hardware store, gas station and a mom and pop grocery. Awesome—not.

273

We made a quick stop at the gas station. I gassed up the Kia with a credit card, *probably stolen*, that Fabio happened to have and then went into the grocery. I winced at the rotting fruit and vegetables as I headed for the frozen and canned aisles. Ten frozen pizzas, two tubs of ice cream, and fifteen cans of brand-less spaghetti later, I got in line at the checkout behind the hottest guy I'd ever seen.

What in the hell was the Goddess's gift to women doing in Buttcrack, West Virginia? Maybe this place wasn't so bad. His ass in his jeans was enough to make my mouth water and he smelled like heaven.

Nine months in the magic pokey were enough to make any girl horny, but this guy was something else. I made a couple of girly sounds hoping to get his attention, but failed—so I touched his butt. Not grabbed—kind of brush-touched accidently on purpose.

"You could have asked first," a deep sexy voice informed me without even turning around.

"I'm sorry," I said politely to his back. "I have no idea what you're talking about."

"You could have requested to cop a feel of my ass." He turned around and I almost dropped to the floor. He wasn't just pretty, he was redonkulous gorgeous. Dark wavy hair, blue eyes, lashes that belonged on a girl, a body to die for and a face that would make the Angels weep. Oh. My. Hell.

"It was in my way. Consider yourself lucky. I almost slapped it."

His laugh went all the way to my woowoo. I nearly crushed the can of Spaghettios I was clutching.

"Well, beautiful girl," he drawled in a Southern accent that made my brain short out, "I'd suggest you watch your ass. If it gets in my way I'll do much more than slap it."

"Promise?" I challenged.

He considered me for a long moment and then winked. "Promise."

I held on to the counter as I watched him walk out of the store and realized I didn't even know his name. Whatever. I didn't need to get into any messy relationship. Hell, I'd never maintained a relationship in my life. I'd always had lots of boyfriends, but the minute it got serious I was out of there. Fast. Plus, I rarely dated mortals. Mr. Fine Ass didn't really look like relationship material. However, he did look like awesome one or two or three night stand material... Crap. I supposed I'd have to grocery shop on a regular basis. I grabbed my bags and went back to my new reality.

"Diiiiid you get my pasta?" Fabio inquired. He'd moved back to the front seat as he was clearly done attending to his gonads.

"Yep."

"Annnnd fresh tomatoes, baaaaasil and garlic?"

"Yep." He'd find out soon enough he was going to be eating Spaghettios. That was the price he'd have to pay for cleaning his Johnson for three hours, plus the fresh stuff would have killed him more certainly than my car had. "You ready to check out our new digs?"

"Asssss ready as I'll ever beeeeeee," he said with disgust.

"I'm not really buying that you didn't know Hildy," I said dryly. "You seem to be having an awful lot of issues here."

"It's heeeeer reputation," he shot back. "I don't liiiike this."

"Well buddy, neither do I, but if I don't figure out why I'm here Buttcrack Yoogiemamma will turn me into a mortal on Halloween. So we're going to the house and we are going to fucking like it. You got it?"

"Yesssssss," he answered morosely. "Gotttt it."

Available Now##

275

Excerpt from READY TO WERE

Chapter 1

"You're joking."

"No, actually I'm not," my boss said and slapped the folder into my hands. "You leave tomorrow morning and I don't want to see your hairy ass till this is solved."

I looked wildly around her office for something to lob at her head. It occurred to me that might not be the best of ideas, but desperate times led to stupid measures. She could not do this to me. I'd worked too hard and I wasn't going back. Ever.

"First of all, my ass is not hairy except on a full moon and you're smoking crack if you think I'm going back to Georgia."

Angela crossed her arms over her ample chest and narrowed her eyes at me. "Am I your boss?" she asked.

"Is this a trick question?"

She huffed out an exasperated sigh and ran her hands through her spiked 'do making her look like she'd been electrocuted. "Essie, I am cognizant of how you feel about Hung Island, Georgia, but there's a disaster of major proportions on the horizon and I have no choice."

"Where are you sending Clark and Jones?" I demanded.

"New York and Miami."

"Oh my god," I shrieked. "Who did I screw over in a former life that those douches get to go to cool cities and I have to go home to an island called Hung?"

"Those douches *do* have hairy asses and not just on a full moon. You're the only female agent I have that looks like a model so you're going to Georgia. Period."

"Fine. I'll quit. I'll open a bakery."

Angela smiled and an icky feeling skittered down my spine. "Excellent, I'll let you tell the Council that all the money they invested in your training is going to be flushed down the toilet because you want to bake cookies."

The Council consisted of supernaturals from all sorts of species. The branch that currently had me by the metaphorical balls was WTF—Werewolf Treaty Federation. They were the worst as far as stringent rules and consequences went. The Vampyres were loosey goosey, the Witches were nuts and the freakin' Fairies were downright pushovers, but not the Weres. Nope, if you enlisted you were in for life. It had sounded so good when the insanely sexy recruiting officer had come to our local Care For Your Inner Were meeting.

Training with the best of the best. Great salary with benefits. Apartment and company car. But the kicker for me was that it was fifteen hours away from the hell I grew up in. No longer was I Essie from Hung Island, Georgia— *and who in their right mind would name an island Hung*—I was Agent Essie McGee of the Chicago WTF. The irony of the initials was a source of pain to most Werewolves, but went right over the Council's heads due to the simple fact that they were older than dirt and oblivious to pop culture.

Yes, I'd been disciplined occasionally for mouthing off to superiors and using the company credit card for shoes, but other than that I was a damn good agent. I'd graduated at the top of my class and was the go-to girl for messy and dangerous assignments that no one in their right mind would take... I'd singlehandedly brought down three rogue Weres who were selling secrets to the Dragons—another supernatural species. The Dragons shunned the Council, had their own little club and a psychotic desire to rule the world. Several times they'd come close due to the fact that they were loaded and Weres from the New Jersey Pack were easily bribed. Not to mention the fire-breathing thing...

I was an independent woman living in the Windy City. I had a gym membership, season tickets to the Cubs and a gay Vampyre best friend named Dwayne. What more did a girl need?

Well, possibly sex, but the *bastard* had ruined me for other men...

Hank "The Tank" Wilson was the main reason I'd rather chew my own paw off than go back to Hung Island, Georgia. Six foot three of obnoxious, egotistical, perfect-assed, alpha male Werewolf. As the alpha of my local Pack he had decided it was high time I got mated...to him. I, on the other hand, had plans—big ones and they didn't include being barefoot and pregnant at the beck and call of a player.

So I did what any sane, rational woman would do. I left in the middle of the night with a suitcase, a flyer from the hot recruiter and enough money for a one-way bus ticket to freedom. Of course, nothing ever turns out as planned... The apartment was the size of a shoe box, the car was used and smelled like French fries and the benefits didn't kick in till I turned one hundred and twenty five. We Werewolves had long lives.

"Angela, you really can't do this to me." Should I get down on my knees? I was so desperate I wasn't above begging.

"Why? What happened there, Essie? Were you in some kind of trouble I should know about?" Her eyes narrowed, but she wasn't yelling.

I think she liked me...kind of. The way a mother would like an annoying spastic two year old who belonged to someone else.

"No, not exactly," I hedged. "It's just that…"

"Weres are disappearing and presumed dead. Considering no one knows of our existence besides other supernaturals, we have a problem. Furthermore, it seems like humans might be involved."

My stomach lurched and I grabbed Angela's office chair for balance. "Locals are missing?" I choked out. My grandma Bobby Sue was still there, but I'd heard from her last night. She'd harangued me about getting my belly button pierced. Why I'd put that on Instagram was beyond me. I was gonna hear about that one for the next eighty years or so.

"Not just missing—more than likely dead. Check the folder," Angela said and poured me a shot of whiskey.

With trembling hands I opened the folder. This had to be a joke. I felt ill. I'd gone to high school with Frankie Mac and Jenny Packer. Jenny was as cute as a button and was the cashier at the Piggly Wiggly. Frankie Mac had been the head cheerleader and cheated on every test since the fourth grade. Oh my god, Debbie Swink? Debbie Swink had been voted most likely to succeed and could do a double backwards flip off the high dive. She'd busted her head open countless times before she'd perfected it. Her mom was sure she'd go to the Olympics.

"I know these girls," I whispered.

"Knew. You knew them. They all were taking classes at the modeling agency."

"What modeling agency? There's no modeling agency on Hung Island." I sifted through the rest of the folder with a knot the size of a cantaloupe in my stomach. More names and faces I recognized. Sandy Moongie? *Wait a minute.*

"Um, not to speak ill of the dead, but Sandy Moongie was the size of a barn…she was modeling?"

"Worked the reception desk." Angela shook her head and dropped down on the couch.

"This doesn't seem that complicated. It's fairly black and white. Whoever is running the modeling agency is the perp."

"The modeling agency is Council sponsored."

I digested that nugget in silence for a moment.

"And the Council is running a modeling agency, why?"

"Word is that we're heading toward revealing ourselves to the humans and they're trying to find the most attractive representatives to do so."

"That's a joke, right?" *What kind of dumb ass plan was that?*

"I wish it was." Angela picked up my drink and downed it. "I'm getting too old for this shit," she muttered as she refilled the shot glass, thought better of it and just swigged from the bottle.

"Is the Council aware that I'm going in?"

"What do you think?"

"I think they're old and stupid and that they send in dispensable agents like me to clean up their shitshows," I grumbled.

"Smart girl."

"Who else knows about this? Clark? Jones?"

"They know," she said wearily. "They're checking out agencies in New York and Miami."

"Isn't it conflict of interest to send me where I know everyone?"

"It is, but you'll be able to infiltrate and get in faster that way. Besides, no one has disappeared from the other agencies yet."

There was one piece I still didn't understand. "How are humans involved?"

She sighed and her head dropped back onto her broad shoulders. "Humans are running the agency."

It took a lot to render me silent, like learning my grandma had been a stripper in her youth, and that all male Werewolves were hung like horses… but this was horrific.

"Who in the hell thought that was a good idea? My god, half the female Weres I know sprout tails when flash bulbs go off. We won't have to come out, they can just run billboards of hot girls with hairy appendages coming out of their asses."

"It's all part of the *Grand Plan*. If the humans see how wonderful and attractive we are, the issue of knowingly living alongside of us will be moot."

Again. Speechless.

"When are Council elections?" It was time to vote some of those turd knockers out.

"Essie." Angela rolled her eyes and took another swig. "There are no elections. They're appointed and serve for life."

"I knew that," I mumbled. Skipping Were History class was coming back to bite me in the butt.

"I'll go." There was no way I couldn't. Even though my knowledge of the hierarchy of my race was fuzzy, my skills were top notch and trouble seemed to find me. In any other job that would suck, but in mine, it was an asset.

"Good. You'll be working with the local Pack alpha. He's also the sheriff there. Name's Hank Wilson. You know him?"

"Yep." *Biblically. I knew the son of a bitch biblically.*

***

"You're gonna bang him."

"I am not gonna bang him."

"You are so gonna bang him."

"Dwayne, if I hear you say that I'm gonna bang him one more time, I will not let you borrow my black Mary Jane pumps. Ever again."

Dwayne made the international "zip the lip and throw away the key" sign while silently mouthing that I was going to bang Hank.

"I think you should bang him if he's a hot as you said." Dwayne made himself comfortable on my couch and turned on the TV.

"When did I ever say he was hot?" I demanded as I took the remote out of his hands. I was not watching any more *Dance Moms*. "I never said he was hot."

"Paaaaleese," Dwayne flicked his pale hand over his shoulder and rolled his eyes.

"What was that?"

"What was what?" he asked, confused.

"That shoulder thing you just did."

"Oh, I was flicking my hair over my shoulder in a *girlfriend* move."

"Okay, don't do that. It doesn't work. You're as bald as a cue ball."

"But it's the new move," he whined.

Oh my god, Vampyres were such high maintenance. "According to who?" I yanked my suitcase out from under my bed and started throwing stuff in.

"Kim Kardashian."

I refused to dignify that with so much as a look.

"Fine," he huffed. "But if you say one word about my skinny jeans I am so out of here."

I considered it, but I knew he was serious. As crazy as he drove me, I adored him. He was my only real friend in Chicago and I had no intention of losing him.

283

"I know he's hot," Dwayne said. "Look at you— you're so gorge it's redonkulous. You're all legs and boobs and hair and lips—you're far too beautiful to be hung up on a goober."

"Are you calling me shallow?" I snapped as I ransacked my tiny apartment for clean clothes. Damn it, tomorrow was laundry day. I was going to have to pack dirty clothes.

"So he's ugly and puny and wears bikini panties?"

"No! He's hotter than Satan's underpants and he wears boxer briefs," I shouted. "You happy?"

"He's actually a nice guy."

"You've met Hank?" I was so confused I was this close to making fun of his skinny jeans just so he would leave.

"Satan. He's not as bad as everyone thinks."

How was it that everyone I came in contact with today stole my ability to speak? Thankfully, I was interrupted by a knock at my door.

"You expecting someone?" Dwayne asked as he pilfered the remote back and found *Dance Moms*.

"No."

I peeked through the peephole. Nobody came to my place except Dwayne and the occasional pizza delivery guy or Chinese food take out guy or Indian food take out guy. *Wait. What the hell was my boss doing here?*

"Angela?"

"You going to let me in?"

"Depends."

"Open the damn door."

I did.

Angela tromped into my shoebox and made herself at home. Her hair was truly spectacular. It looked like she might have even pulled out a clump on the left side. "You want to tell me why the sheriff and alpha of Hung Island, Georgia says he won't work with you?"

"Um…no?"

"He said he had a hard time believing someone as flaky and irresponsible as you had become an agent for the Council and he wants someone else." Angela narrowed her eyes at me and took the remote form Dwayne. "Spill it, Essie."

I figured the best way to handle this was to lie—hugely. However, gay Vampyre boyfriends had a way of interrupting and screwing up all your plans.

"Well, you see…"

"He's her mate and he dipped his stick in several other…actually *many* other oil tanks. So she dumped his furry player ass, snuck away in the middle of the night and hadn't really planned on ever going back there again." Dwayne sucked in a huge breath, which was ridiculous because Vampyres didn't breathe.

It took everything I had not to scream and go all Wolfy. "Dwayne, clearly you want me to go medieval on your lily white ass because I can't imagine why you would utter such bullshit to my boss."

"Doesn't sound like bullshit to me," Angela said as she channel surfed and landed happily on an old episode of *Cagney and Lacey*. "We might have a problem here."

"Are you replacing me?" Hank Wilson had screwed me over once when I was his. He was not going to do it again when I wasn't.

"Your call," she said. Dwayne, who was an outstanding shoplifter, covertly took back the remote and flipped over to the Food Channel. Angela glanced up at the tube and gave Dwayne the evil eye.

"I refuse to watch lesbians fight crime in the eighties. I'll get hives," he explained, tilted his head to the right and gave Angela a smile. He was so pretty it was silly—

piercing blue eyes and body to die for. Even my boss had a hard time resisting his charm.

"Fine," she grumbled.

"Excuse me," I yelled. "This conversation is about me, not testosterone ridden women cops with bad hair, hives or food. It's my life we're talking about here—me, me, me!" My voice had risen to decibels meant to attract stray animals within a ten-mile radius, evidenced by the wincing and ear covering.

"Essie, are you done?" Dwayne asked fearfully.

"Possibly. What did you tell him?" I asked Angela.

"I told him the Council has the last word in all matters. Always. And if he had a problem with it, he could take it up with the elders next month when they stay awake long enough to listen to the petitions of their people."

"Oh my god, that's awesome," I squealed. "What did he say?"

"That if we send you down, he'll give you bus money so you can hightail your sorry cowardly butt right back out of town."

Was she grinning at me, and was that little shit Dwayne jotting the conversation down in the notes section on his phone?

"Let me tell you something," I ground out between clenched teeth as I confiscated Dwayne's phone and pocketed it. "I am going to Hung Island, Georgia tomorrow and I will kick his ass. I will find the killer first and then I will castrate the alpha of the Georgia Pack...with a dull butter knife."

Angela laughed and Dwayne jackknifed over on the couch in a visceral reaction to my plan. I stomped into my bathroom and slammed the door to make my point, then pressed my ear to the rickety wood to hear them talk behind my back.

"I'll bet you five hundred dollars she's gonna bang him," Dwayne told Angela.

"I'll bet you a thousand that you're right," she shot back.

"You're on."

Chapter 2

"This music is going to make me yack." Dwayne moaned and put his hands over his ears.

Trying to ignore him wasn't working. I promised myself I wouldn't put him out of the car until we were at least a hundred miles outside of Chicago. I figured anything less than that wouldn't be the kind of walk home that would teach him a lesson.

"First of all, Vampyres can't yack and I don't recall asking you to come with me," I replied and cranked up The Clash.

"You have got to be kidding." He huffed and flipped the station to Top Forty. "You need me."

"Really?"

"Oh my god," Dwayne shrieked. "I luurrve Lady Gaga."

"That's why I need you?"

"Wait. What?"

"I need you because you love The Gaga?"

Dwayne rolled his eyes. "Everyone loves The Gaga. You need me because you need to show your hometown and Hank the Hooker that you have a new man in your life."

"You're a Vampyre."

"Yes, and?"

"Well, um…you're gay."

"What does that have to do with anything? I am hotter than asphalt in August and I have a huge package."

While his points were accurate, there was no mistaking his sexual preference. The skinny jeans, starched muscle shirt, canvas Mary Janes and the gold hoop earrings were an undead giveaway.

"You know, I think you should just be my best friend. I want to show them I don't need a man to make it in this world…okay?" I glanced over and he was crying. Shitshitshit. Why did I always say the wrong thing? "Dwayne, I'm sorry. You can totally be my…"

"You really consider me your best friend?" he blubbered. "I have never had a best friend in all my three hundred years. I've tried, but I just…" He broke down and let her rip.

"Yes, you're my best friend, you idiot. Stop crying. Now." Snark I could deal with. Tears? Not so much.

"Oh my god, I just feel so happy," he gushed. "And I want you to know if you change your mind about the boyfriend thing just wink at me four times and I'll stick my tongue down your throat."

"Thanks, I'll keep that in mind."

"Anything for my best friend. Ohhh Essie, are there any gay bars in Hung?"

This was going to be a wonderful trip.

***

One way in to Hung Island, Georgia. One way out. The bridge was long and the ocean was beautiful. Sun glistened off the water and sparkled like diamonds. Dwayne was quiet for the first time in fifteen hours. As we pulled into town, my gut clenched and I started to sweat.

This was stupid—so very stupid. The nostalgic pull of this place was huge and I felt sucked back in immediately.

"Holy Hell," Dwayne whispered. "It's beautiful here. How did you leave this place?"

He was right. It was beautiful. It had the small town feel mixed up with the ocean and land full of wild grasses and rolling hills. How did I leave?

"I left because I hate it here," I lied. "We'll do the job, castrate the alpha with a butter knife and get out. You got it?"

"Whatever you say, best friend. Whatever you say." He grinned.

"I'm gonna drop you off at my Grandma Bobby Sue's. She doesn't exactly know we're coming so you have to be on your best behavior."

"Will you be?"

"Will I be what?" God, Vamps were tiresome.

"On your best behavior."

"Absolutely not. We're here."

I stopped my crappy car in front of a charming old Craftsman. Flowers covered every inch of the yard. It was a literal explosion of riotous color and I loved it. Granny hated grass—found the color offensive. It was the home I grew up in. Granny BS, as everyone loved to call her, had raised me after my parents died in a horrific car accident when I was four. I barely remembered my parents, but Granny had told me beautiful bedtime stories about them my entire childhood.

"OMG, this place is so cute I could scream." Dwayne squealed and jumped out of the car into the blazing sunlight. All the stories about Vamps burning to ash or sparkling like diamonds in the sun were a myth. The only thing that could kill Weres and Vamps were silver bullets, decapitation, fire and a silver stake in the heart.

Grabbing Dwayne by the neck of his muscle shirt, I stopped him before he went tearing into the house. "Granny is old school. She thinks Vamps are…you know."

"Blood sucking leeches who should be eliminated?" Dwayne grinned from ear to ear. He loved a challenge. Crap.

"I wouldn't go that far, but she's old and set in her geezer ways. So if you have to, steer clear."

"I'll have her eating kibble out of my manicured lily white hand in no time at…holy shit!" Dwayne screamed and ducked as a blur of Granny BS came flying out of the house and tackled my ass in a bed of posies.

"Mother Humper." I grunted and struggled as I tried to shove all ninety-five pounds of pissed off Grandma Werewolf away from me.

"Gimme that stomach," she hissed as she yanked up my shirt. Thank the Lord I was wearing a bra. Dwayne stood in mute shock and just watched me get my butt handed to me by my tiny granny, who even at eighty was the spitting image of a miniature Sophia Loren in her younger years.

"Get off of me, you crazy old bag," I ground out and tried to nail her with a solid left. She ducked and backslapped my head.

"I said no tattoos and no piercings till you're fifty," she yelled. "Where is it?"

"Oh my GOD," I screeched as I trapped her head with my legs in a scissors hold. "You need meds."

"Tried 'em. They didn't work," she grumbled as she escaped from my hold. She grabbed me from behind as I tried to make a run for my car and ripped out my belly button ring.

"Ahhhhhhgrhupcraaap, that hurt, you nasty old bat from Hell." I screamed and looked down at the bloody hole that used to be really cute and sparkly. "That was a one carat diamond, you ancient witch."

Both of her eyebrows shot up and I swear to god they touched her hairline.

"Okay, fine," I muttered. "It was cubic zirconia, but it was NOT cheap."

"Hookers have belly rings," she snapped.

"No, hookers have pimps. Normal people have belly rings, or at least they used to," I shot back as I examined the wound that was already closing up.

"Come give your granny a hug," she said and put her arms out.

I approached warily just in case she needed to dole out more punishment for my piercing transgression. She folded me into her arms and hugged me hard. That was the thing about my granny. What you saw was what you got. Everyone always knew where they stood with her. She was mad and then she was done. Period.

"Lawdy, I have missed you, child," she cooed.

"Missed you too, you old cow." I grinned and hugged her back. I caught Dwayne out of the corner of my eye. He was even paler than normal if that was possible and he had placed his hands over his pierced ears.

"Granny, I brought my..."

"Gay Vampyre best friend," she finished my introduction. She marched over to him, slapped her hands on her skinny hips and stared. She was easily a foot shorter than Dwayne, but he trembled like a baby. "Do you knit?" she asked him.

"Um...no, but I've always wanted to learn," he choked out.

She looked him up and down for a loooong minute, grunted and nodded her head. "We'll get along just fine then. Get your asses inside before the neighbors call the cops."

"Why would they call the cops?" Dwayne asked, still terrified.

"Well boy, I live amongst humans and I just walloped my granddaughter on the front lawn. Most people don't think that's exactly normal."

"Point," he agreed and hightailed it to the house.

"Besides," she cackled. "Wouldn't want the sheriff coming over to arrest you now, would we?"

I rolled my eyes and flipped her the bird behind her back.

"Saw that, girlie," she said.

Holy Hell, she still had eyes in the back of her head. If I was smart, I'd grab Dwayne, get in my car and head back to Chicago...but I had a killer to catch and a whole lot to prove here. Smart wasn't on my agenda today.

Chapter 3

The house was exactly the same as it was the last time I saw it a year ago. Granny had more crap on her tables, walls and shelves than an antique store. Dwayne was positively speechless and that was good. Granny took her décor seriously.

"I'm a little disappointed that you want to be a model, Essie," Granny sighed. "You have brains and a mean right hook. Never thought you'd try to coast by with your looks."

I gave Dwayne the *I'll kill you if you tell her I'm an agent on a mission* look and thankfully he understood. While I hated that my granny thought I was shallow and jobless, it was far safer that she didn't know why I was really here.

"Well, you know…I just need to make a few bucks, then get back to my life in the big city," I mumbled. I was a sucky liar around my granny and she knew it.

"Hmmm," she said, staring daggers at me.

"What?" I asked, not exactly making eye contact.

"Nothin'. I'm just lookin'," she challenged.

"And what are you looking at?" I blew out an exasperated sigh and met her eyes. A challenge was a challenge and I *was* a Werewolf…

"A bald face little fibber girl," she crowed. "Spill it or I'll whoop your butt again."

Dwayne quickly backed himself into a corner and slid his phone out of his pocket. That shit was going to video my ass kicking. I had several choices here…destroy Dwayne's phone, elaborate on my lie or come clean. The only good option was the phone.

"Fine," I snapped and sucked in a huge breath. The truth will set you free or result in a trip to the ER… "I'm an agent with the Council—a trained killer for WTF and I'm good at it. The fact that I'm a magnet for trouble has finally paid off. I'm down here to find out who in the hell is killing Werewolves before it blows up in our faces. I plan to find the perps and destroy them with my own hands or a gun, whichever will be most painful. Then I'm going to castrate Hank with a dull butter knife. I plan on a short vacation when I'm done before going back to Chicago."

For the first time in my twenty-eight years on Earth, Granny was mute. It was all kinds of awesome.

"Can I come on the vacation?" Dwayne asked.

"Yes. Cat got your tongue, old woman?" I asked.

"Well, I'll be damned," she said almost inaudibly. "I suppose this shouldn't surprise me. You are a female alpha bitch."

"No," I corrected her. "I'm a lone wolf who wants nothing to do with Pack politics. Ever."

Granny sat her skinny bottom down on her plastic slipcovered floral couch and shook her head. "Ever is a long time, little girl. Well, I suppose I should tell you something now," she said gravely and worried her bottom lip.

"Oh my god, are you sick?" I gasped. Introspective thought was way out of my granny's normal behavior pattern. My stomach roiled. She was all I had left in the world and as much as I wanted to skin her alive, I loved her even more.

"Weres don't get sick. It's about your mamma and daddy. Sit down. And Dwayne, hand over your phone. If I find out you have loose lips, I'll remove them," she told my bestie.

I sat. Dwayne handed. I had thought I knew everything there was to know about my parents, but clearly I was mistaken. Hugely mistaken.

"You remember when I told you your mamma and daddy died in a car accident?"

"Yes," I replied slowly. "You showed me the newspaper articles."

"That's right." She nodded. "They did die in a car, but it wasn't no accident."

Movement was necessary or I thought I might throw up. I paced the room and tried to untangle my thoughts. It wasn't like I'd even known my parents, but they were mine and now I felt cheated somehow. I wanted to crawl out of my skin. My heart pounded so loudly in my chest I was sure the neighbors could hear it. My parents were murdered and this was the first time I was hearing about it?

"Again. Say that again." Surely I'd misunderstood. I'd always been one to jump to conclusions my entire life, but the look on Granny's face told me that this wasn't one of those times.

"They didn't own a hardware store. Well, actually I think they did, but it was just a cover."

"For what?" I asked, fairly sure I knew where this was going.

"They were WTF agents, child, and they were taken out," she said and wrapped her skinny little arms around herself. "Broke my heart—still does."

"And you never told me this? Why?" I demanded and got right up in her face.

"I don't rightly know," she said quietly. "I wanted you to grow up happy and not feel the need for revenge."

She stroked my cheek the way she did when I was a child and I leaned into her hand for comfort. I was angry, but she did what she thought was right. Needless to say, she wasn't right, but...

"Wait, why would I have felt the need for revenge?" I asked. Something was missing.

"The Council was never able to find out who did it, and after a while they gave up."

Everything about that statement was so wrong I didn't know how to react. They gave up? What the hell was that? The Council never gave up. I was trained to get to the bottom of everything. Always.

"That's the most absurd thing I've ever heard. The Council always gets their answers."

Granny shrugged her thin shoulders and rearranged the knickknacks on her coffee table. Wait. Did the Council know more about me than I did? Did my boss Angela know more of my history than I'd ever known?

"I knew that recruiter they sent down here," Granny muttered. "I told him to stay away from you. Told him the Council already took my daughter and son-in-law and they couldn't have you."

"He didn't pay me any more attention than he did anyone else," I told her.

"What did the flyer say that he gave you?"

"Same as everybody's—salary, training, benefits, car, apartment."

"Damn it to hell," she shouted. "No one else's flyer said that. I confiscated them all after the bastard left. I couldn't get to yours cause you were shacking up with the sheriff."

"You lived with Hank the Hooker?" Dwayne gasped. "I thought you just dated a little."

"Hell to the no," Granny corrected Dwayne. "She was engaged. Left the alpha of the Georgia Pack high and dry."

"Enough," I snapped. "Ancient history. I'm more concerned about what kind of cow patty I've stepped in with the Council. The *sheriff* knows why I left. Maybe the Council accepted me cause I can shoot stuff and I have no fear and they have to hire a certain quota of women and…"

"And they want to make sure you don't dig into the past," Dwayne added unhelpfully.

"You're a smart bloodsucker," Granny chimed in.

"Thank you."

"You think the Council had something to do with it," I said. This screwed with my chi almost as much as the Hank situation from a year ago. I had finally done something on my own and it might turn out I hadn't earned any of it.

"I'm not sayin' nothing like that," Granny admonished harshly. "And neither should you. You could get killed."

She was partially correct, but I was the one they sent to kill people who broke Council laws. However, speaking against the Council wasn't breaking the law. The living room had grown too small for my need to move and I prowled the rest of the house with Granny and Dwayne on my heels. I stopped short and gaped at my empty bedroom.

"Where in the hell is my furniture?"

"You moved all your stuff to Hank's and he won't give it back," Granny informed me.

An intense thrill shot through my body, but I tamped it down immediately. I was done with him and he was surely done with me. No one humiliated an alpha and got a second chance. Besides, I didn't want one… Dwayne's snicker earned him a glare that made him hide behind Granny in fear.

"Did you even try to get my stuff back?" I demanded.

"Of course I did," she huffed. "That was your mamma's set from when she was a child. I expected you'd use it for your own daughter someday."

My mamma...My beautiful mamma who'd been murdered along with my daddy. The possibility that the Council had been involved was gnawing at my insides in a bad way.

"I have to compartmentalize this for a minute or at least a couple of weeks," I said as I stood in the middle of my empty bedroom. "I have to do what I was sent here for. But when I'm done, I'll get answers and vengeance."

"Does that mean no vacation?" Dwayne asked.

I stared at Dwayne like he'd grown three heads. He was getting terribly good at rendering me mute.

"That was a good question, Dwayne." Granny patted him on the head like a dog and he preened. "Essie, your mamma and daddy would want you to have a vacation before you get killed finding out what happened to them."

"Can we go to Jamaica?" Dwayne asked.

"Ohhh, I've never been to Jamaica," Granny volunteered.

They were both batshit crazy, but Jamaica did sound kind of nice...

"Fine, but you're paying," I told Dwayne. He was richer than Midas. He'd made outstanding investments in his three hundred years.

"Yayayayayayay!" he squealed.

"I'll call the travel agent," Granny said. "How long do you need to get the bad guy?"

"A week. Give me a week."

Available Now##

299

Book Lists (in correct reading order)

HOT DAMNED SERIES
Fashionably Dead
Fashionably Dead Down Under
Hell on Heels
Fashionably Dead in Diapers
Fashionably Hotter Than Hell

SHIFT HAPPENS SERIES
Ready to Were
Some Were in Time
No Were To Run

MAGIC AND MAYHEM SERIES
Switching Hour
Witch Glitch
A Witch In Time

HANDCUFFS AND HAPPILY EVER AFTERS SERIES
How Hard Can it Be?
Size Matters
Cop a Feel

If after reading all the above you are still wanting more adventure and zany fun, read *Pirate Dave and His Randy Adventures*, the romance novel budding novelist Rena was helping wicked Evangeline write in *How Hard Can It Be*.

Warning: Pirate Dave Contains Romance Satire, Plot Spoofing, and Pirates with Two Pork Swords. Enough said.

About Robyn Peterman

Robyn Peterman writes because the people inside her head won't leave her alone until she gives them life on paper.

Her addictions include laughing really hard with friends, shoes (the expensive kind), Target, Coke Zero Cherry with extra ice in a Styrofoam cup, bejeweled reading glasses, her kids, her super-hot hubby and collecting stray animals.

A former professional actress with Broadway, film and T.V. credits, she now lives in the South with her family and too many animals to count.

Writing gives her peace and makes her whole, plus having a job where you can work in your underpants works really well for her. You can leave Robyn a message via the Contact Page and she'll get back to you as soon as her bizarre life permits! She loves to hear from her fans!

** Visit **www.robynpeterman.com** for more information.**

Made in the USA
Columbia, SC
31 December 2021